Hero of Mine

By Codi Gary

The Rock Canyon, Idaho Series
Bad For Me
Return of the Bad Girl
Bad Girls Don't Marry Marines
Good Girls Don't Date Rock Stars
Things Good Girls Don't Do
The Trouble with Sexy (a novella)

The Men in Uniform Series
Hero of Mine
One Lucky Hero
I Need a Hero (novella)

Hero of Mine

A MEN IN UNIFORM NOVEL

CODI GARY

AVON IMPULSE
An Imprint of HarperCollinsPublishers

Hero of Mine

A Men in Uniform Novel

This is a work of fiction. Names, characters, places, and incidents are products of the author's imagination or are used fictitiously and are not to be construed as real. Any resemblance to actual events, locales, organizations, or persons, living or dead, is entirely coincidental.

Excerpt from *The Virgin and the Viscount* copyright © 2016 by Charis Michaels.
Excerpt from *Love On My Mind* copyright © 2016 by Tracey Livesay.
Excerpt from *Here and Now* copyright © 2016 by Cheryl Etchison Smith.

EPub Edition AUGUST 2016 ISBN: 9780062372284
Print Edition ISBN: 9780062372291

Avon, Avon Impulse, and the Avon Impulse logo are trademarks of HarperCollins Publishers.

AM 10 9 8 7 6 5 4 3 2 1

This one is for my brothers—blood or not, you're still family; Wyatt, Brian, Randy, Chris, Jason, Mark, Doug, and Dave. Love you all.

Chapter One

TYLER BEST DIDN'T believe in fate.

Fate was an excuse people who'd experienced really bad shit or really astounding luck used in order to explain how their lives tended to twist and turn. Fate was a fantasy.

Tyler was a realist. He didn't rely on some imaginary force to direct him. He'd taken chances and gotten knocked on his ass a few times, but he kept going because that's what life was. You didn't give up when it got hard.

Even in the face of devastating loss.

Tyler stared at the picture of Rex, his military dog, and the ache in his heart was raw, even eight months later. Rex had been his for three years before getting killed in combat. While Tyler was overseas, away from his family and friends, the dog had been his best friend, bringing him great comfort. When he'd lost Rex, he'd almost quit working with dogs. It had been difficult to be around them.

Yet, here he was, waiting to be led back to the "last day" dogs at the Paws and Causes Shelter. It was his first time here, as it was relatively new. Most of the time he visited Front Street Animal Shelter or the one off of Bradshaw, but new rescues and shelters were being added to the program every day. Ever since he'd become the head trainer for the Alpha Dog Training Program, a nonprofit created to help strengthen the connection between military personnel and their community, he'd become the last hope for a lot of dogs. If they passed their temperament test, they'd join the program. Not all of them did, and on those days it was hard to remember all the lives the program saved. It was hard to walk away from a dog's big soulful eyes when Tyler knew the only outcome was a needle filled with pink liquid death, but he couldn't save them all.

Just like he couldn't save Rex.

"Sergeant Best?" a woman called from behind the reception desk.

Tyler stood up and slipped his phone back into his pocket. "Yes, ma'am."

"You can go on through. Our tech, Dani, is waiting in the back to show you around. Just straight back; you'll see the double doors."

"Thank you." Tyler opened the door, assaulted by high-pitched barks of excitement and fear. As he passed by the kennels, he looked through, studying the dogs of all shapes and sizes. He wasn't sure why he was so melancholy today, but it had been coming on strong.

He pushed through the double doors and immediately realized the man and woman inside were arguing. Loudly.

"No, he has more time. I talked to Dr. Lynch, and he promised to give him until the end of the day in case his owners claim him." This was shouted by the woman with her back to him, her blonde ponytail swinging with every hand gesture.

"Don't be naïve. You've been here long enough to know that he won't be claimed." This was said by the thin, balding man in the lab coat, who was pushing sixty and had the cold, cynical look of someone who'd been doing his job too long. Tyler had seen it on the faces of veterans who had found a way to steel themselves against the horrors that haunted them. But once you shut that part off, it was hard to find it again. "Even if they come looking, they'll just tell you to put him down anyway. If they had the money to pay for his care, then they could afford a proper fence. All you're doing is putting off the inevitable and wasting valuable pain meds."

He tried to sidestep the blonde, who was a good head shorter, but she planted herself right in his path. When she spoke, her voice was a low, deadly whisper. "If you make one more move toward that cage, I will body check you so hard you'll forget your own name."

Tyler's eyebrows shot up, and he crossed his arms, hoping like hell the guy tested her. He really wanted to see her Hulk out.

"I will have you fired and sue you for everything you have if you touch me, you disrespectful little bitch."

Tyler opened his mouth to defend her, but Blondie beat him to it by laughing. "Good luck with that. Of course, I could always say that you were being an über-perv, like with Mandy in reception. I'm guessing that if you have another complaint filed against you, you'll be the one they ask to leave."

The older man paled, and his lips compressed into an angry white line.

"Yeah, I thought that would get your attention," she said, sounding rather smug. "Now, I suggest you leave this room, because even if I have to camp here until five o'clock, I am not leaving. And if you try to put Fugly down again before his time is up, I'll have a camera phone and a news story with your name right in the headline."

Fugly? She was protecting an animal named Fugly?

The man made a sound of disgust and headed toward another door away from Tyler. Once he was gone, Tyler stood there for a moment, waiting for her to notice him.

She ran her hands over her face and released a shaky sigh before she turned around.

And froze when she spotted him.

Tyler took in her heart-shaped face and pointed chin, the green of her darkly lashed eyes, and her rosebud mouth wrapped into an O of surprise. She had a sweet girl-next-door look to her, and suddenly, his day brightened a bit.

"Don't you know it's rude to eavesdrop?" she asked.

Damn, that was a boatload of hostility in one pint-sized bundle.

"I didn't mean to, ma'am. I was told to come on back. Wasn't expecting to almost break up a brawl." He gave her his best smile, the one his friends said would disarm even the angriest woman alive.

All she did was blink at him several times before she groaned. "You're the guy from Alpha Dog?"

Tyler held out his hand to her. "Sergeant Tyler Best."

She took his hand, and he was surprised by the firm grip. "Danielle Hill, but everyone calls me Dani."

"You can call me Tyler or Best, whatever you prefer."

All she did was nod, so either she missed the flirtatious edge in his tone or she just wasn't interested. Either way, Tyler was a little disappointed by her reaction.

Dani pointed to the far wall of cages, oblivious to his disgruntlement. "Those are all the dogs whose time here expires. Feel free to take them out into the holding room"—she indicated a white door that had a sign reading HOLDING ROOM— "and do whatever you gotta do."

Turning her back on him, she squatted down in front of a large cage and opened it. Tyler bent down to see a massive gray dog with black spots and stripes. The dog lifted his head slightly, his floppy ears pricking as she cooed.

"Hey, Fugly, how you doing, bud?" Dani's hand glided over the dog's head and neck, and he relaxed back on his side with a whimper.

"What happened to him?" Tyler asked.

"Someone hit him with their car. A yard crew behind them stopped and picked him up, brought him here, but there's only so much I can do. The X-rays show he needs leg surgery, but my regular doctor is off today, and the prick subbing for him won't do a damn thing to help."

Tyler came closer, squatting behind her. The dog lifted his head and met Tyler's gaze with soft green-gray eyes. Rex's eyes had been a dark brown, nearly black, but the expression in this dog's eyes was still the same—filled with trust. This dog wasn't afraid of humans; he expected them to help him, to ease his pain.

Tyler's chest clenched. Although he'd trained several dogs since Rex, he hadn't experienced this pull, this kinship. This big, gray dog was calling to him, and he couldn't ignore it, no matter how crazy it seemed.

"Release him to me."

Dani spun his way so fast, she nearly knocked him back. "What?"

"Release him to me, and I'll run him down to my veterinarian. They'll go over the extent of his injuries and let me know what he needs."

Dani stared at him, her gaze wary. "Why would you do that? And what about the dogs you're supposed to evaluate?"

What the hell *was* he doing? He wasn't even sure the dog was trainable, let alone what his injuries were.

But he could still remember Rex's body as it cooled and stiffened in his arms. There had been nothing he could do to help Rex, but he could help this dog.

"If you will run interference for me with that guy, I'll drive…" Tyler hesitated to call the dog the bullshit name. "I'm sorry; he needs a better name than Fugly."

Dani laughed, but her voice shook a bit as though she might cry. "The workers that brought him in were calling him that."

"Not anymore. Whatever his name is, I'll drive him up there, drop him off, and come back here. If his owners show up, you can give me a call."

"I don't have your number." She closed the cage door and stood up.

"The front desk has it, but do you have your phone on you?" he asked.

"Yeah, I'll go get it." She left the room, and Tyler studied the dog. He was probably a good hundred and fifty pounds, which wouldn't be a problem to carry, but if he had more injuries they couldn't see, Tyler was concerned about jostling him around and doing more damage. He'd ask Dani if they had a stretcher when she got back.

She came back through the doors and handed him her phone. "Here."

Tyler stood up, staring at the screen saver of a smiling toddler with his arms wrapped around Dani's neck. Well, shit, that sent whatever attraction he'd had crashing to the ground. He had three rules for hooking up: Be honest from the get-go, no sleeping over, and definitely no repeats within the same week. And then there were the types of women he steered clear from.

No crazies. No attached or married women. And definitely no single moms.

No ifs, ands, or buts about it. He had watched his own mom get screwed over enough times to know that if you weren't ready, just stay far away.

Clearing his throat, he swiped his thumb over to her contacts and put in his information. "Cute kid."

"Thank you."

"He yours?" he asked.

"Yes, he's mine."

Was it just him, or did she sound defensive?

"How old is he?" Tyler handed the phone back to her, disappointed that she was off limits.

"He's almost two." Dani slipped her phone into her pocket. Her curt responses told him she didn't want to discuss her child with a complete stranger, and he couldn't blame her.

Apparently, he was just a nosy, interfering bastard today.

"About Fugly. I was going to just carry him out, but I'm afraid of causing more damage."

"He doesn't have internal bleeding, at least not that showed up on the X-rays. Most of the impact from the car occurred on his back end. Plus, I gave him a dose of pain meds when he first came in, and it should last him a while."

"Okay then, you get the door, and I'll get the dog."

Dani unlocked the cage again and unhooked the dog's IV, wrapping the tubing over the mobile pole by the cage. As gently as he could, Tyler reached in and picked up the dog, who tried to thrash for half a second before Tyler spoke firmly. "Stay."

The dog stilled, and Tyler stood up with him in his arms. "It's gonna be okay, boy."

Dani opened the doors as they went, but once they got to the lobby, Lab Coat Guy spotted them and spluttered, "What do you think you're doing?"

Dani puffed up. "He's taking the dog to his vet, since you won't do anything to help him."

Tyler had to admire the set of balls on Dani as every eye in the room swung on Lab Coat, pinning him with accusation.

"I didn't say anything like that. I told you his prognosis wasn't good and he was suffering."

"And I wanted a second opinion, so we're getting one."

Tyler grinned, following Dani out the door. Pausing for half a second, Tyler gave Lab Coat a warning look. "I haven't had a chance to evaluate the dogs yet. They'd better all be there when I get back."

Lab Coat swallowed hard, and as she closed the door, Dani laughed. "I think he just pissed himself."

Tyler liked her laugh, light and tinkling, like Christmas bells. "You're pretty terrifying yourself."

"I don't let bullies push me around," she said. "Where are your keys?"

"Right pocket."

When the warmth of her hand pushed into his pocket and grabbed his keys, he couldn't help his physical reaction. It was just too close to the groin, and the way she pressed with seeking fingers against him was enough to give him a semi. Despite it being October, it was still in the mideighties in Sacramento, and Tyler could feel beads of sweat dribbling down the sides of his face as she continued her search; he told himself it was just the heat getting to him.

Luckily, she hadn't seemed to notice, and once she found the keys, she unlocked the doors and pulled open the back door of the Alpha Dog van.

"Hang on." She ran back inside while Tyler waited, the dog's weight making his arms burn.

Suddenly, she was back and climbing past him into the backseat of the van.

"What are you doing?" he asked.

"Isn't it obvious? I'm coming with you. You're going to need someone to hold onto him while you drive, and besides," she said, her expression a soft mask of worry, "I don't want him to be alone and scared."

Tyler nodded, knowing exactly what she meant. He'd been rescuing dogs his whole life, much to his parents' exasperation. He remembered the first dog he'd brought home at nine, a skinny black dog with matted fur and a rank odor. When his mom had told him he couldn't bring the dog inside, he'd teared up and told her, "But, Mom, he's so hungry and scared." His mom had caved like a big old softy, and his dad left, coming back with food, bowls, and a collar and leash. He'd named the dog Barney, and he'd been the start of Tyler's love of dogs.

The fact that Dani appeared to have the same passion made him like her more. Cute, funny, didn't take shit from anyone? Plus, he'd bet his last dollar she was great in bed.

But the tiny, smiling little boy on her phone screen was like a big fat stop sign. He didn't do single moms—at least, not when he knew about the kid.

Laying the dog gently into the back, he watched her settle his head in her lap and begin stroking his gray coat. Suddenly, she looked up at Tyler, those green eyes filled with gratitude and…Hell, he had no idea, but it was a first for him.

"Thank you."

Tyler slammed the door to the van without responding, grabbing the keys out of the passenger door.

Tyler Best, bleeding-heart dog rescuer.

He climbed up into the driver's seat, preparing to take off.

"Really, why are you doing this?" she asked from behind him.

Adjusting the mirror so he could see her, he gave the only answer that made sense. "Why not?"

Chapter Two

DANI HILL HAD never been easily won over by any man. Could they get her into bed? Sure, but she never had any delusions about who she was sleeping with. She was a magnet for jackasses and always had been. Until she'd gotten pregnant, and her boyfriend had decided he couldn't handle being a dad and had taken off.

Angel Ramirez had been all that a twenty-one-year-old girl could desire. Muscular with a jealous streak and hazel eyes, he'd been everything her mom and dad had hated. But she'd loved him—or, at least, she'd thought it was love.

They hadn't been together very long when she'd found out she was pregnant, and she'd been terrified to tell him. He'd been pissed and told her he would take her to the clinic, but she'd refused. He'd disappeared for days, but just as she was sure he was gone for good, he'd popped up again. She'd been relieved, thinking he was back for her and the baby, but he had just wanted her to know that he was moving south to Los Angeles. He was taking a job with his cousin, and if she wanted to keep the baby, that was fine, but she shouldn't expect anything from him.

In that moment, Dani had finally realized that her parents had been right about everything. That there was a reason bad boys should be avoided at all times. That she was about to have a baby with a man who had never cared about her, but she'd been too stupid to realize it.

And although she couldn't fully regret being with Angel, she had learned from her wild and reckless dating history. She'd grown and was more determined than ever to live her life right and give her son, Noah, the best of her.

Which meant she didn't go out with guys with easy smiles and killer blue eyes. Even if he was carrying an injured dog into a veterinary clinic and willing to pay for the charges, despite the fact that it wasn't his.

So what? Other guys would do this. He's a dog lover, that's it. Don't make a big deal out of it and start looking at him like he's some kind of hero. You feel nothing, do you hear me?

Dani heard it, but it was hard to listen when he told the vet tech, "Just call me with your game plan, and use this card for what he needs. I want updates, though."

A guy who offered carte blanche medical care for a stray dog? It was hard not to want to throw her arms around him and give him a massive hug. Or, at the very least, sigh dreamily.

Get ahold of yourself, or I swear I am going to haul off and slap you silly. Then everyone will think you are crazykins.

A vet tech by the name of Darius took Fugly from Tyler, assuring him he'd call when he knew something.

Tyler watched Fugly disappear through the doors, and Dani's heart fluttered at the concern on his face.

"We should get back so I can evaluate the dogs before Dr. Horrible decides to exact his revenge on us," he said, turning back to face her.

"Dr. Horrible?"

Tyler seemed embarrassed. "*Dr. Horrible's Sing-Along Blog*. It's a three-part web series by Joss Whedon."

"So it's a musical?" she asked. They had pushed open the front door of the vet's office and were walking toward his van.

"No, I mean, yeah, it's a musical, but it's Whedon. Anything Whedon does is awesome." He actually beat her to the passenger door and opened it for her. Dani couldn't remember the last time a guy had put in the effort.

"What else has he done?" she asked.

He actually stood in the door opening as she climbed into the front seat, his jaw hanging open. "Are you serious?"

"I don't watch a lot of TV, unless it's on Netflix or something." Why did it sound like she was apologizing for not knowing who some obscure web series creator was?

"He's on Netflix! *Firefly, Dollhouse, Buffy the Vampire Slayer*—"

"Whoa, you watch something called *Buffy the Vampire Slayer*?" She broke out into peals of laughter, and he slammed the door. She was still guffawing when he climbed into the driver's seat.

"Whedon also wrote and directed the Avengers movies and *Agents of Shield*."

"Well, you should probably lead with that and not that other stuff," she said smartly.

"Unless you've been living under a rock, you should know who Whedon is and what Buffy is."

"Oh, God, I can't take you seriously when you say things like that."

"What, just because of the name of the show? I'm trying to school you on one of the most ingenious writers and directors of a generation."

"And I'm listening, but I'm sorry, it's a little hard to imagine."

"You should be apologizing to the great Joss Whedon, not me," he said.

She glanced his way and caught the smile he'd been fighting. "As soon as I get home, I'll write an extensive apology and post it to my mommy blog."

"You have a mommy blog?"

"No, but it would be funny if I did. Mine would be 'what not to do as a parent.' " *Shit, why had she said that to him?*

"I'm sure most women feel like that."

Dani knew his comment was supposed to be comforting, but he didn't know her or her situation. So far, she'd just been doing her best, but nothing ever felt like it was good enough, especially compared to other moms. Moms who had waited until they had a career, had picked the right guy and gotten married. The freaking Pinterest moms who put all their amazing cupcakes and DIY birthday party decorations up for everyone to ooh and ahh over.

She hated those moms. There wasn't a crafty bone in her body, and staring at all of those perfectly creative ideas and handmade awesomeness left her feeling even more like a failure.

"So, how long have you worked at the shelter?" Tyler asked.

She was grateful for the change in subject and the escape from her pity party. "Only a few weeks. I actually work the night shift at Fairview Animal Hospital so I can be home during the day with my son. I only usually do a few hours in the morning at the shelter, but today one of the other women called in to say she'd be a little late, so I agreed to stay."

"Where is your son?" he asked.

Was he accusing her of something? "He's with my mom, not that it's any of your business."

"Hey, no need to get hostile. I was just asking," he said.

"I'm not hostile; I just don't appreciate the insinuation that I'm neglecting my son."

"Whoa, no insinuation! Geez, are you always this defensive?" he asked.

Dani didn't say anything, partly because she was embarrassed. She was constantly taking flak from her mom about how she was raising Noah, and it had just become instinct to immediately go on the defensive. Even with a total stranger who was just being inquisitive. She shouldn't have jumped down his throat. Especially since he was helping out Fugly.

"What are you going to do with Fugly if he makes it?" she asked.

"I figure I'll see what his injuries are, and depending on how he does during his temperament evaluation, I'll find something for him to do. The first item on the agenda is to give him a better name."

"What if he doesn't pass?"

She saw it, even if it was just a flicker. The grim downturn of his mouth that said exactly what would happen if he didn't pass.

"I like to think positively," he said.

Dani had a feeling he was avoiding the question for her benefit. *He's probably scared you'll rip his face off if he says the wrong thing.*

"How many dogs are you looking for?" she asked.

"I have four open kennels, but if I find more that are a good fit, I'll usually foster them or one of the other trainers will take them in."

"Isn't it hard doing that? Testing a dog, and when he fails, knowing he's most likely going to die?" she asked.

"It's the way it is, and until we can come up with a better system, I can only save the ones I can train as police, military, search and rescue, and therapy dogs. We are trying to grow, and the goal is to have an Alpha Dog program in every city, but it's just us for now."

Dani swallowed back the sour taste his cold, matter-of-fact explanation had created in her mouth. "It's not fair. Some of these animals have never known kindness or been trained—"

"And it sucks, believe me, but I can't take every dog. There are too many good ones to waste time on the ones who might bite a child one day. If I don't do my job right, and one of our dogs attacks someone, the whole program could get shut down. And then we aren't helping any dogs."

Dani understood, she did, but having him act so casual about it rubbed her the wrong way. How could he be so callous?

He parked the van in the same spot as before, and as he killed the engine, he turned.

"Look, I'm sorry if I'm coming off like an asshole, but if I can't hold it together and make the tough calls, then I can't do this job. I have a friend who's a vet, and he worked in shelter medicine for years. He told me once that in shelter medicine you get hard or you get out, because otherwise, all the bad shit you see is going to haunt you."

"You honestly think that people in shelter medicine no longer care about helping the animals?" she asked.

"It's not that they don't care, it's that the system has worked against them for so long, they've learned to triage, just like a doctor in the emergency room. Just like your lab coat guy."

"Wait, so you agreed with him about euthanizing Fugly?"

"No, that is not what I'm saying. I am saying that I understand how some people get to the point where it's less heart-wrenching to essentially turn off their humanity."

Dani opened her door and got out, turning to face Tyler. "Maybe that works for people like you, but I don't have an on and off switch. I feel things and I empathize, and if that makes me weak to some people, then they can go to hell."

She slammed the door with a bang and headed for the front of the building, waiting for the sound of his van door opening or the heavy tread of his boots.

But he didn't come after her, at least not in the time it took her to get inside and find Suzy had made it in for her shift.

"Oh, thank God you're here," Dani said. "There is a guy from Alpha Dog Training Program, and he's going to be evaluating the dogs scheduled for euthanasia today, but I need to get Noah before my mom has a meltdown."

"Yeah, yeah, go, I'll handle the guy." Suzy was an average brunette a few years older than Dani. "Hey, is he cute though?"

Cute? Cute was for puppies and kittens, not six-foot-tall men with broad shoulders and male-model faces.

Dani grabbed her purse out of the locked desk drawer and glanced out the front office window. Tyler was just getting out of the van, looking a little bewildered. He probably wasn't used to women yelling at him and then running away from all that sexiness.

"Cute is not the word I would use," she said.

Suzy's shoulders slumped as she misinterpreted Dani's meaning, and she used the opportunity to sneak away. The last thing she wanted was another interaction with Tyler.

Dani exited through the back door and got into her car. As she turned the key, the engine sputtered, an issue it had been having lately, and she groaned. Running her hands over the dash, she tried to coax it in a low, husky voice. "Come on, baby, work for me, and I promise I'll get you a tune-up soon."

Several seconds ticked by, and Dani tried the engine again. As the car came to life, Dani gave a little thank-you to the car gods and headed out toward Carmichael, a suburb of Sacramento next to Citrus Heights. Her parents had lived in the same house since they got married, and she knew the way there even on autopilot. Which meant that her mind wandered a bit as she tried to imagine where she was going in the next few years.

If it was up to her mom, Dani would go out and eventually marry one of the nice, sensible men she'd been trying to set her up with, but Dani wasn't interested in men, let alone blind dates with men her mom spoke highly of. The only boyfriend her mom had ever liked was Dwight, who was a super-smart, clean-cut guy who'd asked her to homecoming junior year. But Dwight had just been an asshole in a nice-guy exterior, constantly putting Dani down about her looks, how she wasn't as intelligent as he was, how she had no direction. After six weeks, Dani realized she was dating her mom, and she dumped his ass in the middle of the quad after he'd asked her if she really wanted her personal pizza.

But her mom had been disappointed and always cited Dwight as the one who got away. In her own way, her mom's taste was just as bad as Dani's—with the exception of her dad—and therefore she could not be trusted to find Dani a man.

Twenty minutes later, Dani pulled into the driveway, and as she climbed out, she heard screaming coming from inside the house. Noah's screaming.

Racing to the front door, she burst inside and found her mom rocking Noah as he cried.

"What happened?" Dani wasted no time crossing the room and holding her arms out to her son. When he reached for her, she saw the swelling lump on his forehead and gasped.

"He was running and ran right into the doorjamb. He's got a nasty bump, but he's okay, I think—"

"Did he lose consciousness?" Dani realized she was shouting at her mom, but it was only to be heard over Noah's cries.

But in true Laura Hill form, she stood up with her hands on her hips, her green eyes narrowed. "Danielle Louise, do you really think I wouldn't take my grandson to the emergency room if he had knocked himself out?"

"No, of course not, I'm sorry." Dani held Noah against her, rubbing his back and humming. As his sobs started to subside, she said, "I think I'm going to take him anyway, just to be sure. That is quite a goose egg on his head."

"Can you really afford to do that? I'm sure he's fine. Kids are tough," her mom said.

Dani didn't respond; there was no point. Her mom and dad were older than her other friends' parents and were big fans of saying "shake it off" and "rub some dirt in it."

Whereas Dani would rather take on another hospital bill if it meant peace of mind.

"You're earlier than I was expecting. Did something happen?" her mom asked.

"Nope, the girl I was covering for finally showed up, that's all."

"So what are your plans, then?" she asked.

After the emergency room, you mean?

"Noah and I will probably take it easy. Make some food. Watch cartoons."

"You shouldn't let him watch too much TV."

Why was it her mom couldn't go one minute without giving her unsolicited advice?

"I don't, but thank you for watching him." Dani carried a sniffling Noah over to the couch and picked up her diaper bag.

"I only tell you these things to help. I saw this study the other day on television and the effects it has on—"

"Mom! Noah is fine."

"I don't want to fight with you, Danielle. You're young, and I just thought you'd be interested in what I've learned from raising you, but that's fine."

Danielle didn't mention that she hadn't exactly grown up to be a perfect, functioning adult. What was the point? Her mother had given her an out, and she was going to take it.

"I appreciate your advice, Mom, just let me ask for it. Okay?"

Her mother nodded regally. "I'll try, but it's hard to break old habits."

Dani shook her head. Her mother wasn't going to change, but at least she was being reasonable.

Wait...

A reasonable mother meant she wanted something.

As if on cue, her mother said, "By the way, I wanted to make sure you're coming to church with us on Sunday."

Uh-oh, here we go again. "I haven't been to church in years, Mom."

"Well then, it's time to start back up. It's good for the soul, you know."

Despite the innocence in her voice, Dani knew there was something else afoot. "Why now?"

"Because I want you to meet a few people. You're always saying you don't have time to meet men your age, but there are several very nice ones who go to church with us, and I want to introduce you."

"Mom, when are you going to give up? I am not looking for a husband."

"Well, you should be," she snapped.

"And thousands of feminists' heads just spun around in horror."

"Your father and I won't be around forever to help you with Noah, and it's expensive to pay for childcare and housing and other bills. You get by because we help you, but you need a partner. Someone to take on the burden. And honestly, you need to stop all this volunteering and wasting your time. You should be working more. You can't afford to give your time away, not now."

Dani took a deep, cleansing breath. "Mom, I volunteer one day a month at the spay and neuter clinic, and it is something that is needed. We are all doing fine, and as far as the future goes, we'll see how everything shakes out, but I am not going to chase down man after man just because you think I should. When I'm ready, and I don't know that I will be, I will start dating."

"Yes, because you've shown just what a good judge of character you can be."

Her mom's sarcasm swirled like a bitter brew in her stomach, confirming her own thoughts. "We'll see you later, Mom."

"I'm only trying to help you," her mom called after her.

Dani shut her parents' front door, thinking about Tyler and his words of wisdom as well.

"Everybody's just so helpful today."

Chapter Three

TYLER SAT ACROSS from Sergeant Dean Sparks on Monday morning, waiting for him to say something. He'd known the minute he told Sparks about the dog he was going to have a meltdown, but what could Tyler do? He couldn't leave the dog to die.

"You don't even know if we can use the dog for the program?"

"Nope," Tyler said flippantly.

Sparks sat back in his chair, sighing heavily. "Best, I know that we've had a couple of dogs we ended up not being able to train for the program, but we can't spend thousands of dollars on a dog that *might* be a good fit."

"Alpha Dog isn't paying for him. I am. Once he's out of the vet and healed, I'll temperament test him and go from there. The program doesn't need to be affected unless he passes his test and doesn't have any long-standing injuries."

"What exactly was so special about *this* dog?" Sparks asked.

Tyler wasn't sure how to describe it, the undeniable connection between him and the big gray dog. *I had to help him* sounded stupid, and Dean would never be able to understand that it was the truth.

Plus, having that pretty tech Dani looking at you like you hung the moon wasn't half bad, either.

Well, for a little while at least, before he managed to piss her off again. Tyler wasn't going to mention the girl, though, and have Sparks give him more shit. Especially since Tyler wasn't really into her.

Then how come she keeps popping up in your head?

Because he hadn't gotten laid over the weekend?

"Look, it's on my dime, and if he doesn't work out, I'll find him a home."

"Still, this program needs to be functioning in order to succeed. You brought six dogs back with you from the shelter, and we only have four kennels."

"If a dog passes his evaluation, then I'm bringing him back here. If you have a problem with that, replace me." Tyler wasn't going to back down on this. Leaving behind dogs who couldn't pass their evaluation was one thing, but there was no way he wasn't going to find room for every dog who did.

Sparks shook his head. "Just when I think you don't have a heart, you do something like this."

"I never said I don't have a heart; I just keep it heavily guarded."

Sparks ran his hands over his face and close-cropped dark hair. "Best, I want to save them all, believe me. But we don't have enough kids in here to handle all the dogs you're bringing in, let alone trainers." Sparks paused to look over one of the other dog's descriptions. "I mean, this dog Bosco is only thirty pounds and looks like a stuffed animal a child would snuggle. Is he going to be a therapy dog?"

"No, he's too high energy, and it would be a waste. The dog is fast as hell, and I guarantee with the right training, I can have him taking down men like a hundred-pound rottie."

"Meanwhile, where are two of these dogs going to go?" Sparks asked.

"Apollo and Zeus are ready for training, so I'll graduate them from basic. The kids working with them can take over these new ones."

"So, does that mean you're going to be taking Apollo and Zeus home with you?" Dean grinned evilly. "Casey misses Apollo so much. I think he's actually convinced Violet he needs a dog, but if I tell him you've got Apollo at home, he might forget about it for a while and just start showing up at your place."

Casey was a graduate of the Alpha Dog Training Program and was Sparks's girlfriend's little brother. Tyler liked Casey, and the kid liked him. His sister Violet wasn't Tyler's biggest fan, probably because he'd slept with her best friend and never called her again. That tended to make women think he was a jerk, but he wasn't out to hurt anyone. He just liked having fun.

"You tell him he's welcome anytime, just text me first in case I have…company."

Dean rolled his eyes at the innuendo. "Get the hell out of my office, player. You've got a date at the pediatric wing this afternoon."

Tyler left the office and headed back toward where Apollo and Zeus were held. Most of the trainers took turns visiting local hospitals and nursing homes. It gave the dogs excellent exposure and usually brightened the patients' spirits.

Tyler liked visiting the kids, but there was another patient he usually swung in to check in on. Henry Coleson was a sixty-four-year-old Marine with no family or friends to speak of. They had met by chance, and Tyler had started visiting him whenever he could. Henry's body was riddled with cancer, and although he could be a pissy son of a bitch, he never turned Tyler away when he visited.

Tyler passed by one of the moms being led out by a trainer and nodded at her with a smile. "Ma'am."

She returned his smile, and Tyler started whistling, feeling good. It didn't matter if they were young or old, women liked Tyler, always had. Only a handful had ever shot him down or stood immune to his charms. One of them had been Dani.

Which is good for you because not only is she a single mom, she obviously has some issues.

It was true; she'd been angry, defensive, and rude. In other words, drama. And he definitely didn't need any of that.

You're better off sticking to the lonely and uncomplicated.

DANI STOOD IN her kitchen making coffee, her eyes burning with fatigue. The whole weekend had been a disaster. It was bad enough that she'd picked Noah up on Thursday with the bump on his forehead, but after trying and failing to get in with his pediatrician, they'd ended up at the urgent care clinic. The doctor there had assured her Noah would be fine, but she'd overheard the nurses saying that one of the other little boys in the waiting room had been dehydrated from throwing up for days. Dani had prayed hard that Noah wouldn't get it, but sure enough, Noah had spent most of yesterday throwing up, and she had hardly been able to sleep, worried he'd start up again. She'd slept on the couch, with Bella lying across her feet snoring. She loved the fat pug, really, but her loud snores hadn't helped Dani's insomnia.

The coffee dripped slowly, and Dani tapped her foot impatiently. She'd called in sick for tonight, just to be on the safe side, and her boss had been understanding. It was the first time Noah had ever experienced the stomach flu, and watching his tiny body convulse and retch had been heartbreaking.

Finally, the pot filled up, and Dani pulled down one of the mismatched mugs from the cupboard. The rich aroma made her mouth water as she started to pour.

The soft sound of Noah's feet on the carpet, followed by the trampling of Shasta, their shepherd mix, made Dani put down the coffeepot reluctantly. She turned with a smile, her heart swelling as her son stumbled down the hallway, his brown curls mussed from sleep. Although he still slept in his crib, he had started to be able to climb out. Shasta padded along beside him, pushing her nose into his hand for head pats, but the little boy ignored her, surprisingly. She had brought the dog home the same time she'd found out she was pregnant with Noah, and from the moment he was born, Shasta had attached herself to him, and he adored her. He still must feel pretty crummy if even her demand for affection couldn't make him smile.

"Hey, buddy, you feeling any better?"

Noah shook his head as he climbed up onto the couch next to Bella, who still snored loudly.

"Do you want me to get you some crackers or something?"

Noah didn't answer. Dani went to grab the saltines anyway and heard the unmistakable sound of Noah throwing up. She flipped on the light as she rushed to Noah's side. There was a large puddle of dark vomit on the floor, and Dani stared at it for a moment, puzzled. Noah hadn't had anything to eat in over twenty-four hours except a little chicken broth last night. Why was his vomit so dark?

And then she saw the reddish brown tinge and what looked like…What was that congealed junk? Dani glanced up into Noah's pale face, saw the burnished smears in the corner of his mouth and chin, and knew.

Blood. Her son was puking blood.

Dani ran to grab her purse from the kitchen and her hard-soled slippers from the bedroom, panic propelling her like a whirlwind. Finally, she scooped a crying Noah up in her arms and raced out the door.

"It's okay, baby. Mama's got you. We're just going to the doctor."

Noah sobbed into the crook of her neck as she threw open her car door. Buckling Noah into his car seat, she kissed his cheeks and forehead before closing the door.

When she turned the key in the ignition, there wasn't even a click.

"No, this cannot be happening." She tried again, begging and pleading with her car, but still, nothing happened.

Noah started gagging again, and Dani grabbed her phone from her purse. As she dialed her parents' home, she turned in time to watch Noah cover the whole front of his pajamas and seat with blood.

Ending the call, she dialed 911 instead. "Hang on, baby. We're going to take a ride in a spaceship."

Chapter Four

HENRY COLESON GLOWERED at Tyler as he held out the spoon of Jell-O to him.

"I'm not a fucking child. So why the hell are you trying to feed me like one, dipshit?"

"Because the nurse said you won't eat and I should try to convince your stubborn behind to take a bite." Tyler had limited patience for most people, but Henry was different. The battle-scarred Marine had seen a tour in Nam and Desert Storm, served his country forty-five years, and, six months after retirement, found out he had stage four prostate cancer. They'd taken his prostate but found the cancer had already spread to his liver and lungs. He'd gone through chemo and even a few experimental trials, but nothing had worked. He'd finally said enough.

Henry took a few deep, labored breaths, the tubes in his nose fogging. "I'm trying to starve myself, you dumb fuck. Why won't you just let me die?"

"I get that, but here's the thing. I'm not ready to let you bite it yet. I still need you around."

"For what? The only shit I was ever good at was being stupid and screwing. And you don't got a problem with either of those things." Henry's laughter turned into a hoarse round of coughing that ended in a few painful wheezes.

"Shouldn't crack yourself up like that. Karma's a bitch."

"Fuck you," Henry said weakly.

"See, if you can still cuss me out, I know you aren't ready to die yet."

"Tyler…" Henry's voice was hoarse, and Tyler met his foggy gray eyes.

"Yeah?" he asked.

"You…need to get yourself a life."

Tyler took a piece of the roast beef off Henry's plate and fed it to Apollo, who sat next to his chair at attention. He was a young dog, but he and his brother, Zeus, were going to make wonderful therapy dogs. Tyler enjoyed bringing them by the children's wing of the hospital and watching the kids' faces light up. He was going to miss them when they graduated from the therapy program and became someone's sidekicks.

"I have a life. I have my place, my job, training the dogs. I even rescued a dog last week—"

"I'm talking about something you can leave behind. Someone who will be there for you when you're an angry old bastard being eaten up with cancer. Who cares if you live or die and cries at your funeral."

"I care, Henry. And I promise to pour a shot of whiskey on your grave when you go," Tyler said, trying to lighten the mood.

"Are you deliberately missing the point? You're young now, but eventually you're going to wake up and realize you spent your whole life serving your country and you have nothing to show for it except a broken dick and a lot of bad memories."

Tyler patted the older man's shoulder. "I'll get married, eventually. Don't worry about it. I'm more concerned with Nurse Hatchet coming back and seeing that you didn't touch your food. She looked like the type that would strap you to the bed and force-feed you."

"Just let me be, kid." Tyler had never heard Henry so dejected, and for the first time, he realized that Henry meant it. He wasn't just being a martyr to start an argument.

He was done fighting.

The doctors had given him six months a year ago, but he'd proved them wrong. He'd been beating the odds for a while.

Tyler set the Jell-O on the tray and, unsure of how Henry would respond, took his friend's hand and gave it a gentle squeeze. "Okay."

"Don't you got some kids to entertain?" Henry didn't shake him off or call him a pussy, like he would have a few weeks ago. It made the grief squeezing Tyler's chest hurt worse.

"I'll get to them soon. Right now, I figured I'd talk you to sleep."

"What else is new? You can't tell a decent story to save your life. You should try something with bloodshed, intrigue, adventure, forbidden love—"

Tyler scoffed. "When have you ever told a story about forbidden love?"

"That girl I met when I got back from Operation Desert Storm."

"What girl? You mean the hooker?"

Henry's face turned beet red. "She was not a hooker; she was an exotic dancer."

"Yeah, I hate to break it to you, but if they accept money and actually let you touch them, they're no longer just a stripper."

Henry mumbled something under his breath, and Tyler chuckled. "Usually you deliver your insults at a roar."

"At least I found someone to love. Not everyone does, and some of us don't have all the time in the world, you know."

It was far too true, and Tyler stared at Henry, the silence between them thick enough to cut with a knife.

Tyler didn't like to talk about the day he got shot, but with Henry...Well, he felt like the old guy could empathize. Besides, he'd heard all his battle stories. Might as well share his before Henry was gone.

"Did I ever tell you about when I got shot?"

Henry opened both of his eyes and sat up a bit. "No, haven't heard that one."

"Wanna hear it now?"

Henry nodded. "Sure, kid."

Tyler started talking, staring at the wall as he remembered. "I was patrolling with my dog, Rex. He was this big German shepherd, about ninety pounds and smart as hell. We were just walking, and then there was this slicing pain. There were bullets flying everywhere; it took me a second to even realize Rex wasn't moving. I radioed for help and just kept holding Rex as I waited. And then when I was in the hospital, my friend brought me a plastic container full of ashes and told me they belonged to Rex. That they'd burned him and thought I'd want to take him home with me. Corny, right? But I did, even bought an engraved urn and everything. It sits up on the shelf in my room."

Henry's gaze was heavy, belying his lighthearted insult. "You're still a crap storyteller."

"I know." He gave his friend a little salute as he stood up. "I'll see you tomorrow, okay?"

Henry didn't respond, just stared at him for a few seconds. Finally, he returned the salute. "Thank you for making my time here not so shitty."

Tyler hated how much the words sounded like good-bye.

SEVERAL HOURS LATER, Dani stood in the hallway of Mercy San Juan Hospital, outside of Noah's room, talking to his doctor. After X-rays, blood tests, and a mountain of tears from both Noah and Dani, Dr. Barrick finally had answers.

"We believe that Noah got a tear in his esophagus while vomiting yesterday, and it bled into his stomach. At this point, we don't think we'll have to repair it surgically, as these tears usually heal on their own. However, we'd like to keep him a day or so for observation."

Despite the doctor's almost casual, no-big-deal tone, Dani still had a lump of panic lodged in her throat. "Is there anything I need to watch for?"

"Other than if the vomiting continues, no. He's being monitored by the machines and getting fluids. You might want to grab a couple of things from home to make him more comfortable, but otherwise, I assure you, he's in good hands."

"Thank you." Dani could tell that the doctor was anxious to move on, and she wanted to be back in the room with Noah. She could see her mom sitting next to his bed, giving Dani hand cues and mouthing *What's he saying?* while Noah watched *Mickey Mouse Clubhouse*, his thumb in his mouth. Dani had been trying to break him of the habit, but today she would let it slide.

She entered the room, walked straight to the head of Noah's hospital bed, and began brushing back his curls. He didn't take his hazel eyes from the screen, but he did reach up with his IV-free hand to hold hers.

"What did the doctor say?" her mom demanded.

"That they want to keep him overnight for observation, but he should be fine." Dani gave her mom a warning look when she opened her mouth again. She didn't want to discuss what the doctor had said in front of Noah. "Do you mind going to my place and packing a bag for Noah and me? And feed the dogs for me?"

"Of course I can, but I want to know—"

"Mom, I'll tell you a little later, okay?"

Huffing loudly, her mom finally took the hint. "Fine, just text me. Do you want me to bring you back something to eat?"

"No, I'll just grab something from the cafeteria," Dani said.

"Well, all right then." Her mom leaned over and kissed Noah's hand. "Mapa will be back soon, handsome boy."

Noah looked up at Dani, squeezing her hand hard. Reading the panic in her son's eyes, Dani smiled reassuringly. "I'm staying. Mapa is just going to get some things for us. Is there anything you want her to bring back?"

"Shasta."

Dani laughed. "She can't bring Shasta back, sweetheart. Anything else?"

"Pig."

Pig was Noah's favorite stuffed animal. Dani had grabbed it for five bucks at some department store with the purchase of the matching book before Noah was born. He dragged that thing around everywhere, so it was no surprise it was the second thing he picked.

"All right, I'll be back in an hour or so."

Once her mom left the room, Dani let go of Noah's hand to go around and take the chair her mom had been sitting in. Once she was settled, she reached out to put her hand over Noah's, trying to let go of some of the fear that had been suffocating her ever since she had seen the blood. The nurses and doctors had been kind to her, even after she'd yelled at the X-ray technician for making Noah stand for another X-ray after he puked again. She had tried to keep it together so Noah wouldn't see how scared she was, but she had never been very good at holding back her emotions.

And feeling helpless had only made things worse.

Suddenly, there was a knock on the open door.

"Puppy!" Noah cried excitedly.

Dani glanced toward the door and blinked several times as she recognized Tyler Best from Alpha Dog, holding the leash of a black puppy with large floppy ears.

"Hey there, sorry to interrupt, but I have someone who wanted to meet you." Tyler looked away from Noah and seemed to do a double take when his eyes met hers. "Oh, hi."

"Hello." Clearing her throat to get rid of the squeak, she added, "How are you?"

"Fine, just bringing Apollo by to greet the kids. He's in training and needs the socialization."

Noah was trying to sit up but stopped with a painful grimace, clutching his stomach with a whimper.

"Noah, honey, are you okay?" Dani stood up, the fear once more clawing up and squeezing her chest.

"I didn't mean to upset him," Tyler said.

"No, he's having stomach problems, so I think it just hurts." Dani knew it wasn't his fault, yet there was just a thread of irritation in her voice.

Tyler brought Apollo closer and picked the young dog up. "How about I bring this big guy to you…" Tyler looked up at Dani expectantly.

"Noah."

"Noah, meet Apollo. If you're very gentle, you can stroke his ears." Noah reached out cautiously, running his hand down the puppy's neck. "Doesn't he just have the softest fur?"

Noah nodded and started to stretch closer but hesitated. As if sensing her son's desire, Tyler put the pup on the bed next to Noah gently and said, "Stay."

The dog stilled, even when Noah cuddled closer, his hand drifting over Apollo's head and down his back.

Dani's whole body relaxed, warming from the inside out as Apollo turned his head and ran his pink tongue over Noah's wrist, causing her son to giggle softly. Ashamed that she'd been thinking unkindly of Tyler, she had a hard time meeting his eyes as she commented, "Wow, he's really well behaved. There is no way my dog would be that still, especially if she was getting love."

"He's been training for months and had two different kids working with him. It's just something that takes time and patience."

As she watched Noah stroke the puppy's shiny black coat, tears pricked her eyes. There were kids a lot sicker than Noah in the hospital, so she shouldn't take up too much of Tyler's time, but it was the first smile she'd seen from her son all day.

"Thank you," she said softly.

When she met Tyler's eyes again, there was a charge of awareness. The blue depths were the color of those tropical ocean pictures, so bright and clear, and although she'd never really noticed a man's lips before, his were really quite nice and soft looking.

"You're welcome. Like I said, we're just making the rounds."

Horrified by her thoughts, she stammered, "Oh, well, we...We shouldn't keep you."

"You're not, really. I've been here for hours and already said hi to everyone else today. We've got just one more stop after you before we head home."

"If you're sure you don't want to get going—"

"Do you want us to leave?" he asked.

Yes! "No, of course not." Dani glanced toward Noah and saw that he was turned on his side with his arm wrapped around Apollo, whose head was down on the hospital bed. "Is he asleep?"

Tyler craned his neck and nodded. "They both are."

Dani ran her hands over her face. "Thank God."

"If you don't mind me asking, what's going on with Noah?" Tyler asked.

"He had the flu, and they think he tore his esophagus while he was vomiting. He started throwing up blood this morning, and we've been here since about seven."

"That must have been really scary."

His expression was filled with such sincere empathy, and it was comforting. "It was. He's my whole world, you know?"

Realizing that tears were spilling down her cheeks, she laughed. "I'm so sorry, I don't mean to cry and make you uncomfortable." Sniffing softly, she asked, "How's the dog?"

"Good, I'm picking him up Friday. Luckily, just his leg was injured. They did surgery, pinned the break, and put a cast on it, but he's great. He still has to take it easy, but the healing time is only six weeks or so. Hopefully, we'll be able to evaluate him and see where he fits in the program."

"What if he doesn't fit in the program?" she asked.

"If he doesn't fit and he passes his temperament test with flying covers, then I'll just find him an awesome home." That wide, charming smile came out again, and her heart did a little stutter. The guy was pretty lethal; she imagined that women fell all over themselves to get with him.

But not Dani. She could think he was drop-dead gorgeous, but she wasn't interested. Especially when adding the wrong man to their lives could have devastating repercussions for Noah.

Why are you even thinking about this? It's not like the guy has asked you out or anything.

"How long have you been at the program? I'm sorry; I don't know much about it."

"I've been there since it opened, so about seven months. If we can get one of these programs set up near every military base, we'd be helping a lot of dogs, but it all depends on how it goes here."

"So, you're active military, but you train and evaluate dogs?"

"Yes, but the kids at the program do most of the basic obedience training. Once the dogs graduate from basic obedience, they will be placed into specialty training."

"And the kids that are there? Is it like a camp or something?"

"No, they're juveniles who've been charged with non-violent crimes. Instead of spending two weeks to six months in juvie, they come to us."

Dani thought her jaw would hit the floor. "You let criminals handle these dogs?"

"They're kids who have had a little trouble; just like with the dogs, the kids are monitored for behavior. This program is helping to give these kids an outlet and a skill set so that they don't end up in prison as adults. But even adult prisoners have benefitted from a program like this inside the prison. They put the dog in the cell with the prisoner, and it not only gives the dog a home, but it gives the prisoners a lifeline."

Thoroughly scolded, Dani blushed. "Sorry, that probably came out pretty judgmental."

"Didn't you mean it to be that way?" he asked bluntly.

"No, not really. I was just surprised, because you hear so many stories about teenagers hurting animals, and—"

"You can't go by what you see on the Internet and the news. I work with these kids, and although they might have problems, they would never torture the dogs."

"Again, I'm sorry. I didn't mean to upset you."

"You didn't. I just get defensive of my kids, I guess."

The way he said it left Dani with the same gooey feeling she'd had when he'd offered to pay carte blanche for Fugly's care.

Dani gently ran her fingers over Noah's back. "I know the feeling."

Chapter Five

TYLER PICKED UP Fugly from the veterinarian on Friday after work. He brought with him a new leash and collar with the name Duke on the ID tag and Tyler's phone number on the back. Tyler had decided to rename him after a late-night viewing of *G.I. Joe*. As he paid his bill, the tech handed him his yellow microchip tags and the information he needed to register him online. Tyler had put up a Craigslist ad for a found dog and put Duke's picture in several pet groups on Facebook, but even if the owners claimed him, Tyler's info would still be on the chip. Just in case he got out again.

The tech led Duke out to him, and the minute the dog laid eyes on Tyler, he started to pull on the leash, dragging the bright orange cast behind him with a screech as it rubbed across the linoleum.

"Whoa, easy, Duke. I swear I'm not going anywhere." Tyler laughed as he rubbed Duke's ears before taking the leash. He and Duke walked out the door, and Tyler kept glancing down at the huge dog, a little concerned the extra-large dog crate he'd bought wouldn't be big enough. He popped the back of his Tahoe open and unlocked the crate's door. Tyler lifted Duke into the back, and the dog settled inside with his leg cast. All in all, it was just about perfect.

Tyler noticed a definite twinge in his knee as he came back around to the driver's side and climbed behind the wheel. He needed to go back to stretching it when he got home at night.

Apollo and Zeus were locked in their crates on his backseat, and with all of the supplies he'd grabbed at PetSmart on the way to pick up Duke, his car was stuffed pretty full.

Pulling out onto the road, he saw a blonde zip by in a little black car, and his mind flashed to Dani and Noah. He'd ended up staying at the hospital an hour later than he'd planned, talking to Dani about the program and his group of kids while Apollo and Noah had slept. The Dani in the hospital room had been easier to talk to than the one he'd initially met. Maybe it was because her guard was down or she was more vulnerable because she was worried about Noah, but Tyler had enjoyed it. If Apollo hadn't woken up whining, who knows how long he would have stayed. Noah slept through his departure, and as he'd said good-bye to Dani, he'd been tempted to ask for her phone number. The only thing that had stopped him was the voice in his head silently shouting the three types of women he avoided.

Yet, he still couldn't get that soft look in her green eyes out of his mind. The one she had whenever she glanced at Noah's sleeping form.

The one she'd shared briefly with him.

It was the same one he'd seen on his mom's face when she looked at his stepdad, and it had scared the hell out of him.

Having been raised by a single mother himself, he still remembered a few of the losers who had used and ditched his mom before she'd met his stepdad, Gareth Best. His mom had been lucky to find a guy like Gareth, someone who accepted her kid as his and treated her with respect and love. Gareth had never treated Tyler like a burden or a pest the way a few of his mom's boyfriends had. The first time Gareth met Tyler, he had taken his mom and him to the batting cages. It had been the most fun he'd ever had, and when Gareth had asked him how he'd feel about Gareth asking his mom to marry him, Tyler hadn't hesitated. Once they were married, Gareth had adopted Tyler, and even after Tyler's brother, Dereck, and sister, Zoe, were born, Gareth never treated him any differently.

Tyler remembered that every time Gareth had done something for him, whether it was bringing him a new mitt or taking him camping for the first time, his mom had gotten this soft, sweet look on her face.

Tyler knew that he wasn't ready to be a dad to anyone; he had too much more to do. Maybe once he retired, he'd think about settling down, but he liked his life the way it was. Why complicate things?

*Even if you see her again, you can just smile, say hi,
and move on. Why sweat something that hasn't even happened yet?*

Tyler turned into the driveway of his house, hitting
the garage opener so he could pull inside. After months
in the hospital and all the physical therapy he'd needed
because of his gunshot wound, he'd been more than content to settle in once he'd been placed with Alpha Dog.
He'd started researching VA loans, and at twenty-eight,
he had his own four-bedroom, two-bath in a Natomas
neighborhood. It had been a foreclosure, so it had needed
some work, but it was in good shape overall and less than
ten minutes from work. Plus, the backyard was .18 of an
acre, bigger than most, with a back patio for his barbeque.
His mom kept hassling him about why he needed such a
big house if he wasn't going to settle down, and he'd told
her it was so he could house all of them if they ever came
to visit. His parents still lived in the Bay Area, while his
brother went to Berkeley and his sister was still in high
school. But really, Tyler just liked his space.

Letting the pups out of their crates and leading them
out to the backyard, he went back for Duke. He'd bought
an extra-large cage for Duke to rest in, which he'd set up
in the living room next to Apollo's and Zeus's cages. The
vet had wanted him to rest as much as possible, but constantly carrying a single crate from the car to the house
wasn't going to work.

Opening the crate, Tyler carried Duke in as gently
as he could. Setting him up on the cushiony bed in his
cage, he rubbed his hands over his head and his ears.

Duke looked up at him with that same trusting look, and Tyler's chest squeezed.

"I got you, buddy."

Duke laid his head down and snuggled in just as Tyler's cell rang.

"Best."

"Hey, man, I need your help."

Tyler grinned at the sheer panic in his friend Blake Kline's voice.

"Wow, you sound like you're almost begging, man."

"Asshole, I'm serious. These people I go to church with want me to meet their daughter for coffee tonight, and I didn't know how to refuse—"

Tyler shook his head. Kline had *nice guy* written all over him, and people were always throwing their daughters, sisters, and best friends at him. "You say, 'No. N. O.'"

"Look, they put me on the spot, and I thought I could do it, but…but I have to cover for Sparks tonight with the kids, so I thought maybe you'd go in my place."

"You want me to go on your date?" Tyler didn't do blind dates; he liked to know what he was getting into. "Dude, no. I'll just cover your shift at Alpha Dog."

"No, just…I'm not ready, man, okay? Can't you do me a solid? I'll owe you."

Tyler grimaced, understanding ripping through him. Tyler had met Sparks, Kline, and their friend Oliver Martinez in group therapy, and when they'd all been assigned to Alpha Dog, they had grown closer. Tyler knew that Kline had lost his wife in a shooting at the Base Exchange where Kline had been stationed two years ago, and as far as Tyler knew, he hadn't been involved with anyone since.

"Why don't you just call her and tell her you can't make it?" Tyler asked.

"Because they didn't give me her number. Just told me to be at the Starbucks on Watt at seven."

"You always get the digits, man." Tyler couldn't believe this was actually happening. "This is the craziest thing I've ever heard. Who the hell sets their daughter up without giving her—"

"Look, yes or no, Best? Since you're every woman's type, I figured you'd be a good replacement. You just have to sit down, talk to her for an hour—"

"Half an hour. I have an injured dog at home."

"Forty-five minutes."

Tyler groaned as he smoothed his fingers over the tension headache building in his forehead. "Fine, but when you say you owe me, that isn't just an empty statement. You're going to actually *owe* me, so be aware, I'll come a-calling sooner or later."

"Fuck it, I'll do whatever you want. I'm desperate."

"Yeah, I got that."

"Be at the Starbucks on Watt and Highway 80 at seven and just tell her I couldn't make it."

Kline ended the call, and Tyler shook his head. He checked the clock; he had forty-five minutes to get changed and be at the Starbucks. Damn it, he hadn't even had dinner yet.

The things he did for these guys.

DANI WALKED INTO the Starbucks on Watt Avenue at five to seven, still fuming from her mom's ultimatum. When she'd sprung the fact that she'd set up a coffee date for Dani with some guy from her church earlier, Dani had told her to cancel it. That she had no right to try to manage and control her life.

Unfortunately, that hadn't worked, and her mom had asked her to go on this one date and she would stop pestering her.

For a while, at least.

Still, Dani had refused, until her mom had threatened not to watch Noah anymore. Dani knew it was a bluff, but if her mom went through with it, Dani would have to find someone to watch him, and day care and babysitters weren't cheap.

So now here she was, ordering a grande nonfat chai latte, waiting for some stranger to show up. Why couldn't people just leave her alone? Even her friends talked about setting her up on blind dates; if she wanted to go out, she'd start online dating.

Dani snagged a table for two by the window and set her smartphone on the table, noting the time. If the guy wasn't there in five minutes, she was taking off. And if he was there...well...in a half an hour, she'd fake an emergency and go home.

The door opened, and a middle-aged man with a goatee and glasses stepped inside. Dani assumed he was her date and held up her hand in greeting, but he didn't even glance around, just headed straight for the counter to order.

Smoothing her hand over her head, she tried to act cool, keeping one eye on the door. A couple of teenagers came in next, and Dani started counting down the minutes until she could leave.

The door swung open, and to Dani's surprise, Tyler Best walked inside. He glanced around the busy room, and when his gaze met hers, his beautiful eyes widened.

Dani's heart pounded as he approached.

"Hey, there." His hands gripped the back of the empty chair across from her.

"Hi. How are you?"

"I'm good, just meeting someone. How about you?" he asked.

"The same." God, she did not want to tell this gorgeous guy she was waiting for a blind date. "Who are you meeting?"

"Actually, it's kind of a funny story. My friend got suckered into a blind date with some woman by her parents. He ended up having to work and didn't have her number to cancel, so he sent me instead."

A horrifying suspicion snaked through Dani. "Oh, wow, well it's nice of you to take over so she doesn't sit around like an idiot."

"Yeah, but I don't see any women sitting alone except…" Suddenly, Tyler grinned. "It's you, isn't it."

Heat burned Dani's cheeks. "I was blackmailed."

Tyler laughed and slapped the table. "Let me grab my coffee, and you can tell me all about it. You want a pastry or something, since you already got yours?"

"No, I'm fine, thanks."

"All right, be right back."

He winked as he walked up to the counter with a cocky swagger, as if he knew she was checking out his ass. Dani noticed the pretty barista toss her dark hair back as he approached, and there was some definite eyelash fluttering going on.

This could not be any more humiliating.

When he finally came back and sat across from her with his cup, she noticed the name and phone number on the side of his cup.

"Aw, how cute. She dots her *i*'s with a heart."

"You don't?" he teased.

"No, I'm an adult."

"Ah, which explains why your parents are in charge of your dating life."

Dani's hackles went up. "Like I said, I was blackmailed into this date. Believe me, if I was interested, I could find my own dates."

"I believe it. You're beautiful, kind, caring…I imagine there's a lot of guys who would love to take you out."

Thunderstruck by his compliment, all she could say was, "Thank you."

"Which begs the question, why aren't you out there, finding your own dates?"

Dani wasn't interested in getting into her sordid and messy dating history, so she tried to keep it vague. "I'm too busy to date."

"And yet, you're here."

"Why are *you* here?" she snapped. "You obviously have no problem meeting girls."

"I was bribed, but we were talking about you. Why do your parents feel the need to set you up when you can obviously find your own man?"

Dani wasn't sure how much to say to him, so she chose a little vague honesty. "I don't exactly have the best track record with picking men and don't really trust my own judgment. Especially since I have Noah to consider. So, I just figure it's easier to not date than to make a mistake."

Tyler leaned over the table, his expression seductive. "And what's your judgment say about me?"

Her answer popped out before she could stop herself. "That you're a player and I'd be smart to get my ass up and walk out."

Tyler's eyes sparkled with humor. "I wouldn't use the word *player*…"

"Then what word would you use?"

"Flexible?"

"Your body?" *Holy shit, had she really just asked that?*

"No, but if you want to find out—"

"I don't." She knew she was red all the way down her neck, but there was nothing for it. "You shouldn't tease me, especially since I'm not your type."

His smile dissolved. "What makes you think you aren't my type?"

"Well, I have a child, for one thing. I noticed the way you reacted after you saw his picture on my phone. It's okay. Most guys run for the hills once they find out you're a single mom."

"Only because they know they can't handle the responsibility and don't want to waste your time," he said.

Her hand gripped her coffee cup so hard she felt it start to give. "My son is more than a responsibility. He's my light, my joy, and my world." Taking a drink of her coffee to hide her anger, she added, "Any man who looked at Noah as a chore he didn't think he could handle wouldn't be worth my time anyway."

Tyler stared at her so hard and long that she started to squirm. What was he thinking? That she had a big mouth? Or that she was just being defensive again?

"You're right. That's exactly how my mom felt before she married my stepdad."

He'd been raised by a single mom? Interesting.

"How old were you?" she asked.

"About eight. I was lucky, though; my dad always treated me the same as my half brother and sister. Some kids aren't so fortunate."

That was her constant fear. That she'd let someone in their lives who wouldn't love Noah as his own. She'd rather be alone forever than have her son hurt by another man's rejection.

"That's exactly why I don't date," she said.

Uncomfortable silence stretched between them, and finally she broke it by asking, "How's the dog? Did you ever rename him?"

"I'm calling him Duke."

"Duke. It's a good name."

"I just picked him up from the vet a couple of hours ago, so I need to get back soon."

"Oh, of course."

He seemed to hesitate before asking, "Okay, I know you barely know me, and I promise, I have no nefarious plans afoot, but if you want to see him, you're more than welcome to come over. I'm just in Natomas, about ten minutes up the freeway."

Going back to the house of a man she barely knew? What a ludicrous idea.

"Sure. I'd like to see him."

You are an idiot.

"Great, just follow me." He stood up and held the door for her as they left Starbucks with their drinks.

As she climbed into her car, the voice in her head silently scolded her.

We need to talk about your decision-making skills.

Chapter Six

TYLER STILL COULDN'T believe he'd invited her to his place, but it wasn't as if he could change his mind. Not when she was standing on his doorstep with him, waiting as he unlocked the door. She was so close, he could feel her body radiating heat amid the cool autumn breeze, and it was so distracting, he'd almost dropped his keys twice.

Get a grip, man; it's not as if you've never brought a woman home before.

Not that it was like that; he really had just invited her over to see the dog. Although, he had to admit, when he'd walked through the door and seen her sitting there, even if she hadn't been Kline's mystery date, he would have sat down anyway. There was something about her that intrigued him, and damned if he could figure out what it was.

"Do you need some help?"

He glanced over his shoulder at her, taking in her amusement. "I can get it."

"Before I'm thirty?" she asked.

"How long before you're thirty?" he asked, just as the lock turned.

"Six years."

Opening the door wide to let her in, he winked. "I think we're safe, then."

She chuckled as she passed by, and he shut the door, watching her glance around his bare house.

"Did you just move in?" she asked.

"A few months ago."

She shot him a look of disbelief, and he tried to see what had her so surprised. So the only furniture in the living room and kitchen were his couch and entertainment center. He didn't need much.

"Not a big nester, huh?" she said.

"What the hell is a nester?"

"Someone who settles in, decorates. Makes his place homey."

He had never been big for posters and stuff on his wall, and all his pictures could fit in his wallet. "Yeah, sorry, I flunked out of 'nester' school."

"That's okay. I forgive your lack of style."

He snorted, trying to bite back a smile. He liked her sass. "Duke is over there behind the couch."

"Did you name him after Duke Orsino?"

"Who?" Tyler squatted down in front of Duke's cage, ignoring Apollo and Zeus's whimpers. The big dog tried to stand up, but Dani crooned for him to stay down as she opened the cage.

"Duke Orsino from *She's the Man*."

"Is that a chick flick?" he asked.

"I guess so." She rubbed Duke's ears lovingly, and the dog gave a happy groan.

"Then, no. I named him after the *G.I. Joe* character."

"Well, you should watch it. It is hilarious," she said.

"I don't watch chick flicks."

Her mouth dropped. "You've never seen one…ever?"

"Why would I?" *I have a penis.* He didn't say that, though; he had some tact.

"Maybe with your mom or a sister or a girlfriend—"

"My mom and I watched Disney movies together when I was little, my sister is twelve years younger than me, and I've never had a girlfriend."

Why was she staring at him like he was an alien? "Not even in high school?"

"I dated. We hung out." *We fucked.* "But no, I've never had someone I'd willingly watch crap for."

"They aren't crap. They are funny, entertaining awesomeness, and you are missing out." She scooted in closer to him, and their thighs touched, sending a jolt of awareness through him. "How are you feeling, buddy?" she asked Duke. "You don't think that rom-coms are crap, do you?"

Duke made some kind of whimpering growl, and Tyler could have sworn the dog glared at him, clearly choosing sides.

"See, Duke gets it."

"Only because he's had his balls snipped."

Tyler expected her to act like a typical woman and call him sexist or whatever, but she just laughed. "Maybe, or maybe he just likes getting rubs and scratches."

Unfortunately, her words didn't play as innocently in his mind as she'd probably meant them, and he imagined letting Dani give him all kinds of rubs and scratches. Just the flash of Dani in his head, her mouth open in a little O as her nails raked down his back, his dick buried inside her warmth, left him with a semi pressing against the front of his jeans.

"How long will his recovery be?" she asked.

Trying to think of anything besides his dirty thoughts, he stood up and took a few steps away from her. "About six to eight weeks."

"Poor guy. That's a long time to chill out in a cage."

"He won't be stuck in there all the time. He has a cast on, so he should be able to get around okay once the leg heals a bit."

Dani closed the door and stood up. The way she was looking at him with those deep green eyes made him feel taller, stronger. No one had ever looked at him like that.

"Thank you for what you're doing for him."

"It was just a broken leg. He deserved better than to be put down for something that wasn't his fault."

Before he knew it, she'd stood up on tiptoe and kissed his cheek. "You can shrug it off, but it proves there's more to you than you let on."

She rocked back on her heels, and the heat of her mouth on his skin lingered. His gaze was fastened to those pink, plump lips, and if she had been any other woman, he'd be taking the invitation those parted lips offered.

But nothing had changed. He was the guy with nothing to lose, and she was a mom. Nothing was simple or easy, not where them hooking up was concerned.

"Well, um…I should get home. I have work tonight," she said.

The moment over, Tyler didn't know whether to feel relieved or to curse.

"How is Noah feeling?"

"Good, actually. No further complications."

"That's great. He's a cute kid."

"Thanks. It's hard, with it just being the two of us. My parents help out, but for the most part…" She trailed off, and her face flamed. "I have to go. Take care of Duke."

She just about raced for the door, and he caught up before she could fully close it, pausing in the open doorway, flummoxed. He'd never been so confused by a woman, but there he stood, puzzling and puzzling until his puzzler was sore.

What are you, the Grinch? Just be thankful your stupidity didn't get the best of you. The last thing you want to do is lead that poor woman on.

Still, her reaction to his comment was interesting. Almost as if she was afraid of telling him too much.

It was getting harder and harder to remember why he didn't want to get involved with her. Why couldn't he remember she was off limits?

DANI WANTED TO curse her own stupidity. The poor guy was just trying to be nice, and she'd started off on a *woe-is-me* speech. He was so sweet with her that sometimes she forgot he walked into a room and women fell at his feet.

Not that it was his fault he was handsome and charming, but that didn't mean she needed to be one of the simpering masses. Just thinking about the number on his coffee cup from that girl, how he'd tossed it in the trash like it wasn't a big deal…It made her want to hate him. How easy it was for him to get and discard attention.

She didn't, though. She might be jealous of how easy it was for him to pick up women, but she definitely didn't hate him.

No, for a split second before she'd kissed his slightly roughened cheek, she'd thought about kissing him on the lips. A simple peck of thanks.

Or so she told herself.

She'd chickened out, though, and after running out of there as if she'd had hellhounds on her heels, she was glad she hadn't gone there. It would have been a big slipup, and starting something up with a guy who was obviously a lady's man would have just been her making the same mistakes over again.

She needed someone who would not only accept Noah as his own, but also care for her. Be her partner in life.

If only she actually believed a man like that existed.

Chapter Seven

THE NEXT DAY at Alpha Dog, Tyler stood frustrated in front of his group of teenagers, who hadn't been listening to him since they'd assembled for training.

"What in the hell is wrong with you this morning? Fall in!"

His loud boom sent most of them scattering back into formation, save one. Carlos Mendez had been pushing back against their authority since he arrived at Alpha Dog a week ago, and nothing Tyler did, from making him do burpees to extra work, had seemed to curb his attitude.

"Mendez, get up here."

Carlos and his dog, Lucky, walked toward Tyler, with Lucky leading Mendez. Tyler nearly started yelling again about letting the dog lead, but he held his tongue. When the sullen kid finally stood before him, his dark hooded eyes narrowed and his mouth set in a stubborn line, Tyler rolled his shoulders and decided to try something a little different.

"Who's the boss, you or him?"

"Shit, I'm the boss."

Tyler nearly rolled his eyes at the kid's bravado. "You think so, huh? Fine." Waving his hand out, he said, "Then I want you to teach the rest of us how to train a dog."

Mendez's hard expression slipped a bit, but Tyler just took Apollo and went to stand next to Hank Osbourne, one of the youngest kids at Alpha Dog. The teenager was staring at Mendez with what appeared to be exasperation.

At least Tyler wasn't the only one fed up with the little punk.

"Okay, Mendez, show us something."

The hotshot actually swaggered as he and Lucky got into position. Lucky, a muscular boxer mix, had a strong, dominant personality, but he was trainable. Tyler had high hopes for the dog, which was why he'd paired him with Mendez.

But if the kid didn't get his shit together, he was going to find himself back in juvie, serving out his sentence there for trying to steal a car.

"Lucky, sit," Mendez said. There was no treat or ball in the hand he held above Lucky's head, not that the dog was watching him. He was actually looking at Tyler as if to say, *Is this kid for real?*

Several snickers throughout the group of boys rose up, and Mendez jerked his head toward them, scowling.

"Sit, you stupid dog."

Still, Lucky ignored him. As more murmurs and chuckles rose up from the other boys, Mendez turned an ugly shade of red. Then Tyler watched Mendez's body language change. Apprehension shot through Tyler, filling him with adrenaline. Without saying a word, he dropped Apollo's leash just as Mendez kicked out at Lucky, catching the dog in the chest.

The dog yelped at the same time Tyler yanked Mendez by the arm and pulled him away. "You're done here."

"Motherfucking dog—"

Tyler grabbed the kid by the front of his shirt, his fist trembling with barely restrained rage. He wanted to pummel him to a bloody pulp, but he was a minor under Tyler's care. He could restrain him, but other than that, he'd have to rely on the system to do its job.

"We have a policy here to keep these animals, who have already been through more than they should, safe. You've had plenty of chances to change your behavior, but you've done nothing but show your disdain for what we do. All of that could be forgiven, but not this."

Mendez spit in his face, the slimy ball oozing down Tyler's cheek. "Fuck you."

Tyler shoved Mendez to the ground and took the cuffs from his belt, securing them on his wrists. When Tyler stood up, Mendez rolled over onto his side, a long string of curses exploding from his mouth. Tyler wiped his face with his shirt while the kid glared at him from the ground, but Tyler was done letting him be macho. "You really blew it; you know that, right?" Pulling out his walkie-talkie, he held the button down.

"Kline."

"Sergeant Kline, Carlos Mendez will no longer be staying with us. Can you please come out and retrieve him? And let the judge know he's a violent little prick who likes to kick dogs."

"Ten-four."

While Mendez struggled to get to his feet, Tyler spoke to the rest of the teenagers. "Let this be a lesson to all of you. Any abuse allegations will be dealt with swiftly and harshly. If you do not report it, you will be removed from the program for being complicit. We are these animals' last hope, and they deserve to be treated with respect." Staring directly at Mendez, Tyler added, "Lucky didn't respect you because he knew you were a coward, too scared to be his leader."

Mendez cursed him, but Tyler ignored the little shit. Approaching Lucky slowly and calmly, he knelt down in from of the dog. He tried to shy away, and Tyler spoke softly. "It's okay, Lucky. You're safe."

The dog's brindled head dipped as he approached. When he finally stopped and sat before Tyler, Tyler rubbed his ears and fed him a treat from his bag.

"Good boy."

The dog reacted excitedly, practically crawling onto his lap. Laughing, Tyler started to stand up, and one of the guys shouted, "Look out!"

Pain exploded in the middle of his back, and he was propelled forward. Lucky moved out of the way swiftly as Tyler hit the ground with a heavy weight on his back.

"You still think I'm a coward, *puta*?"

Dazed and with the wind knocked clear the hell out of him, it took Tyler a second to throw his weight to the side and come out on top of Mendez. His back throbbed with the pain of where Mendez's head had hit his spine, and his knee protested as he dug it into Mendez's back, but he ignored it all.

"Somebody grab Lucky!" Tyler shouted. It wasn't as if the dog could go anywhere besides the fenced yard, but Tyler didn't want him thinking he could just take off.

Dwayne Harlow handed off his leash to Olsen Meyers and ran after the loose dog.

Mendez lay on the ground, still talking shit, and Tyler finally addressed him.

"You asked if I still thought you were a coward? The answer is yes. I think only a coward would attack someone when his back was turned."

"Yo, everything okay out here?" Kline called from the fence.

Tyler stood up gingerly. "Yeah, just get him the fuck out of my sight."

Kline grabbed Mendez and lifted him nearly off his feet. "No problem."

Mendez kept shouting curses at him as Kline hauled him off, and Tyler grimaced. Turning back to face the rest of his guys, his tone was harsh. "Anyone else want to piss me off today?"

No one said a word. Dwayne, who always seemed to be smiling and was one of Tyler's favorites, came back to the group with Lucky, as stone-faced as the rest of them. Tyler went to retrieve Lucky from him.

"Thanks for grabbing him, Harlow."

Dwayne gave him that gamin grin. "You're welcome, boss."

Walking the length of the group to grab Apollo, Tyler said, "Why don't you guys take the dogs for a run around the fence perimeter, and the fastest team without cutting corners"—Tyler gave Hank a warning look, as the kid liked to cheat if he got the chance—"gets an extra privilege."

The group of teenagers and dogs took off like a flash, and Tyler finally gave into the groan of pain he'd been holding in. As soon as they went into class, he was going to take some Tylenol and ice his back.

Not exactly a stellar start to the day.

"Yo!" Sparks called from behind him, drawing him out of his pity party.

"What's up?"

"How come I saw Kline hauling Mendez out of here?"

"Because I kicked him out. The little prick attacked Lucky and me." The kids were coming back at full speed with Dwayne in the front, a wide grin on his face. His dog Charlie's lips flapped up like a set of wings as he ran. The hound mix was all wrinkles and ears, but he was going to make a fantastic search-and-rescue dog.

Dwayne whipped past them, followed closely by Olsen and his Border collie mix, Rambo. The rest of the group stampeded past, and Tyler hollered, "Harlow wins. Now get your dogs some water and head inside. Go straight to study hall; I'll be there in a few minutes. If I arrive and any of you are not there, it's gonna be a bad day for you, too."

Once the kids were out of earshot, Sparks gave him a raised eyebrow. "You okay?"

"I'm fine except I had a buck-fifty kid ram me right in the middle of my spine."

"Didn't you cuff him after he attacked the dog?" Sparks asked.

"Yeah…He got back up and used his head."

He could tell Sparks wanted to laugh; his mouth was doing that twitchy thing. "Well, the good news is he's gone, and the better news is we got a new transfer who can take over Lucky's training. I think he's going to work out."

"It's my job to place the dogs with the kids." Although, maybe if he'd done a better job reading Mendez, Lucky wouldn't have been kicked.

"Whoa, easy, I am not trying to take your job, but I think you're going to mesh well with this kid. Judge Haskins just faxed me his file, and I thought you might like to read it."

Tyler took the file, holding the dogs' leashes in one hand so he could open it. Jeremiah Walton. Age: Fourteen. Charges: Vandalism and destruction of property.

Tyler turned over the page to read the crime report, his eyes narrowing. His mom's husband, Neil Kenetti, had been beating her, and when Jeremiah tried to step in, Neil knocked him around. Afraid he would kill them, Jeremiah ran outside and took a baseball bat to Neil's car and then several cars down the block, setting off alarms all over the neighborhood. Neil started to chase Jeremiah down the street, and when people came out asking what was going on, Neil took off.

"Why didn't the kid call the cops? Or go to a neighbor's house and have them call?"

"Check the address. It's one of those neighborhoods where people don't want to get involved…unless it somehow affects them. And he didn't have a cell phone."

"Still, why the hell is he being charged with anything?"

"Because the mom wouldn't testify against her new husband, and several of the neighbors' cars had minor damage."

Tyler's hands clenched around the file as he nodded. His mom had never been beaten, but she'd been taken advantage of before his dad had come into the picture. He'd been too young to help, to know what was going on, but if anyone had laid a hand on her…

For some reason, Dani's pretty face flashed through his mind. He could never imagine fierce, protective Dani letting anyone hurt her, let alone Noah.

"You're right. I want him."

Sparks slapped him on the back. "I thought you might."

Sparks started to turn away, but before he even knew what he wanted to ask, Tyler blurted, "Were you ever freaked about hooking up with Violet? I mean, once you found out she was raising her brother and sister?"

Sparks paused and seemed to consider his answer. "Yeah, I had reservations. I mean, Violet is essentially a single mom. It's a big commitment, because if things go south, it's not just the two of you, but also the kid you have to consider."

Tyler nodded. It was exactly what he'd thought. There was no way around it; no matter how much he may be attracted to Dani, she was in the small percentage of women who were off limits.

"Why do you ask?"

Tyler just shrugged off Sparks's question. "You know, just curious is all."

"You finally thinking of settling down or something?"

Tyler cracked up. "Me? Dude, you know me. I'm not ready to stop living yet."

And then Sparks said something that was like a gut punch. "I thought the same thing, but honestly? I realized I wasn't really alive until I met Violet."

As Tyler followed Sparks back inside, he thought about his life. About his bare house and his weekends filled with beer, women, and late nights, and he wondered for the first time if Sparks might be on to something.

Chapter Eight

TYLER AND HIS friends were out at Mick's, a military bar in Old Town, shooting pool and drinking beer. Although they used to hang out several times a week, with Martinez and Sparks both in serious relationships, they had cut it down to just once, maybe twice. It sucked for Tyler, because this time out with his friends was almost cathartic. They talked about all the shit going on personally and at the program; anything he needed to get off his chest, he could do on nights like this.

He stood at the edge of the pool table, drinking from his beer glass, and realized that this time was coming to an end. Tyler was twenty-eight, and already his group of single friends was down by half. It wouldn't be long before Kline got back out there and met someone new, and then he'd be the last man standing.

Sure, there were other trainers he could hang with, but these were the men he'd been through some shit with. And not just group therapy—he knew he could call on them anytime, and they would have his back.

Friends like that were hard to find, and it sucked to lose them.

"Yo, Best, mind if we join you?" a woman asked behind Tyler. He turned around and found Megan Bryce, one of the newest Alpha Dog trainers, standing with Slater Vincent. Slater had been assigned to Alpha Dog right before Bryce and was a silent dude, hardly the social type with anyone except Bryce.

Tyler couldn't blame the man. Bryce's thick brown hair, clear blue eyes, and compact body were definitely attractive.

Damn, Tyler was going to have to add another type of woman to avoid: the coworker. Because every fiber of his being was tempted to flirt with her.

"No, you're both welcome, but you get the next round," Tyler said.

Tyler's phone started buzzing in his pocket, and when he pulled it out to check the screen, an unknown number flashed at him. He was tempted not to answer it, but he found himself sliding his thumb across the green phone icon.

"Hello?" Damn, it was hard to hear in the loud bar. "Hang on a second; I'm having trouble hearing you." Pushing his way up the stairs through the throng of bodies, he finally made it outside onto the planked walkway. "Sorry, who is this?"

"Is this Tyler Best?" a woman asked.

Tyler started to get antsy, wondering if this was a former lover calling with bad news. "Yeah, that's me."

"Mr. Best, this is Fiona McCarthy at Mercy San Juan. I'm calling about Henry Coleson. He has you listed as his next of kin, is that right?"

Ah, no.

"Yes, that's correct."

"I am very sorry to call like this, but Henry passed away forty-five minutes ago," she said.

"What do I need to do?" he asked.

"Well, his instructions include being cremated, and he left detailed instructions for you, as well as a private letter. If it's a bad time, you can come by and pick up everything tomorrow, and we can release him to the crematorium then—"

"I'll come now," Tyler said.

"Oh, all right. Well, I'll have everything waiting for you."

"I appreciate that. Thanks."

Tyler hung up the phone and swiftly sent a text to Kline, letting him know where he'd gone. Tyler hadn't talked about Henry to anyone but Blake. Not because he didn't trust his other friends, but because…Hell, he just hadn't.

Damn, he couldn't believe he was gone. He'd been preparing for this moment since the first day he met Henry, but he hadn't actually ever pictured how he'd react. For someone he hadn't even known a year ago, Henry had touched something inside him.

But when Henry had told him he had nobody, Tyler hadn't realized what he'd actually meant. That Tyler was the only person in the world he could release his body to. A guy he had only known six months.

How fucking sad was that?

TYLER STOOD AT the top of the scenic overlook on Highway 50 several days later, looking out over the view. The blue of Lake Tahoe was almost crystalline in the early morning sunlight, the rays twinkling off the surface from a distance.

Tyler held the urn that held Henry Coleson's ashes and a bottle of whiskey in the other. Henry's letter was stuffed into his back pocket, but the instructions were burned into Tyler's brain.

No one was traveling this early on a Friday, so Tyler dumped the container of ashes over the side of the mountain, watching them float down like a gray cloud into the fog below. Setting the container by his feet, he opened up the bottle of Jack Daniel's and held the bottle up.

"Henry, if you're looking down right now, I want you to know that I could get arrested for this."

He could practically hear the wheezy chuckle on the wind. *Just shut the fuck up and get it done, you pussy.*

Tyler took a swig, letting the liquor light a fire down his throat and blamed it for the tears in his eyes. After pouring some over the side after the ashes, Tyler replaced the lid and went back to his car, shivering against the cold.

On his passenger seat sat a box of Henry's things, and the rest Tyler had put in his place while he figured out what to do with them. It had been a little funny that Henry's small, one-bedroom apartment had been better furnished than Tyler's big house, but it was going through Henry's personal items that had really gotten to him.

Tyler pulled the letter out of his pocket and sat there on the shoulder for a moment. Henry had left him all his worldly possessions and the money left in his savings and checking accounts, which hadn't been a ton but was still enough to pay for Henry's cremation with some left over.

He didn't care about the money, though. He unfolded the letter, reading Henry's words again with a sad smile.

Tyler,

We both knew this was coming, and I wanted to be prepared before I got called home. I know it's weird putting the responsibility of my aftercare on your shoulders, but like I said, I was only ever good at two things, and keeping friends wasn't one of them. I lost them to war or suicide or because I slept with their wives. I was a pretty shitty guy, and I have a feeling I'm not meeting Saint Peter at the pearly gates.

From the minute I bumped into you on the way to radiology, I've looked at you like the son I could have had, if I'd ever pulled my head out of my ass and settled down. And I see the path you're headed for. You're a good man. Hell, you'd have to be to visit this old asshole in and out of the hospital for six months.

But you gotta have more to your life to make it meaningful. Meet a nice girl, and get married. Pop a couple of kids out, and be good to them. That way, when it's your time to say good-bye, someone really cares.

When I was pushing forty, I met this beautiful girl named Vicky. I was stationed in San Diego, and she was working as a waitress at this restaurant my friends and I used to haunt. She was going to college part-time for her degree. She wanted to be a teacher, have a bunch of kids, and I loved her, at least, as much as I could have. But I started to doubt myself, especially watching how many of my friends sank into a shit hole of drugs and drink. When the chance came for me to serve in the Gulf War, I took it and told her I was leaving. When she asked what it meant for us, I told her not to wait. And she listened to me. I tried to track her down when I got back, but I had missed my chance. She married and had the kids she wanted, and she's still alive, living in Arizona.

The point of the story is, don't miss yours. Watch for every sign the universe throws your way. I know I sound like a fucking sentimental idiot, but you can learn from me. Don't spend your life looking for the next thing that's going to make you feel good for a few minutes; look for something that is going to make you happy for decades.

That's it. That's all I can leave you with, besides all the shit I collected over my life. Throw it away or pack it up to show your kids someday that you knew this guy once who did a few things.

Take Care,

Henry Coleson

Tyler put the letter in the box and started his car up, then headed down the grade toward Lake Tahoe, thinking about the letter. Just because he liked his life the way it was didn't mean he was going to end up alone. He had plenty of time to settle down. Besides, he didn't screw his friends over.

And how many women have you screwed and never called again? Doesn't exactly make you a good guy.

Tyler ignored the voice and kept driving toward salvation. He'd booked a room for two nights in Tahoe, and Blake was going to meet him later. Gambling, drinking, and dancing were exactly what he needed.

But as the hotels of the strip came into view, Henry's words played through his head.

You gotta have more to your life to make it meaningful... Don't ignore the signs.

DANI WAS IN the kitchen making breakfast for Noah when her best friend, Lana Davison, called. Lana and she didn't talk very often, maybe once every couple of weeks, but they were still close. Things had changed when Dani had become a mom. Lana would call up and ask her to go dancing or to lunch, but Dani either couldn't because of Noah or needed to bring him along. After a while, the invitations had become less frequent, and when Lana had celebrated her twenty-fourth birthday with a trip up to Tahoe, Dani had tried not to be hurt that she wasn't even invited.

They'd finally talked about what was going on and were in a good place again, but Dani couldn't deny that their friendship was forever changed.

"Hey, Lan, how are you?"

"I'm engaged!" Lana screamed.

Dani spilled the milk she'd been pouring on the counter with a cry. "Oh my God, congratulations! Nick proposed? When?"

"Last night. He took me out to dinner and tied the ring to a glass of champagne."

"That is romantic! I am so happy for you." Dani ignored the twinge of jealousy stirring in her gut.

"Thank you! And as my oldest friend, I need you to be my maid of honor!"

Dollar signs flashed across Dani's eyes as she thought about all the responsibilities. Organizing the bridal shower and bachelorette party, buying the bridesmaid dress and shoes. Hair appointments, nail appointments, gifts.

Swallowing down the bile of panic, she said, "When is the wedding?"

"We're thinking of June but haven't nailed down an exact date yet."

Relief seeped through her. She could build up her savings and be able to work with that.

"Okay, I should be able to handle that."

"What do you mean?" Lana asked.

"Well, I just took on a second job a few weeks ago, and my car bit the dust the same day that Noah had to spend the night at the hospital because he was puking blood. Thank God he didn't have to have surgery, but I'm going to have some hefty bills hitting me this month, and I was just panicked for a moment, but I think it will all work out great."

Lana was silent on the other end.

"Lana? Did I lose you?"

"No, I'm here." Her tone was curt, and Dani wondered what in the hell she'd said.

"Is something wrong?"

"I called to share something wonderful with you, and you act as if I'm inconveniencing you."

Dani was completely floored. "That's not what I was doing! I said I could do it but was just telling you, my friend, about the horrible week I've had. And did you miss the part about my son *puking blood*?"

"Yes, I heard you, and he's obviously fine. I just can't believe how self-centered you've become. Every time I call you, no matter what is going on with me, it always gets turned around to you and that kid."

Now Dani's skin prickled with fury, and her voice came out tight. " 'That kid' is my son. And I'm sorry that I don't have anything more stimulating for you besides talking about him, but this is my life. I work and I come home and love my kid."

"Well, that's just sad."

The sneer was evident without Dani even seeing it, and Dani's eyes stung with tears of hurt and anger.

"You know what, Lana? You should pick someone else, because I'm obviously not the right person to be your maid of honor."

"Fine."

The call ended with a beep as Lana hung up, and Dani put her cell down, silently saying good-bye to the last friend she had outside of work. All of her other high-school buddies had drifted off after she'd quit the party scene, but Lana had stuck with her.

Was she self-centered? Dani didn't think so, but looking back on conversations she'd had with Lana or the few times they'd gone out, she couldn't totally ignore the fact that the conversation would often come back to Noah. Noah getting his first tooth, his first steps, and all the other amazing things he did. At least, amazing for her.

But even if she talked about Noah a lot, Lana was wrong. She'd slowly been easing Dani out of her life, and this apparently had been the final test: Would Dani choose Lana?

As sad as it was to say good-bye to the last piece of her past, Dani also felt a tremendous amount of relief. She deserved friends whose values and place in life matched her own. For too long, Lana and she had been trying to stay friends even though it almost came out forced, as if waiting for things to go back to the way things were.

But life was forever changing, and people drifted apart.

Lana's words still ate at her, though. *That kid.* It reminded her of Tyler and his wisdom about how some men just weren't ready for the responsibility of becoming a parent. Just like some people couldn't understand how the needs of her child were more important than a three-hundred-dollar dress and a night out with strippers. Those kinds of people were the ones she should be avoiding anyway.

"Mama?" Noah toddled into the kitchen, finally giving up on his Duplo block tower.

"Hey, sweetie, wanna help me with breakfast?" She picked him up in her arms and kissed his temple.

No more distractions or other people getting in the way. It was time to get back to just Noah and her against the world.

Chapter Nine

One Week Later

DANI PULLED INTO the parking lot of the park, smiling as Noah squealed excitedly from the backseat. Dani had been working her butt off all month to pay off the repairs she'd needed on her car, and it felt like she'd hardly seen her baby at all. But today was the first day of her two weeks of paid vacation from the clinic, and although she only worked at the shelter twice a week, she'd gone ahead and taken the time off from them as well. She planned to spend as much time as she could with her son.

Climbing out of her door, she went to the back of the car first and grabbed the dogs' leashes. Both of them nearly bolted away from her in their excitement to see the green grass, but she quickly got control of them and went to pull Noah out of the car. First, she struggled to get him into his warm, puffy jacket and mittens; then she placed his little knit cap with bear ears on top of his head. Finally, balancing him on her hip, she grabbed the diaper bag, and now that she was officially loaded up like a pack mule, she kissed Noah's cheek.

"You ready to play?"

"Yay! Play!"

Once they were safely on the grass, Dani let Noah down to walk beside her and the dogs. They were the only ones in the park right now, probably because of the definite nip in the air, or maybe it was just too early for most people. Whatever the reason, the cooler temperature didn't seem to bother Noah as he rushed toward the playground.

"Hang on, Noah, wait for Mama." Dani found a good spot and drilled her two anchors into the ground. Hooking Shasta's and Bella's long leashes onto them, she spread out the quilt from her diaper bag and left the bag on the blanket to catch up to her toddling son, who had ignored her directive and was making his way toward the stairs.

"Hey!" she said in her loud mom voice. Noah stopped in his tracks and turned around, his thumb in his mouth. Dani knelt in front of him and spoke a little softer. "When Mama tells you to wait, you wait. Got it?"

Noah nodded, and Dani smiled. "Okay, climb."

Popping his thumb out of his mouth with a grin, he started climbing. Dani followed along beside him all the way to the top of the smaller slide. Dani's heart still climbed up and lodged itself in her throat every time, but she knew it was good to let him explore, to test his limits and gain confidence.

She didn't need to transfer any of her fears onto Noah. She wanted him to be braver, stronger...

Better than she could ever be.

Suddenly, Shasta let out a guttural snarl and started barking. Dani caught Noah as he came down the slide and carried him over to the blanket to see what was bothering the dog.

In the parking lot was a tall man in a dark poofy jacket and beanie. In his hand was the leash of a large gray dog walking with a definite limp.

No way. It couldn't be.

But as the pair moved closer to where Dani stood, she recognized Tyler's handsome face and nearly groaned with frustration. As the only people in the park, it wasn't as if she could ignore him.

What are you obsessing about? Because you got defensive? Or that you almost lost your mind and kissed him?

She knew by the expression on his face that he recognized her and held up her hand. "Hey there."

"Hi." He stopped a few feet from her, Duke at his side. In the weeks since she'd seen the dog, he'd put on weight, and although he was still dragging a cast along on his back leg, he looked good.

"Duke looks healthy."

"So does Noah."

Dani looked over at Noah, who was climbing back up to the top of the smaller slide. He slid down with a squeal, and before Dani could run over and catch him, he hit the ground on his butt.

His big eyes shot to hers in surprise, and she almost giggled at his expression. Except she could feel Tyler's gaze on her and wondered if he was judging her.

"Whoa, buddy, was that fast!" Tyler's tone was excited and jovial, and the toddler instantly responded by laughing.

"Yeah!" Climbing to his sneakered feet, he came over to stand next to Dani, never taking his eyes off Tyler. "Puppy?"

Dani couldn't believe Noah remembered the puppy from the hospital.

Tyler knelt down, and she admired his attempts to avoid Duke's tongue. "Hey, Noah. I'm Tyler. I don't think we were ever properly introduced."

Shasta and Bella whined and whimpered, straining at the end of their leashes, and Shasta growled as Tyler leaned toward Noah with his hand out.

"It's okay," Dani said. The dog quieted, but Dani took comfort in her protectiveness.

When Noah ignored his hand, Tyler took it in stride. "The puppy I brought to see you got a new home, and so did his brother, Zeus. They were adopted by a couple of kids with special needs, and the puppies are going to help them. Isn't that great?"

Noah nodded, and in a flash, he was headed back to the playground equipment.

"Well, he's obviously really broken up about not seeing the puppy," Tyler joked.

"Yeah, kids tend to have a short attention span."

"You don't say?"

"Oh yes." Dani ran over and picked up a cigarette butt just before Noah bent over. "And they're quick."

"Do you mind if I introduce myself to your dogs?"

Dani lifted Noah up and came over. "Sure, the big cautious one is Shasta, and the pug is Bella. They're fine. Shasta just gets a little protective of Noah."

"Good with other dogs?" Tyler held his hand out to her dogs, and Shasta sniffed him excitedly.

"They both love other dogs, although Bella can get a little bossy." Noah struggled in her arms, wanting back down.

"You like to be the boss, huh?" Tyler cupped the sides of Bella's face and scrunched up his own, making Dani laugh. She liked that he was a dog person; so many people didn't get her love of animals.

Duke and the girls sniffed at each other as Tyler stood up, and she noticed him wince. "Are you okay?"

"Yeah, my knee just aches sometimes," he said.

"What happened?"

"I was shot."

Dani was just letting Noah back down, and her gaze jerked up to his. "Shot?"

Tyler chuckled. "What did you think I did before Alpha Dog?"

"I don't know. I mean, I knew you were in the military, but I never imagined that you..." She trailed off, unsure of what else to say.

"It was just part of the gig."

Dani studied him and saw the pain in his eyes, knowing there was more to the story, but it wasn't her place to ask.

Tyler looked away, putting Duke into a down-stay, and Dani, realizing that she'd stared at him too long, jerked her gaze away to find Noah back on the play structure, heading toward the highest area.

Panic seized her, tightening her chest. "Noah, no! Come back down, please."

The toddler paused for half a second and glanced at her before he kept crawling up. Fear and anger bubbled within her as she ran toward the structure, taking the steps at full speed. She stepped onto the top of the first level just as Noah reached out for the large pole.

"Noah!"

Her son jumped at her harsh tone, and all she could do was watch in horror as her baby pitched forward off the structure toward the ground.

TYLER SAW THE kid lose his balance as if in slow motion, his little arms flapping in the air like a bird. Tyler didn't even realize he was moving until he caught Noah in his arms, bringing the kid in close to his chest. The blood pounded in his ears as his adrenaline rushed through, and he barely registered Dani's terrified cries, he was so focused on the trembling kid in his arms.

"Oh my God, Noah!" Dani was suddenly in front of him, tears streaming down her pale cheeks as she reached for her son.

Tyler passed Noah over, and Dani squeezed him, burying her face into his neck as she sobbed. Noah burst into loud wails as Dani rocked him in her arms, murmuring soothingly.

Tyler checked on the dogs; Shasta and Bella were straining at the end of their leashes once more, while Duke still lay there. After his temperament test, Tyler had been working on his training and found he was already accomplished in obedience. The dude was completely chill, and Tyler had done everything he could to find his owners, but no one had responded to his Craigslist ad. Tyler had decided to keep it up until the cast came off, but at this point, Tyler already felt as if Duke had always been his.

His focus once again on Dani, he could tell she was experiencing an emotional roller coaster when she pulled away from Noah and scolded, "When Mama tells you to stop, you stop! Do you know how badly you could have been hurt?"

Followed by another crushing hug that was probably cutting off the kid's air supply, but Tyler wasn't going to interfere. He'd experienced enough of them from his own mom to know that when a mother was scared or her baby was hurt, you did not mess with her.

Dani's wet green eyes met his, her lip trembling. "You must think I'm the worst mother in the world."

"Are you kidding? My mom once turned her back, and I hid in the Macy's men's department for ten minutes. She was in such a panic, and I came out laughing, 'Here I am, Mommy!' "

"Oh, God, I would have died. How old were you?"

"Four, I think? She still says that took years off her life."

"I know the feeling." She kissed Noah's head. "I think that's enough park for Mama."

Noah surprisingly didn't protest, but Tyler realized that he didn't want them to leave.

"What if I took Mommy and Noah out for a hot chocolate and a muffin?"

Noah poked his head up at the mention of hot chocolate, but Dani looked like she was about to decline.

"You really don't have to do that—"

"You don't like muffins?" Tyler asked innocently.

"Of course we do; everybody likes muffins."

"Then it's no problem. We can head up to LaBou and sit outside with the dogs."

He could tell she was still hesitant, but Noah seemed to be watching her with pleading eyes.

"Okay, sure. We would love to have muffins with you."

"Chocolate," Noah whispered.

Tyler's heart skipped at the sweet smile she gave her son, their cheeks still wet from their tears.

Clearing his throat, he said, "You handle him, and I'll help you get packed up."

She didn't argue with him, and he went about folding up their quilt, surprised at himself. If he was so hell-bent on steering clear of Dani and Noah, why hadn't he just said hi and moved on? What was going on with him?

Maybe Henry's advice got to you more than you realized.

Picking up her diaper bag and the dogs leashes, he stood up with a laugh. Just because he hadn't hooked up with a woman for a while, even in Tahoe, didn't mean he was looking to settle down.

"I think we're all packed up," he said.

She looked a little embarrassed, with her cheeks stained red and her eyes slightly downcast. "I'm sorry; we were planning to make a morning of it, so I always pack more than I need."

"You don't have to apologize, really." As they started walking back to the cars, the dogs all fell in line beside them, although the dog she'd called Shasta kept turning her head to check on her humans. It was exactly how Rex had been with him.

When she opened up the back for him, he loaded her dogs and shut the door. Standing alongside her car, he waited as she buckled Noah in. When she finally pulled her head back out and reached for her bag, he handed it to her slowly, their hands brushing. Tyler resisted the urge to wrap his fingers around hers, so delicious was the shock between them.

Instead, he released the strap quickly, holding tight to Duke's leash.

"So, should I just follow you?" she asked.

Standing so close to her, with her looking up at him expectantly, he was tempted to kiss her. To see if she tasted as sweet as she looked.

Backing toward his car slowly, he decided any sudden movements might lead him down a rabbit hole of stupidity. "Yeah, you can follow."

Chapter Ten

DANI SAT AT the outside table with Noah and all three dogs, staring in the window at Tyler ordering their food. The young barista behind the counter smiled at him with definite interest, and Dani wished it didn't bother her so much.

"Game?" Noah asked.

Knowing what Noah was asking for, Dani prodded, "What do you say?"

"Pwease."

Dani bent into the diaper bag and pulled out his Leap-Frog tablet. She didn't let him have it often, mostly for trips in the car, but it was a nice little distraction.

Tyler came outside holding a drink carrier and a white food bag. "All right, I've got the good stuff." As he sat down, he placed cups in front of all of them. Before Noah could reach for his cup, Dani took it and tasted it, making sure it wasn't too hot. With a smile, she handed it back to Noah. "Perfect."

"I told them it was for a little kid and not to make it too hot."

"Thank you." Dani took a sip of the chai latte he'd bought her with a sigh. "This is heaven."

"Wow, your pleasure bar is set pretty low," Tyler said teasingly.

Dani's cheeks burned at the term *pleasure*. "Considering I've been working fifty hours a week or more for the last three weeks, I haven't had a lot of time to enjoy the little things."

"Does that mean I crashed a mother and son date?" Tyler pulled out half a muffin and set it on a napkin for Noah. "I could have gotten a whole one for each of you."

She'd told him they'd split a muffin and was happy he'd listened. "He won't eat it all. And no, you didn't crash the date. Noah and I have two weeks of fun planned."

"Oh yeah, you on vacation or something?"

"Yeah, we can never really afford to go anywhere, so I just take my two weeks and we do day trips. The beach, the zoo, Apple Hill…things I think he'll enjoy."

"That's good. Quality time is important."

She raised her eyebrow at him. "I thought you didn't know a lot about kids."

"I don't, but I have a great mom. She worked full time until she married my dad, well stepdad, but before that, she always spent her days off with me. It meant a lot, and I never questioned that she loved me."

Hearing Tyler speak so openly and warmly about his mom made her heart stutter.

"Oh man, I blew it, huh? You think I'm a mama's boy now."

"No! No, I think it's sweet." Running her hand over Noah's soft curls, she admitted, "I hope someday that Noah talks about me like that."

Tyler handed her the other half of the muffin. "He will, trust me."

And then he pulled out two foil-wrapped croissant sandwiches.

"Are those both for you?" she asked.

With a wink, he opened one up and took a bite. "I'm a big guy with a healthy appetite."

"Apparently."

"Hey now, it isn't nice to call someone a pig."

Her cheeks burned. "I didn't!"

"You insinuated."

Dani grinned sheepishly. "I did, I'm sorry."

"You're forgiven." Wiping his hand on a napkin, he moved closer to Noah. "Hey, dude, what are you watching on here?"

Noah held the tablet out to him, and Tyler squinted at the screen. "Who is this guy?"

"Mickey," Noah said.

"Mickey, huh? Is he cool?"

Noah nodded, his gaze straying back to the tablet.

"Noah, why don't we put the tablet away—"

Tyler glanced up at her and said quietly, "It's okay with me. Besides, I want to know if Mickey finds all the sheep, don't you, Noah?"

Could ovaries really explode? Because Dani was pretty sure hers just had.

ONCE THE EPISODE was over, Tyler let Dani take Noah's tablet back. They had only watched about five minutes of the episode, but it turned out taking an interest in Noah's favorite show had endeared him to the toddler. In fact, when Noah had offered him a slimy piece of muffin with an earnest expression on his sweet face, Tyler hadn't been able to refuse.

He'd taken the soggy piece and pretended to put it in his mouth, chewing with closed-mouth gusto. Noah, delighted, tried to share some more, but Tyler said, "Oh, no thanks, buddy, you eat it. I'm full."

He puffed out his cheeks, and Noah giggled, showing muffin-caked teeth, but instead of being grossed out, Tyler laughed along with him.

And then he'd caught Dani watching them, sipping her latte silently. Her expression wasn't the same as the one from the hospital. That one had scared the hell out of him.

Instead, the warm look she gave him made him feel heroic.

It was a crazy notion, but he liked Dani and Noah. This morning had been fun, even with that scary part. He'd relaxed and opened up like he'd never done with a woman. Talking about his mom like that…Any of his friends would have given him all kinds of hell, but Dani had admired him for it.

It was a bit of an ego boost; he wasn't going to lie. He'd had women admire him for his body, his face, or his charm, but no one had ever caught a glimpse of the guy beneath. At least, he didn't think so, but there was an ease with Dani he appreciated.

Suddenly, Noah and Dani started giggling, and Tyler came out of his musings to find his sandwich gone. Staring down at the three possible suspects, he pursed his mouth. Bella stood under Duke as if trying to catch any scraps being dropped, while Shasta sniffed at Duke's mouth.

"After all I've done for you, you steal my breakfast?"

Duke licked his chops in response.

"Shasta is just sad she didn't get to it first. She's notorious for snatching food off the table when my back is turned."

"So you're saying we both have dogs that are sneaky thieves?" he said.

"Most definitely."

Tyler picked up his second sandwich and took a bite, making happy noises as he watched the three dogs staring at him.

"Okay, now you're just teasing them," Dani said.

"Damn straight, think they can just take my sandwich—"

Tyler jerked his sandwich back just as a giggling Noah reached for it.

"You trying to swipe my food now, too?"

"Noah—" Dani started to say, but Tyler interrupted her.

"You're gonna take the dogs' side, huh? I see how it is." Shoving the sandwich into his mouth and holding it there, he reached out to tickle Noah. The little boy squealed as Tyler's fingers attacked his ribs.

"Mama!"

"I'm coming, Noah." Dani's voice was filled with laughter as she came around the table behind Tyler to help her son.

The sandwich fell onto the table, and Tyler swallowed the bite in his mouth. "You two are tag-teaming me now?" He grabbed Dani when she tried to get by and pulled her onto his lap. "That's fine, I'll get you, too!"

But with Dani's mouth just a hairbreadth from his, her soft round ass pressing into him, both of them stilled. Their breath mingled, and Tyler's eyes locked with her bright green ones.

"Mama."

Noah had crawled out of his chair and was struggling to climb on top of Dani. Once the toddler had put himself between them, he wrapped his chubby arms around her neck. "My mama."

The spell broken, Tyler helped them both off of his lap, trying to ignore the hard-on that had sprung to life.

"Sorry, I got carried away," Tyler said.

Dani's cheeks and neck were scarlet. "No, it's fine. It was fun. I don't know why you say you aren't good with kids. You're a natural."

Words that should have sent prickles of warning down his spine. Instead, he held out his hand and changed the subject. "Do you have your phone on you?"

THAT NIGHT, DANI stood in her kitchen, sipping a glass of wine and staring at the number in her phone. She'd already carried Noah to bed after watching two episodes of *Mickey Mouse Clubhouse* with him and having him fall asleep snuggled into her lap. Now, with the place so quiet, she was really tempted to press the little phone icon and call Tyler.

Are you crazy? You just saw him earlier today! You do not want to freak him out.

God, was it wrong to like him so much? Despite every warning bell ringing in her head that he was a player and a jerk, the way he was with Noah today…playing with him, making him laugh.

But it wasn't just that. The fissions of electricity between them had made her almost lose her mind and kiss him. *In front of Noah.* She knew enough from reading the stack of parenting books and magazines her mom gave her that you never introduced your kid to anyone you weren't serious about.

This situation is a little different. He met Noah by accident twice. You can always keep them separated until you figure out if he's playing you.

Just the thought of putting herself out there again, of trusting someone with not just her heart but Noah's, too, made her palms sweat buckets.

Setting her phone facedown on the counter, she took her glass of wine and went to sit on the couch. She had time. She didn't have to decide right now what she wanted to do with that number.

TYLER WAS AT Mick's Bar playing pool downstairs, and against his will, he checked his phone again.

"You waiting on a call or something?" Kline asked as he took his shot, knocking one of Tyler's balls in. "Fuck, I quit!"

"You can't quit until I beat you." Tyler slipped his phone into his pocket, refusing to talk about Dani with Kline or anyone. Hell, he wasn't even sure why he'd given her the damn number anyway, but the ball was in her court.

Besides, it was Thursday night at Mick's, which meant Ladies' Night. The place would be packed with women looking to get drunk and hook up.

So why was he sweating Dani so hard?

"We're out of beer," Sparks said. "Your turn, Best."

Tyler laid his pool cue down and took the pitcher from Sparks. "Don't touch my stick."

"Not even for a million dollars."

Tyler chuckled as he climbed the stairs to the upper level and pushed his way through the throng of people toward the bar. The place was filled with women in skimpy tube and halter tops, their sweet body sprays and perfumes making the air almost cloying.

Since when aren't you into tube tops?

Since he'd seen Dani in her gray oversized sweater today.

The bartender waved him forward, and he held out a twenty. "Pitcher of Bud."

He nodded and went to fill one up. While Tyler waited, he caught the eye of a tall, stacked brunette with red dick-sucking lips. She smiled coyly at him, and it was a message he recognized.

Come on over.

Yet here he stood, not even tempted to make a move.

"Here ya go, man." The bartender took Tyler's money, and Tyler headed back downstairs, not giving the woman at the bar a second thought.

"Holy shit, he came back! Isn't this the time of night where you're ditching us for some chick?" Kline asked.

Yes, it usually was, and he'd had a clear-cut invitation upstairs. So why hadn't he taken it?

Maybe because she wasn't Dani?

Tyler set the beer down with a hard thunk of irritation and picked up his cue stick. "I told you. I can't leave until I kick your ass."

"Whoa, what's got you in a mood? You strike out or something?" Sparks asked.

"No, I didn't. Now shut the fuck up so I can concentrate."

Chapter Eleven

"Mom, I told you, I'm on vacation, so you don't have to take Noah." Dani stood in the kitchen just after five thirty in the evening, gripping the back of a chair to keep a rein on her temper. She'd taken Thursday to Thursday off for two straight weeks of fun with Noah and had even reminded her mom about it. Every other weekend, her parents took Noah; they told Dani it was so she could go out and socialize, but Dani suspected her mom hoped she'd finally take them up on dating one of the men they kept throwing at her.

"Well, I'm already here, so why don't you just enjoy? Sleep in, read a book…maybe call one of those numbers I gave you?"

"Mom…"

"Really, Dani, I am sorry I forgot, but I drove all the way over here. At least let me take my grandson for the night. He loves spending time with his Mapa."

By the way her son had his arms wrapped around her mom's leg, there was no arguing that point.

"Ugh, fine, let me go pack a bag."

"No need, I've got everything. I bought more diapers this week and some clothes to keep at my house, so you don't have to do a thing." Her mom bent over to pick Noah up, exaggerating a groan. "Oh man, you need to stop growing or Mapa won't be able to carry you anymore."

Dani released the chair and walked over to give her mom a kiss on the cheek. She really was lucky that her mom genuinely wanted to spend time with her grandkid. "Thanks, Mom." Laying a smacking kiss on her son's cheek next, she said, "Have a good time, handsome."

"Say, 'You, too, Mommy.' " Leveling Dani with a serious expression, she added, "Really, Dani, why don't you go shower, put some makeup on, and go out with a friend? Be young for a night." To her surprise, her mom patted her cheek. "You are such a good mom, but you aren't *just* a mom."

Most of the time, Dani thought she was screwing everything up, but here her mom was, giving her praise.

Weird.

As Dani watched her mom buckle Noah into her car through the window, she ran her thumb over the screen of her phone, scrolling through the names until she landed on Tyler's.

It was a Friday night. He probably had plans...

Before she realized what she was doing, she'd tapped the call button.

"Shit." Bringing the phone to her ear, she listened to the ring, whispering out loud, "This is so fucking stupid."

"Sergeant Best."

His deep voice sent a shiver along her skin, raising gooseflesh. "Hi, Tyler, it's…it's Dani. Noah's mom." *Oh, geez, as if he doesn't know who you are.*

"Hey, how are you?"

He sounded happy to hear from her, didn't he? "I'm good. How are you?"

"Great, just getting ready to leave work in a little bit."

"Oh, well, I don't want to bother you. I know you're probably busy—"

"No, it's fine. What's up?"

Dani's mouth suddenly dried up, and she could hardly get the words out. "Well, see, my mom has Noah this weekend. Actually, she takes him every other weekend, even though I told her she didn't have to since I'm on vacation…" *Shut up, you idiot.* "That's not important. I was just wondering, if you don't have plans, maybe you'd want to grab dinner and a movie with me?"

The line was quiet, and Dani looked at the screen, but he was still there. "Hello?"

"You've never asked out a man before, have you?" Dani could practically see his smile, and her cheeks burned.

"No, I haven't ever needed to. Most guys ask for *my* number, not just give me theirs."

"Whoa, sounds like you're calling in my man card."

Relaxing at the banter, she went to sit on the couch. "Maybe I am."

"So, how about I try to earn it back by picking you up and paying?"

Fighting back the urge to giggle, she said, "I might be amenable."

"All right. How about seven thirty? Give me a chance to go home, shower, and change?"

Thinking about her woolly mammoth legs, Dani said, "Let's make it eight."

"Eight works. Just text me your address."

"Okay, see you then."

Dani ended the call and flopped back onto the couch, kicking her legs excitedly. When the dogs came over and started showering her with doggy kisses, she spluttered as she got back onto her feet.

Then the heavy lump of doubt settled in her stomach.

Looking at her dogs, she asked aloud, "Is this a really bad idea?"

Shasta sniffed, and Bella snorted.

Shaking her head, she raced upstairs and started tearing through her closet for something to wear, her stomach fluttering. It was the first time in almost three years she was actually excited about something that had nothing to do with Noah. That was okay, right? Her mom had told her that she wasn't just Noah's mother…she was also a woman.

Besides, it was just one date…with a hot, sexy man who radiated confidence and charm. Who rescued dogs and toddlers and loved his mama without it being a huge turnoff.

It was official: She had nothing to wear.

Oh God, she was in so much trouble.

TYLER STOOD ON the porch of the townhouse, double-checking the address Dani had texted him. He had to admit that he might have changed his shirt a couple times. This was actually his first date, besides his junior prom, but considering they'd never made it to dinner and spent most of the night in the backseat of his car, he wasn't really counting it.

He knocked on the door and heard Shasta's deep bark on the other side, followed by Bella's high-pitched howl.

"Coming!"

He smoothed a hand over his short, shaved hair just as she swung the door open.

"Wow." Tyler's gaze roamed over the black sweater dress that hugged her body like a second skin, the cowl neck hanging off her left shoulder to tease him with the line of her collarbone. Her blonde hair fell smooth and straight just past her shoulders, and her eyes were out-lined by dark shadows, making the green seem brighter.

With a husky laugh, she said, "This old thing? You're sweet."

She stepped out onto the porch with her purse in hand and turned her back on him to lock the door. He noticed the white sales tag sticking out the back and smiled. "You planning on taking it back if the date doesn't go well?"

She reached up to where the tag was, and he narrowly missed getting smacked in the nose.

"Balls, I meant to take that off."

"Did you just say 'balls'?" Cracking up, he snapped the tag off and tucked it into his pocket. "There. I have to admit, that is the first time I've ever heard a woman use the term 'balls.' "

She turned to face him, and in the porch light, the blush on her cheeks glowed becomingly. "I tried to stop cussing once Noah was born, but I couldn't do it completely, so I made up my own."

"Wait, you did not make up 'balls.' "

"No, but I figured it was okay to alleviate my frustration."

"Isn't 'balls' just as bad as anything else?"

"He doesn't know it's that kind of balls."

Tyler chuckled. "Until he says it at school and someone enlightens him."

"Please, don't take it from me. All the other bad words really are off-limits. Just this one."

"You got it." They headed down the steps toward his car, and Tyler grabbed the passenger door, holding it open for her.

Just before she climbed in, she said, "You know, you really should thank your mama for teaching you manners."

"I'll leave that to you when you meet her."

She gave him a startled look from the seat, and the moment her foot was in, he slammed the door. Cursing himself, he rounded the front of the car.

Why the hell had he said *that*?

He opened his door with a heavy sigh. "I didn't mean it like that. I was trying to be cute."

Tyler glanced her way, catching her smile, and it nearly knocked him for a loop, it was so bright.

"Mission accomplished," she whispered.

Fuck, he wanted to kiss her. To reach across the seat and grab her by the back of her neck. To mold his lips to hers and strip her down until she was naked and straddling him.

But no, this was different. It would be different.

Clearing his throat, he started the car and pulled out of her drive, heading toward Watt Avenue. "What are you in the mood for?"

"Anything, I am starving. Plus, I wouldn't mind a drink or two. Just to loosen up, you know?"

Jesus, was she trying to kill him?

"Cheesecake Factory or B.J.'s Brewery?" he asked.

"Mmm, Cheesecake Factory, but only if we can skip to dessert."

Why did everything coming out of her mouth sound so dirty?

"Whatever you want."

Suddenly, her hand was on his arm, squeezing it. "You need to lighten up. Am I making you nervous or something?"

Scoffing, he shot her a look of disbelief. "Hell no, I'm calm as a cucumber."

"Really? 'Cause I think Mr. Big, Bad Ladies' Man is scared of little ole me."

Gunning the engine, he weaved over and pulled into the Cheesecake Factory parking lot. He parked in the first available spot he saw, and as soon as he cut the engine, he turned to face her.

"I'm not scared of you."

She leaned over the seat until she was mere inches from him.

"Prove it."

DANI KNEW SHE should not have had those two shots before Tyler picked her up, but she'd been a nervous wreck. After hauling ass to the mall to find something to wear and then speeding back to get ready, she was shaking. She'd actually cut her leg shaving. So, while she was drying her hair, she'd had one tiny shot of vodka and chased it twenty minutes later with a second one while she waited for him in the living room. It had warmed her up and eased the tension in her muscles.

Maybe a little too much. Because right now, she knew she was asking for it—every delicious, forbidden thing Tyler had to offer. From the moment she'd opened that door and caught his appreciative stare, she'd felt her old, wild self coursing through her body. She wanted to have fun and be daring, and most of all, she wanted Tyler to touch her.

Yet each time she was sure he was about to break, he backed away. Granted, the night had only just begun, but she didn't want to admit that beneath all the bravado and slight liquid courage, she was still a nervous wreck. Was afraid that once the adrenaline and alcohol wore off, she'd revert back to who she was now—cautious and scared.

As Tyler leaned closer, her eyes shut, and she waited for his lips to touch hers, but they never did. Instead, he kissed her forehead, and before her eyes even opened, he was out of the car and heading around to her door.

As she stepped out, slightly disgruntled, she asked, "What was that?"

"I'm not going to be goaded into kissing you, Dani." He shut the door at her back and advanced, pressing into her as he stared down at her with heat in his gaze. "I know that you're used to being in control, worrying about everything that could happen. But tonight, I want you to let go and let me lead you." He ran his thumb across her lower lip, and she was tempted to bite the tip. "I guarantee you, once you let me, you're going to have fun."

Tyler took a step away from her, placing his hand at the small of her back as he guided her toward the restaurant door. Dani was still a little dazed by his forceful tone and embarrassed she'd come on so strong.

"If you wanted to lead the whole night, then why ask what I wanted to eat?"

"Because I don't care about where we are or what we do. I just want to be with you, but at my pace." He held the door open for her. "And I want to take things slow."

"You'd be the first," Dani muttered as she passed through into the crowded, noisy lobby.

"What was that?"

"Nothing."

Chapter Twelve

TYLER SAT BACK as the waiter set down two plates, each with a beautifully dressed slice of cheesecake. Since they'd been seated, Dani had actually seemed to relax a little, less on guard and aggressive. He had recognized her attitude earlier for what it was: a defense mechanism. He had the same one, although his was set to indifferent asshole instead of sexual dynamo.

Still, he wouldn't be human if he said he wasn't tempted, but this was him, Tyler Wyatt Best, trying to be the good guy. To do the right thing.

Man, this shit was hard.

He watched Dani take a bite of her cheesecake, some kind of Oreo creation, and her eyes appeared to roll back in her head. "This is amazing. You have to try it."

Picking up his own fork, he scooped up a hefty chunk and slipped it past his lips. "Oh man. Maybe I ordered the wrong thing."

"Let's see." Without asking, she took a small bite of his peanut butter cup one and licked her lips. "Mmm, yours is pretty good, too."

"Maybe we should split them down the middle and share."

"Hell no, you just about took half of mine with that bite of yours. The rest is mine."

"Wow, I never knew anyone could get so possessive over a slice of cheesecake," he teased.

She licked her fork. "Then they did not appreciate the scrumptious goodness."

Taking a bite of his cheesecake, he moaned. "Keep your cookie crap. Mine's better, hands down."

"To each their own." She took another bite as she picked up her phone and started tapping the screen. "Do you know what you want to go see?"

"Definitely not a chick flick."

She flashed a dirty look his way, and he dived back into his cheesecake. Then her face lit up. "How about this?"

She practically shoved her phone screen in his face, and as he took the phone and read the description, surprise shot through him. "You want to see a horror movie?"

"It's a thriller, and yes. I can't watch them unless Noah is at my mom's, and I hate watching them alone. Please."

Shaking his head, he handed the phone back. "I said whatever you wanted."

Secretly, Tyler wanted to veto the idea. With all of the violence and bloodshed he'd seen in real life, he had no desire to watch it for entertainment, unless it was created by dinosaurs or sharks. But he couldn't bring himself to crush Dani's excitement.

Tyler Best putting someone else's feelings before his own? Will wonders never cease.

An hour later, they sat in a nearly empty theater at the very back. The killer on screen stalked the girl about to get killed, hiding in the shadows. When he jumped out at her, waving his knife around so the light glinted off it, Dani screamed.

Tyler burst out laughing, shaking his head. "If these scare you so bad, then why are we watching it?"

"Because in controlled circumstances, I don't mind being scared," she hissed. "As long as it isn't real."

Tyler sobered, thinking about Rex and how scared he'd been that day. It was the only time in his life that he'd ever understood what *frozen with fear* meant.

He'd been patrolling the perimeter with Rex just after three in the afternoon. One of the other guys, Benjamin, kept BS-ing with him over the radio. He hadn't even been paying attention, hadn't realized what had happened until Rex yelped and the bulled tore through his knee, sending him falling to the ground. The shot had probably saved his life, but at the time, he'd felt trapped. Unable to move with the cascade of bullets whizzing over him.

He'd pulled Rex to his chest and held on, trying to stop the blood gushing from his dog's chest.

"It's okay, Rex. It's going to be okay." Grabbing his radio, he'd started screaming, *"Heavy fire, we are under heavy fire. Rex and I are hit."*

Of course, they hadn't made it in time to save Rex. They'd had to pry his dog's body from his arms so they could get him to the hospital. He'd spent the whole flight scared that they wouldn't make it or that he'd end up losing his leg. Hours of terror, and he'd never experienced anything like it since.

It was why he'd been happy to receive the position at Alpha Dog; the last thing he wanted to do was go back over there.

When Dani's hand covered his and she squeezed, he looked over, coming out of his memories.

"Hey, you okay?"

Shaking off the past, he turned his hand over and threaded his fingers through Dani's. "Yeah, I'm good."

DANI TRIED TO squash the giddiness racing through her as Tyler and she exited the theater holding hands. Most of the men she'd been involved with she'd met at parties and clubs. They hadn't been big on romantic displays or real dates. Tonight, Tyler had made her feel special and cared for.

And damn it, she really, really liked it.

"That was terrifying," she said. "Thank you."

"Glad I could make your night. Not really sure I'll ever get feeling back in my hand after you squeezed it so hard, but—"

"Oh, I'm so sorry." Playfully, she brought their clasped hands up to her mouth and kissed the back of his. "All better?"

"Much."

His blue eyes burned into hers, and her breath caught in her throat.

"Dani?" A voice from her past called out from somewhere in the background.

Jerking her gaze away from Tyler, she found herself facing Angel Ramirez. Her jaw dropped in surprise and horror.

So Noah's father was back from LA, and by the looks of him, things had definitely changed for the worse. His hazel eyes were bloodshot and red-rimmed, as if he had allergies, but she was willing to bet it was drugs. His dark hair was greasy and lank, and his once muscular frame was now leaner.

Why the hell was he back?

"Well, I'll be. Damn, girl, you look good."

Dani felt Tyler stiffen next to her as Angel's gaze slid over her from top to bottom.

"Thanks. I wish I could say the same."

His eyes narrowed as understanding dawned. "Now, why you gotta be like that? You still mad at me?"

With a heavy sigh, Dani shook her head. "No, Angel, I'm not mad at you, but we need to be going—"

"Did you have my kid? Was it a girl or a boy?"

Dani scowled at her former lover, who was watching Tyler with a sly grin.

"It's really none of your business. You were the one who told me you wanted nothing to do with us. A couple hundred bucks, and you were done, right?"

"Hey, I was just curious—"

"Well, stop being curious, because it's not going to happen. You stay away from us." With a light tug on Tyler's hand, she started to lead him toward the exits.

Angel's hand gripped her arm. "I'm not done talking, bitch—ow, fuck!"

In a move she hadn't even seen coming, Tyler had released her hand and grabbed Angel's arm, twisting it up his back until he was bent over in pain.

"Do. Not. Touch. Her."

Tyler shoved him away, and as Angel stumbled forward, barely catching his balance, Dani realized that Tyler was standing in front of her like a shield, protecting her.

Placing her hands on his biceps, she squeezed them as she kissed his shoulder. "Let's just go, okay?"

Tyler put his arm around her, still positioning himself between her and Angel. Dani saw a security guard headed their way when Angel said loudly, "This isn't over."

They kept walking silently until they reached Tyler's car. He helped her inside, and after he'd pulled back onto Watt Avenue, heading toward her house, he still hadn't said a word.

"He wasn't like that when I was with him." Why the hell had she said that? Was she defending her choices or Angel?

She saw him nod, yet still he didn't speak.

"I'm really sorry that you had to get dragged into that tonight. I never expected he'd come back from LA, so I didn't think about this being his old stomping ground. I wasn't always the Queen of Common Sense, you know? I liked bad boys and parties, but when I found out I was pregnant with Noah, everything changed. I knew I had to do better, to be better." She couldn't seem to stop talking, just kept filling the deafening silence. "It's why I haven't dated; I couldn't trust myself to make smart decisions. Was afraid I'd end up falling for a guy who was bad for me...bad for Noah." He made the left turn onto her street, and finally, fed up with his stoicism, she cried, "Will you please just say something?"

After what felt like a lifetime, he spoke softly. "Is that why you asked me out? Because you think I'm a nice guy?" He parked in her drive and, shutting off the car, turned to face her. "That I'm not your usual type?"

Her heart slammed against her chest. "I asked you out...because I wanted to. I mean, you're so good with Noah, and I thought—"

"Forget about Noah, and tell me, how do you feel about me?"

Dani's heart lodged in her throat, and she tried to say something, but no words came out.

A bitter laugh escaped Tyler. "I am such an idiot."

"Tyler, you don't understand—"

"I'm not a good guy, Dani. In fact, I am the last guy you should want your kid to model after. Tonight was essentially the first time I've ever just taken a woman out with no intention of sleeping with her. I don't go to dinner and the movies with women I am not related to. I'm an asshole who is only looking for one thing, and once I've got it, I don't call and I don't write. That's who you asked out tonight."

Tyler was breathing hard, and the windows started to fog up around them. As Dani absorbed everything he'd said, she was even more confused about his behavior tonight.

"Then why did you go out with me? Why the big show of being a gentleman and not making a move?"

"Because I wanted to see if I could do it. Because since I met you and Noah, it got me thinking that maybe I've been missing something. But honestly, I don't know if I'm cut out for this…I don't know if I can be what you need."

Despite every reservation, every warning bell going off in her head to cut him loose, she closed the distance between them and brushed his mouth softly with hers.

"You said you wanted to take things slow…Let's do slow."

TYLER COULDN'T BELIEVE he'd poured his heart out like a pussy, and she'd kissed him for it. He'd told her he wasn't sure he could be a part of their lives, and instead of slamming out of the car, she'd done what he'd been dying to do all night.

Cupping the back of her head as she started to pull away, he kissed her back, sliding his tongue between her lips to deepen it. Her fingers dug into his shoulders as their mouths danced, teasing and tasting each other. Tyler's hand trailed down over her round bare shoulder to her waist and stilled, itching to move around and cup her ass, but no.

Ending the kiss, he chuckled roughly when she tried to follow him. "Hang on, baby, I can tell you right now that if we keep kissing like that, there will be nothing slow about what happens next."

In the dim glow from the porch light, he could see the flash of red across her cheeks right before she released his shoulders.

"Do you want to come in for some coffee or something?"

Tyler didn't trust himself alone in the car with Dani; forget about her empty townhouse.

"I better not. I've got to be up early." Reaching out for her hand, he asked, "Have you ever been geocaching?"

"No, what's that?"

"It's fun. Me and a few of the trainers from Alpha Dog are going to go tomorrow"—he glanced at the clock on his car—"well, okay, today. Do you want to go?"

"I have no idea what it even is, but I don't know. I wouldn't want to intrude."

"If you were intruding, I wouldn't have invited you. It's mostly hiking and exploring while searching for containers filled with knickknacks. Like a scavenger hunt."

"What's the point?" she asked.

"Like I said, it's fun. Plus, I'll be less likely to try for more than just kissing in a group. What do you say?"

She hesitated briefly, then nodded. "I'd love to."

"Good. I'll pick you up at eight."

"Eight?" He climbed out of the car at her little squeak and went around to let her out. "You know that is barely seven hours from now."

"Then I'd better make sure you get inside and go right up to bed." He stopped at the bottom of the steps while she climbed to the top.

"Seriously, eight?" She stood on the porch above him, unlocking her door. When she turned back around, her mouth open, he'd stepped up so he was standing right behind her and cut off whatever other protest she had with a hard, hot kiss.

When he pulled back, his voice was so low and gravely, he hardly recognized it. "I promise to make it worth your while."

Chapter Thirteen

DANI HAD GOOGLED geocaching that morning and couldn't believe that this was what Tyler and his friends liked to do in their spare time. Treasure hunting? Seriously? It was so childish and nerdy.

Her doorbell rang just after eight in the morning, and blearily, she answered it. Tyler stood on the front porch, grinning like an idiot with a Starbucks cup in his hands.

"If that's for me, I take back all the mean things I've been thinking about you this morning."

"About me?" He handed off her coffee and bestowed a long, lingering kiss on her mouth that left her swaying. "Don't hate. You're going to have fun."

"So you say, but I haven't been hiking since I was nine."

"It's like riding a bike. Do you want to bring the dogs?" he asked.

After a moment of consideration, she shook her head. "They have a doggie door to go out back, and besides, Bella gets tired after a while, and I don't feel up to carrying around a thirty-pound pug."

"Well, I brought Duke. He gets around pretty well with the cast. We're going back to the vet next week, and once the cast is removed, he'll start his specialty training." Holding his hand out, he added, "Shall we go?"

Dani stepped out, locking her front door with the key. "What is his specialty going to be?"

"I think he'll be excellent in search and rescue. It's not my department at Alpha Dog, but I'm going to train him myself."

When he took her hand and led her down the steps after him, her whole body warmed from the inside out.

"You look very pretty, by the way. Did you go shopping for this last night, too?"

Dani squeezed his hand and shot him a glare. "No, and I did not go out and buy that dress special either. It had just been sitting in my closet, and I'd never worn it."

"Sure. You know, it's okay to admit that you went shopping for our date."

"Please, you already have women falling all over themselves to get to you. The last thing you need is an ego boost."

He spun her around until her back was against his car, and the hand not holding hers rested next to her ear. He leaned over her, his face a serious mask save for the unholy twinkle in his eyes.

"You know, you're one tough customer. Why do you think my ego doesn't need stroking?"

"Because men who look like you always know they're hot."

"Aha, so you admit it. I'm hot."

Pulling him closer, she leaned up toward his mouth. "Pretty is as pretty does."

"Ye havna care fer me tender feelins, lass."

This time his fake Irish accent earned him a smile. "If you're done with your stroking expedition, can we go?"

"One kiss first."

She was happy to oblige, keeping her coffee out of the way. Both of his hands ended up cupping her face as he kissed her so well her toes actually tried curling in her boots. Her nipples hardened against the cups of her bra, and she nearly dropped the cup in her hand, the urge to wrap her arms around him was so strong.

Again, he was the one to pull away, but she took it as a good sign that his dark blue eyes were nearly black with desire.

"We better go. We're meeting everyone at eight thirty." He released her and took a step back.

"Who is everyone?"

"Hop in, and I'll tell you."

"What, you aren't going to get my door this time?" she asked.

"I would, but you're kind of in my way."

Realizing she was still leaning against it, she stood up. "Sorry."

"Don't be. I like that I'm distracting you."

"There you go again."

Once she was in, she was greeted by Duke's wet nose in her ear from the backseat. Laughing as she dodged his tongue, she murmured, "Nice to see you, too."

Tyler glanced her way as he climbed in. "You ready?"

"For fun? Sure, bring on the fun."

"That's the spirit."

TYLER PULLED INTO the Raley's parking lot alongside Sparks's truck. If Dani was nervous about meeting his friends, she didn't show it.

Him? Well, he was wondering what the hell had possessed him to bring her around the bunch of idiots when this was so new. When he wasn't sure what this was besides…

Happiness. Yeah, he could admit that when he was around Dani, it was like he was enjoying a good buzz without the hangover.

He hadn't told anyone he was bringing Dani, and he couldn't imagine what they were going to think. He just hoped they'd keep their mouths shut. The last thing he wanted was anyone to screw with him in front of Dani.

"Okay, full disclosure, my friends don't know you're coming."

"Are they going to be mad?" she asked.

"No, but they've also never had me bring a woman around them, so they might act a little…peculiar. Just ignore them."

Dani laughed. "Whatever you say."

Tyler took a deep, nervous breath and climbed out of the car just as Sparks and his girlfriend, Violet, rounded the back of his truck with donuts in hand.

"Hey, you're here. We're just waiting on Kline, Bryce, Vincent, Martinez, and Eve to get here, and we can get going."

"Whoa, Martinez got Eve to come?" Frankly, Tyler couldn't imagine Eve Reynolds geocaching; she might break a nail or something.

"Yeah, apparently, he made some kind of deal with her…"

Sparks's voice trailed off as Tyler opened Dani's door and she stepped out.

In fact, his friend's jaw seemed to be fixed to his chest, it had fallen so far.

"Sorry, we have a last-minute addition. Dean Sparks and Violet Douglas, meet Dani Hill."

Violet seemed to recover first, wiping her hand on a napkin before stepping around and offering it to Dani.

"It's nice to meet you."

"Likewise."

Awkward silence followed the introduction, as Sparks still stood there looking dumbfounded. When Violet called his name loudly, Sparks finally shook himself out of it and greeted Dani warmly.

"Sorry, but you're the first woman Tyler's ever brought along to geocache with us."

"So I've heard. I'm honored to be included, although I'll admit, I'm not much of a treasure hunter."

"Neither am I, but this is only my second time out, so we can be newbies together," Violet said.

When Kline and Martinez pulled up, Kline glanced toward Dani quizzically as he approached Sparks. Tyler watched with narrow eyes as Kline nodded toward Dani and Sparks replied quietly.

"Shut the fuck up!" Kline shouted in surprise.

Glancing down at Dani in exasperation, Tyler said, "That's Kline. He's a dumbass."

ONCE ALL OF the introductions had been made, they headed up Highway 49 toward the hiking trail Tyler had been telling Dani about. Dani was still floored by his friends' reaction to her, as if she was some kind of alien life-form they'd never encountered before.

"So, when you said your friends might be surprised, you weren't joking."

"Yeah, I'm sorry about that."

"Actually, I'm going to take it as a compliment. Being the first woman you've introduced to your friends is kind of special."

He didn't agree, and she worried she might have said the wrong thing. Especially considering how new this all was. If she really thought about it, this was only her sixth time meeting him, including that first time at the shelter. It wasn't as if they had been dating six months and decided to start introducing each other to the people in their lives. No, they'd had a hostile first run-in, three chance meetings, and two dates... Yet when she was with him, it felt longer.

Especially when he was kissing her.

But she had to remind herself that as good as it felt to be with him, he could bail at any time. She needed to guard her heart and especially guard Noah's. Which meant that whatever this was, she had to make sure it stayed between them until she knew it was something more than just a distraction, for both of them.

As Tyler pulled off into a gravel parking lot, he still hadn't responded to her slip.

"If this is uncomfortable or you want to back out, I completely understand," she said.

"No, it's not that. I wanted to spend more time with you." He reached into the middle console and pulled out two GPS devices. "Only now, I wish I'd just blown them off and taken you geocaching alone, just the two of us."

"Well, as nice as that sounds, it's a little late for that, so show me how these work."

Tyler turned her device on, and when it lit up, she saw a bunch of tiny dots on the mapped screen.

"Whoa, how long are we doing this for?"

"Don't worry; with Eve along, I doubt we'll make it three hours before she'll want to get back in the car."

Dani grinned. His friend's beautiful girlfriend, with her dark hair, perfect red nails, and pinup body definitely didn't look like the outdoorsy type.

"What about Megan? Is she with Blake or Slater?" Dani asked.

"Bryce is not with either of them, as far as I know, and Kline is actually the guy who had me meet you in his place. He's not ready to date anyone, least of all a ballbuster like Bryce."

"What makes her a ballbuster?"

Suddenly, Megan banged on the window behind Tyler. "Come on, Best, get the lead out! We got shit to find."

Tyler held up his hand. "Need I say more?"

"No, you need not." For the first time, Dani didn't wait for Tyler to come around and get her door.

The only person in the group who hadn't been weird around her was Slater Vincent, who, according to Violet, was a new trainer at Alpha Dog. The guy had greeted her warmly, and there had been no loud voice or wide eyes.

Tyler pulled Duke from the back and helped the dog down gently. Violet was holding onto the leash of a black and white stocky pit bull, and Martinez led a dog so big and ugly, Dani almost took a step back. However, when Eve, the girlfriend least likely to get her hands dirty, stepped out in faded jeans and a wool sweater and proceeded to kneel down and give the brute all kinds of hugs and affection, Dani had a feeling that Tyler had misjudged her.

"All right, the first cache we're looking for is the Gold Nugget. Does everyone have it on their GPS?" Sparks asked.

Tyler leaned over and showed her what to press to bring up the cache's details, his warm breath on her neck so tantalizing, she leaned back into him without thinking. When he brushed his lips against her cheek, she caught the wide, meaningful glances that Megan, Eve, and Violet shared.

"All right, troops, let's move out!"

As they headed up the narrow trail two at a time, Dani asked, "So, what exactly am I looking for?"

"This one says it's a tub. So, you're going to look under trees, maybe in a stump or in a cluster of rocks. When we get within thirty feet of it, we are usually just about on top of it."

"What does the person who finds it get?"

"The admiration of the group?" Tyler wrapped his arm around her and squeezed her shoulder. "Do I detect a bit of competitiveness in you?"

"I'm afraid so. If I'm playing a game, I like to win."

"So do I."

The GPS started beeping, and the group began fanning out. Dani spotted a cluster of trees in the direction the arrow pointed and made a beeline for them, with Tyler hot on her heels.

"Hey, since this is my first time, shouldn't you go easy on me?" she asked.

"Now, would it be right of me to just let you win?"

"No, but it would be nice."

"All's fair, baby."

Blake Kline's head jerked their way, and Dani whispered, "Are they going to spend the whole day jumping every time we speak?"

"Hard to say." Suddenly, Tyler let out a whoop and picked up a camouflage-painted tub.

"Hey, you said a tub! You didn't say it was green!"

"I didn't know, but even if I did, home-court advantage."

Crossing her arms over her chest, Dani threw down the gauntlet. "So that's how you want to play it, huh? All right, Tyler Best, get ready, because it is on like Donkey Kong."

Tyler grinned at her as he unscrewed the lid. "Bring it on, newb."

Chapter Fourteen

AT AROUND TWO in the afternoon, the group had settled into the outdoor tables at the local In-N-Out Burger. While the guys all went inside to grab food, Dani was left alone with Violet, Eve, Megan, and the dogs. The three women had been nothing but nice to her, but she was still a little nervous.

Especially when they started asking her questions.

"So, Dani, how did you and Tyler meet?" Eve asked.

"I was working at the shelter where he rescued Duke. I'm a vet tech."

"You guys have been dating for over a month?" This was squeaked by Violet, whose brown eyes appeared to be bugging out of her head.

"No, no, we actually just had our first date last night. Well, *technically* our first date."

"What do you mean, technically?" Megan asked.

"Well, I was supposed to have a date with someone else at Alpha Dog, but when he bailed at the last minute, Tyler took his place. Once we realized we already knew each other, he took me back to his house"—Megan flashed Eve a knowing look, and Dani frowned—"so I could check on Duke, but after that, we said good night. Nothing romantic about it."

"So, what was the turning point?" Violet asked. "When things got romantic?"

"I don't know...I just started to think that maybe he wasn't the player I'd first thought." All three women glanced at each other oddly, and Dani's cheeks burned. They probably all thought she should have gone with her instincts, that she was just being naïve, but they didn't see Tyler the way she did.

At least, that is what she told herself.

Thankfully, the guys chose that moment to return, and as Tyler sat down next to her, she couldn't help relaxing just having him there.

"Your cheeseburger, fries, and root beer," he said.

"Thank you." Dani took her food, and Tyler gave her a funny look. Had she sounded upset? She must have, because he was looking around at the other women, who were avoiding his gaze.

Her phone started vibrating in her pocket, and when she pulled it out, the picture of her mom holding Noah flashed across her screen.

"Sorry, I have to take this." Climbing off the bench, she slid her finger over the answer button. "Hello."

"Hey, honey, how is your weekend?"

Dani stepped away from the group, heading back toward the car. "Fine, how are you and Dad? Is Noah having fun?"

"Yes, but I noticed his ear seems to be bothering him. I was going to take him to the urgent care, but I wanted to let you know."

God, that's all they needed, another ear infection. "Okay, which one are you taking him to? I'll just meet you there."

"Really, sweetie, I can handle this. It's probably just an ear infection—"

"Yeah, but Noah will be scared after his stint in the hospital, so I'd rather just be there."

"All right, well, I'll take him to the one just up the road," her mom said.

"Fine, it will take me about forty-five minutes to get back into town."

"Forty-five minutes? Where are you?"

Dani rolled her eyes. Of course her mom was going to start asking questions. She had probably just let her know about Noah as a ruse to find out if she was just sitting at home.

"I'm in Auburn, geocaching with some friends."

"What the heck is gero crashing?"

"Geocaching, Mom. And it's like treasure hunting for adults."

"Oh, well…Well, that's good. What friends?"

Oh, good Lord, it was like she was sixteen again.

"Just some friends. You don't know them." Well, okay, they knew Blake Kline at least, but she didn't want to get into that with her mom.

"Well, if you're having fun—"

"I am, but I'd rather be there for Noah." Clearing her throat, she added, "I'll see you in a bit."

Dani hung up the call and walked back over to the table, where most of them were done eating. She put her hand on Tyler's shoulder, and he covered her hand comfortingly.

"Everything okay?" he asked.

"Yeah, but do you mind taking me home?"

"Of course."

Bless Tyler. No questions asked, he just agreed.

"You're leaving? But you didn't finish eating," Megan said.

"I'll just take it to go."

"Is someone hurt or something?" Eve asked.

Dani saw Oliver elbow his fiancée, who then gave him a dirty look.

"My mom's just taking my son to the doctor, and I want to be there."

The silence that settled over the group was like a dark cloud, especially when one by one, they each turned their attention toward Tyler. Their expressions ranged from anger to shock.

Finally, Violet said kindly, "I hope he feels better."

"Thanks."

As Tyler picked up her food and put it into the bag, he didn't look at any of his friends, and once they were safely inside the car, she asked, "Was it just me, or did they seem upset with you?"

"It wasn't just you."

"But why would they be? Because you're dating a single mom?"

Tyler tossed her a forced smile as he backed up. "They probably think that I'm taking advantage of you."

Dani laughed at the absurdity of it. "They don't know me very well, or they'd never think that. Or you, for that matter."

Tyler didn't say anything else, just turned up the music, and all the joy and fun of the day seemed to wither as he sang along to a Daughtry song.

TYLER DROPPED DANI off with a kiss on her cheek, leaving her in her doorway with a confused look on her face. What could he say to her? He was humiliated. It was one thing to have doubts about whether he could hack it with Dani, but for his friends to share those doubts?

His friends had thought the worst of him, without even asking him what was going on.

He'd at least expected Martinez, the mother hen of the group, to give him the benefit of the doubt, but even his mouth had been pinched with disapproval.

And that look had quickly popped his happy, delusional bubble.

An hour after he got home, he shouldn't have been surprised that his three best friends came into his place without knocking. Duke barked excitedly until he recognized them, but he didn't relax.

Maybe he sensed the crazy tension in the air.

"What the hell are you doing?" Sparks boomed.

"Having a beer and watching *The Negotiator*. Wanna join me?"

"Dude, be serious. What are you fucking doing?"

Tyler stood up, going toe to toe with his friend. "Like I said, chilling. You're the one who burst into my place with an attitude, so how about you explain to me what your problem is?"

"Okay, okay, put your dicks away, we're all friends here." Kline stepped between them, pushing Sparks back.

"Best, what is the deal with Dani?" Martinez asked bluntly.

"I brought her geocaching. I'm dating her. What part of that is hard to grasp?"

"Except you don't date. You hook up and take off," Sparks snapped.

Tyler glared at him. "Not this girl. Not this time."

"Dude, you were just telling me a few weeks ago that you weren't interested in settling down, and now you're dating a woman with a kid? You should know better."

Before he knew what he was doing, he was holding the front of Sparks's shirt, and their faces were inches apart. "Fuck you. Just because I don't share every thought going through my mind doesn't give you the right to come in here and preach at me."

"It's not fair to lead that poor girl on, make her think you're serious, and then drop her like she ain't shit—"

Putting all his weight behind the blow, Tyler punched Sparks right in the face. He felt his friend's cheek crack against his knuckle painfully, as if it was all happening in slow motion, and still he kept moving, tackling him to the floor. The sound of Duke's barking and his own blood thrumming in his ears flooded his senses, drowning out the inner voice yelling at him that he was attacking his friend. He was too far gone to think straight, shaking with rage and uncertainty.

Martinez and Kline were grabbing at him, trying to pull him off Dean, and he shouted, "You don't call her shit; do you understand me?"

"I didn't, you crazy asshole! I was talking about the way you treat women like toilet paper!"

"Well, she's different!" At this point, Kline and Martinez were holding onto both his arms as Sparks climbed to his feet.

Sparks's hand cupped his cheek, and he wiggled his jaw before answering. "Yeah, I can see that."

All the fight seemed to drain out of Best, and he sagged between Kline and Martinez.

"You good, bro?" Kline asked.

"Yeah, I'm good."

They released him, and Martinez said, "I'll get us some beers."

Sparks and Tyler stood several feet apart, breathing hard and watching each other warily, with Kline standing at the ready to jump in. Sparks was the first to sit down on of the recliners Tyler had brought in from

Henry's place. Actually, most of the furniture he'd added had been Henry's, with a few of his own pieces thrown in. He had to admit, it felt more like home now that he'd nested, versus when it had been just a place to sleep.

Martinez came back in, passing around bottles of Bud before he sat down in the other recliner.

"Jesus, you almost busted my eye socket," Sparks grumbled.

"You're lucky that's all I did."

When Sparks tensed up, Martinez shouted, "Enough." With a nod from Sparks, Martinez took a deep breath and added, "Look, Best, I know we came in here hard, but we were just concerned. We're your friends—"

Tyler released a bitter laugh. "Yeah, great friends. You think I'm an asshole who would take advantage of a single mother just to get a piece of ass."

Martinez jumped in before Sparks could open his mouth. "You're right, we were dicks, and even if we did think that, it was none of our business."

"But, since we're here and you're talking about it, are you serious about this girl? Or are you just searching for something, and she's the first woman to stumble into your path?" Kline asked.

Tyler took a long pull from his beer and sat back into the couch. "She didn't stumble into my path. Believe me, I tried to avoid her, but I kept running into her." Looking right at Kline, he said, "That blind date you bailed on? That was her. When I took Apollo to the hospital to make his social rounds, she was there with her son. I decided to go to a different park one morning, just on a whim, and she was there. At that point, I decided God was either trying to tell me something, or I had the worst timing in the world."

"But do you really like her? Or are you just trying to prove something to yourself?" Sparks asked.

Tyler bristled. "Exactly what would I be trying to prove?"

Sparks grinned then winced. "That you're not a total douche."

The other guys seemed to be waiting on Tyler's reaction, and when he laughed softly, the atmosphere changed. All the anger and tension dissipated, and they were just a group of friends shooting the shit and connecting on common ground.

Just like they used to do in group counseling, where they'd first met.

"I know my track record with women hasn't been great, but I've never deceived anyone. I've never made them believe I was in it for anything more than fun, and they all knew what they were getting into. Dani didn't take my bullshit, not from the moment I met her, and I liked that about her. And yeah, briefly I looked at her as if she was just another notch on my bedpost, but that was before I found out about Noah."

"And that's her kid, right? You've met him?" Martinez asked.

"Yeah, twice. He's cute."

"But are you really ready to date her? Because when you date the mom, you're dating the kid, too, and for a guy who hasn't had a relationship last longer than forty-eight hours…"

Kline trailed off, but they all got the message. Did he really think he was ready to be a dad?

"We're taking it slow. It's only our second date. If things don't work out, we're both adults."

Sparks sat forward, his dark gaze clashing with Tyler's in warning. "You're right, and if that's the way the two of you are going to play it, fine. But you need to stay away from that little boy until you're sure, because you don't want to let him get attached and then have to walk away when things don't work out with his mom."

Tyler knew Sparks was right, and that had been his plan, but that didn't mean he had to like being told what to do. Especially by Sparks, who hadn't followed his own advice with Violet.

Still, Tyler was tired of fighting, so he kept his opinions to himself. "Fine. Now shut the fuck up, or get the hell out so I can finish my movie."

Chapter Fifteen

DANI BRUSHED THE curls back from Noah's forehead while the doctor examined his ear. Her mom sat in one of the empty chairs, watching her like a hawk eyeing its prey.

"So, tell me more about this group of friends. What are their names? How did you meet them?"

"Mom, I don't really think this is the time," Dani said. The words came out slightly muffled due to her clenched teeth.

"Huh." The doctor pulled the otoscope out of Noah's ear and addressed the nurse. "Do you mind grabbing me a pair of alligator forceps?"

Dani knew what forceps were, and worry tightened her chest. "Forceps? Is there something in his ear?"

"Yes, but I don't know what. At first, I thought it was a hard ball of wax, but I noticed something metal in it."

Metal? Oh God.

The nurse came back in, and the doctor said, "All right, Noah, I am going to remove something from your ear, and it might be a little uncomfortable, but your mom is going to sing your favorite song while I remove whatever is in your ear."

Dani took her son's small hands and started humming the *Mickey Mouse Clubhouse* theme song as the doctor pulled the forceps out of the sterile pack. Noah hummed along for a minute and then whimpered as the doctor started the extraction.

"Hey, it's okay, buddy, just look at Mama. It will only be a second, and then Mapa and I will take you out for ice cream."

"I got it, Noah," the doctor said, holding up a small black object. He squinted at it for a moment or two, hmm-ing under his breath. "I think it's a battery."

Dani was floored. She'd never seen anything like it, and when she told him so, he shrugged. "It could have come out of a toy or something. It doesn't seem to have been in there very long. No corrosion. At least he didn't swallow it."

Guilt twisted up Dani's gut. Was the doctor blaming her? Thinking that she wasn't watching her son closely enough?

"How long is not very long?" she asked.

"Maybe a week? It's hard to know for sure."

God, obviously he was right. She'd been distracted, or maybe she would have noticed a broken toy or that his ear was sore. She turned to her mom and spoke more sharply than she'd intended. "Do you have anything that battery might have come out of?"

Her mom immediately went on the defensive. "Are you *blaming* me for this? Because I haven't had Noah all week; you have."

"This is no one's fault," the doctor said loudly. "Accidents happen. I would just make sure to search for any broken toys or electronics that might have a battery like this and be careful what you allow Noah to play with in the future."

Ashamed for starting a fight in the doctor's office, Dani asked, "Is there…is there anything else he needs? Medicine or something?"

"Nope, he should be fine. Like I said, it probably wasn't in there very long." Giving Noah a stern look, the doctor added, "Now, young man, no more putting things in your ears or up your nose. If you find something and you don't know what it is, I want you to show your mom or dad or your grandparents. Understood?"

Dani's cheeks warmed at the mention of a dad, but Noah just nodded for the doctor, his mouth wrapped around his thumb.

"Thank you for getting us in and for all of your help," Dani said.

"It's not a problem; these things happen." The doctor's tone was reassuring and comforting, and Dani realized that she'd probably just been projecting her own guilt. She should have insisted on keeping Noah with her this weekend. It was why she'd taken a vacation, not to go gallivanting around with a bunch of strangers.

"You can just head on up front, and they'll take care of you," the doctor said.

"Thank you." Dani helped Noah down from the table and took his hand, her mom following behind them as they went up to pay. As Dani searched through her purse for her medical card, her mom started talking.

"Accidents happen, honey. There's no use beating yourself up about it. Or me, for that matter."

"I don't blame you, Mom, but I do blame myself." Handing the card over to the receptionist, Dani lowered her voice and said, "How could I not know that my son had a battery in his ear?"

"As closely as we watch him, we're only human. We miss things. And like the doctor said, Noah is fine."

Dani's eyes swam as she took back the medical card and handed over her debit card. She didn't want to have this discussion in front of the receptionist, who handed her back her ATM card with several tissues. God, how embarrassing to get all weepy in front of strangers.

Once they were outside, Dani said, "Noah might be fine now, but it could have been worse. And that's on me."

"Please, do you think that you never took years off my life with your shenanigans? I'll never forget the time you thought you could fly. You were playing in the back-yard and decided that you were going to jump off your play structure. You could have tangled yourself up in the swing or worse, but you didn't. You hit the ground and broke your arm. So, if you think I don't know how you're feeling right now, I do. I felt so guilty taking you into that ER, glancing around at all of the nurses, imagining what they must be thinking, but you know what? It was all in my head. The only thing they thought was that you were just being a kid."

"Mom, I was six when I did that, not under two." Reaching for her mom's back car door, she said, "I'm just going to take Noah home."

"No, you are not. Your dad is making corn bread and beef stew for dinner, and you are more than welcome to join us, but my grandson is going to come back to my house so he doesn't associate it with any of this negativity."

Her mom took Noah's hand from her, and although Dani wanted to protest, she also didn't want to make a scene and upset Noah.

"Mom, he isn't going to associate your house with anything negative." Dani popped open the door and bent inside to help her mom buckle Noah into his car seat. "Is it so crazy that I just want to be home with my son?"

Her mom closed the opposite door without answering, and Dani kissed Noah's cheek. "Hang on, bug, while I talk to your grandma."

Noah just pulled up his LeapFrog tablet off the seat next to him and turned it on.

Dani closed the door and faced off with her mom, shooting daggers at her. "Noah is my son, and the only reason I am not pulling him out of this car and taking him home with me now is that I don't want to upset him. But I am no longer a child, and you do not get to tell me what I will and will not do with my son."

Her mom puffed up like an angry turkey, glaring right back at her. "I told you that I had this under control, and you didn't have to change your plans for us, but you're so obsessed with being the perfect mother that you push aside all the other elements in your life you should be tending to. You won't be twenty-four forever."

"For God's sake, Mom, would you just cut the bullshit? You don't need to manage my life anymore. I'm not the same stupid girl I was three years ago."

"No, you're not the same girl. In fact, you're so far removed from her, sometimes I poke at you just to catch a glimpse of her. As crazy as you made me, you had such a spark in you, so much life. Now, your whole life revolves around Noah." Her mom shook her head at her. "I just think that you've gone from one extreme to another, and you can meet in the middle, you know. You can still make smart choices and be young. Because someday, sooner than you think, Noah is going to have his own friends, and he's not going to want his mom smothering him."

"That's many years off," Dani said.

"Well, for tonight, you're off duty. Go home. I'll bring Noah back after church tomorrow."

"Why do you insist on taking Noah to church? He's not even two, and you force him to sit there for an hour listening to things he doesn't understand."

Her mom's face turned an ugly shade of purple. "Noah does just fine, and besides, it's good for him to learn about his Maker. There is nothing wrong with instilling good moral values in children."

Sure, because it worked out so well for me.

"And before you say anything else to needle me, can we just hug and say our good-byes? Unless, of course, you want to tell me about your new friends?"

Since I'm definitely considering never seeing him again, I think not.

"Good-bye, Mom."

TYLER STARED AT the screen of his phone until it turned black. Then, he slid his thumb across the screen and stared some more. For some reason, he just couldn't bring himself to call Dani. Maybe it was the way he had left her on her porch, cold and without any explanation. Or, perhaps it was that it was nearly eleven o'clock at night, and he was afraid she'd already be asleep.

Besides, he wasn't even sure what he wanted to say to her.

Maybe that you're sorry for being a tool and that your friends are a bunch of dipshits?

Except now, he could see his friends' point of view, and it had him questioning what he was doing with Dani all over again.

Where are your balls, man? Just text her. You already swore to take things slow. What happened to all the brave talk about her being different?

Getting up his nerve, he texted, *Hey, how's Noah?*

Setting his phone down on the table, he got up and walked away from it. His gaze caught Duke's, who was following him across the room with his smoky eyes.

"What? I texted her."

Duke's floppy ears perked up, and he barked at him.

A half a second later, his phone chimed. He didn't even realize he was flying across the room to answer it until he flopped onto the couch. Picking up his phone, he read her message.

He's okay. He had a battery in his ear. Feeling like the worst mother in the world, and to top it all off, my mom wouldn't even let me bring him home. How are you?

What did he say? That he felt like a jerk about the way he'd left things with her? Or was that too honest?

You aren't a bad mom. Shit happens. And he's fine, right? You shouldn't be so hard on yourself.

Look at him, being all supportive and understanding.

Shit, he was losing it.

His phone alerted him of another message, and he had to read it twice.

You're sweet.

No, he wasn't. He was a jerk. A jackass. A douche bag. But he liked that she thought so.

What are you doing right now?

Did that sound pushy? Damn, he was not used to being the insecure one.

Actually, I'm drinking alone and watching Netflix. Pretty pathetic, right?

Glancing down at the mess of beer bottles from the guys earlier, he responded.

No, sometimes we need to drink. Want some company?

Well, fuck, he'd done it. He had put himself out there for rejection, and he wished he could take it back.

And then his phone dinged.

Sure, but I gotta warn you, it's not pretty.

His normal response would have been something cheesy like *You're always pretty,* but it didn't feel right, using something trite on Dani.

I'm on my way.

Tyler grabbed Duke and was loading him up just as his phone rang. He looked down and saw Dani's number flashing.

"Hey, what's up?"

"Maybe this is a bad idea," she said.

Tyler paused in the door of his Tahoe, stunned. "What?"

"Us. Doing this. I mean, you aren't even sure you want to get involved, and after today, with your friends hating me, and Noah—"

"My friends don't hate you. They were pissed at me. They thought I was taking advantage of you."

"Well, I don't think that, but I'm worried about Noah—"

"Wait, wait. I am not going to hurt Noah. In fact, I thought we decided we were going to wait for me to spend time with Noah until we were sure?"

"We were, but this is more about you distracting me *from* Noah."

What the hell did he say to that? An easy quip sat on the tip of his tongue, waiting to be used.

Instead, he stood silent. Had he ever been at a loss for words?

First time for everything.

"Are you still there?" she asked.

He cleared his throat before speaking. "Yeah, look, Dani, if you don't want me to come over, that's fine. I get you not wanting to get involved." He hated how twisted up he was over this girl. "But I don't think you should use me getting between you and Noah as an excuse. No matter how things go between us, Noah will always come first with you; I get that. Just like today. I will never fault you for putting your son before everything. In fact, I admire you for it."

This time, he thought *she* had hung up, it got so quiet on the line.

"Dani? What's it going to be?"

Finally, she said, "I'll see you when you get here."

She ended the call, and he slipped his phone in his pocket. Whatever he'd said had obviously been the right thing.

Funny. All the times he'd ever tried to win a girl over, he'd never considered being sincere.

Chapter Sixteen

DANI FLUFFED HER flat hair in the mirror, but all it did was make the blonde strands staticky. She wished her cheeks weren't so flushed and her eyes so bleary; she'd been halfway through a bottle of wine when he'd texted, which had been another reason she'd tried to cancel with him. She didn't trust herself alone with him.

God, why had she invited him over in the first place? She'd been planning to be really firm about why she didn't want to get involved, but then he'd said all that sweet stuff about not wanting to get between her and Noah and that he respected her.

When the hell had a man's respect ever sounded so hot?

Pulling open the fridge, she grabbed a bottle of water. Drinking water would sober her up, right? Maybe she should start a pot of coffee…

A knock at her door sent Bella flying off the couch, barking hysterically, while Shasta lifted her head, released a loud woof, and laid her head back down.

Too late to do anything but answer, she walked across the living room and pulled the door open. Tyler stood on her front porch in a pullover sweatshirt and jeans, Duke sitting patiently by his side.

"Hey," he said.

"Hey, come on in." Both of her dogs circled and sniffed Duke as he came inside, and Dani had the bizarre urge to do the same to Tyler as his cologne drifted around her like a warm hug.

"So, what are we watching?" He put Duke in a down-stay and sat on the couch, looking totally at ease with a sexy grin. One of his arms draped over the back of the couch, while the other rested on his knees. If she sat down next to him, would he wrap that hard, muscular arm around her shoulders?

Oh, boy.

"I wasn't sure. Why don't you choose?"

"Nope, it's not my house. You pick," he said.

She walked around the coffee table and sat next to him on the couch, but his arm didn't move.

Relaxing slightly, she teased, "Even if I choose a chick flick?"

"Whatever you pick, I promise not to complain."

"You're being awfully accommodating."

"I figure I better be, or you might kick us out. Besides, according to you, I'm sweet, so why wouldn't I let you have your way?"

She laughed as she picked up the remote, already knowing what to pick. "We'll watch *One Small Hitch*."

"What is that?" he asked.

Dani raised an eyebrow at him. "I thought you didn't care what I chose?"

"So I can't be curious?"

"It's a movie about a guy who pretends to be engaged to his best friend's little sister when he finds out his dad is dying. It's funny; you'll like it."

She could practically feel the skepticism radiating from him but chose to ignore it as she pressed play.

About fifteen minutes into the movie, Tyler was indeed chuckling, but Dani was fighting to stay awake. Her eyes fluttered closed a couple times, and she yawned loudly. "Sorry."

"It's okay. Are you too tired? Should I go?"

"No, are you kidding? You just got here, and besides, you want to finish this."

"Then at least come here. I keep seeing your neck jerk every time you doze off, and your head flops forward. It can't be comfortable."

As Tyler pulled her in against his body, his arm wrapping around her, she suddenly wasn't so tired anymore. She snuggled into him, laying her head on his chest so she could still see the TV. The steady rise and fall of Tyler's chest under her cheek was lulling her back to sleep slowly, and before she drifted off, it occurred to her that she hadn't been comfortable enough to fall asleep with a man in years.

TYLER SMILED AS Dani's soft snores reached his ears. She was obviously exhausted from their late night and early morning. He let her continue to sleep while he finished the movie. Dani had been right about this one; he had enjoyed it. Who would have thought he'd actually enjoy a movie his mom and sister would have squealed over?

When the credits finally rolled, he tried to adjust his arms so he could pick her up and carry her to her room, but she groaned and glued herself to him, her mouth now pressing against the skin of his neck.

Oh, fuck. His hard-on pushed against the fly of his jeans, and he wanted badly to adjust it, but he'd hate to have her wake up to find him holding his dick. She might get the wrong idea, and despite current evidence to the contrary, unconscious women did not do it for him.

She stirred as he tried to pick her up. "What are you doing?"

Her voice was soft with sleep.

"I was going to get you settled in bed and then go home."

" 'S'late. Shouldn't be driving."

He knew she probably had no idea what she was even saying, but having Dani trying to get closer to him didn't exactly make him want to run for the door. Besides, it sounded like an invitation to sleep over, even if it was made with a slight slur.

Picking her up in his arms, he carried her up the stairs of the townhouse, being careful of the narrow hallway so he didn't crack her head on the wall. He walked into a dark room, the light from the hallway shining inside and highlighting the queen-size bed and bright floral comforter.

He laid her down on top of it and awkwardly tried to pull it down so he could place her beneath it. Finally, he settled for covering her with the quilt from the end of her bed.

Tucking it around her, he leaned over and kissed her forehead.

"Good night, beautiful."

Suddenly, she sat up. "Where are you going?"

"I was going home."

"Don't go," she whispered.

"Okay," he said automatically.

And then, she flopped back on the bed with a snore.

Tyler wasn't sure if it was the alcohol or her just being tired, but he went downstairs and locked the doors. Crashing on her couch, he turned on a Jason Statham movie and settled in. He could have just gone to bed with her—it wasn't as if he would push his advances on a sleeping woman—but he actually didn't want Dani to wake up and find him in her bed. He wanted her to be clearheaded when she invited him into it, but she was right about one thing. It was late, and he'd rather travel across town in the early morning than after two.

Before the first car chase, Tyler's eyes grew heavy, and he fell asleep with a smile.

Staying the night with a woman before he'd even slept with her? Imagine that.

THE NEXT MORNING, Dani stirred to life with a groan, her head pounding like the dickens. She should have known better than to drink too many glasses of red wine before bed, but last night she'd been throwing herself a bit of a pity party.

Cracking one eye open, she squinted at her surroundings. She was in her bedroom, which was strange because the last thing she remembered was being on the couch with Tyler.

She sat up swiftly, and her head protested at the pain of the movement. Tyler must have carried her upstairs after the movie ended.

Looking in the bed next to her, she half expected to find him, but it was undisturbed. It had been nice of him to put her to bed after she'd passed out on him. She'd have to call him today and thank him.

Stretching as she sat up, she checked the clock on her nightstand. It was just after eleven thirty, which meant her mom would be dropping Noah home soon.

Dani climbed down the stairs and could swear she smelled coffee brewing. Had Tyler set the timer to go off?

As she hit the bottom of the stairs and saw him standing in her kitchen with his back to her, his sweatshirt gone, she stopped short.

Shit, he had stayed the night. Did that mean they…

"Ahem, uh, hey," she said clumsily.

He turned with a smile. "You're up. Here." He set a glass of water and two white pills on the counter. "For the hangover. Coffee is almost up, and I've got pancakes made and keeping warm in your oven."

"Thank you." Sitting at the counter, she downed the pills and half the glass of water. She caught a glimpse of herself in the mirror and nearly groaned aloud at the horrible disarray of her hair. Not to mention her mouth tasted disgusting…

Oh, God, please don't try to kiss me.

"So, you, eh, you stayed over…" How to ask this delicately? "Upstairs?"

He set a cup of coffee on the counter near her elbow with a grin. "Are you trying to ask if we slept together last night?"

His teasing made her face burn. "It's not funny!"

"No, I did not take advantage of the beautiful, passed-out girl in my care. I carried you upstairs, and when you brought up the fact that it was late and not safe to drive, I crashed on your couch. Which, by the way, is incredibly comfortable." He turned his head from side to side, and his neck cracked. "Hardly a crick."

Relief swept through her. "So, no sex?"

"Disappointed?"

"No, believe me"—when he paused, shooting her an affronted look, she rushed on—"I just meant that if I'm going to have sex for the first time in almost three years, I'd at least like to remember it."

His coffee cup stalled on its way up to his lips, and his eyes widened. "Three years?"

With a smirk, she sipped her own coffee. "I've been a little busy."

"Three years," he mused.

"It's not as if I couldn't have gotten some, I just didn't want to fall back onto bad habits. And there's more to consider when you're a mom. I'm not going to go home with some guy I just met and take the chance that he's a serial killer. None of the guys from my past are men I want to go down that road with again, as you've witnessed from my last ex." Running a hand over her messy hair, she sighed. "It was just a better option to be celibate."

By the way he avoided her eyes and turned to pull out a plate piled high with pancakes, she had a feeling his dry spell wasn't as long as hers.

"Where's your syrup?" he asked.

"In the cabinet next to the fridge."

Why wasn't she more freaked out by him being there? Or by the fact that her mom could show up any second with Noah and she was a grumpy disaster in the morning?

Because he put you to bed last night, and instead of taking advantage, he slept on the couch? Or perhaps you like the way he looks in your kitchen.

"Glass measuring cup?"

God, why did she think he was so cute bustling around her kitchen? "Under the silverware."

He poured syrup into the measuring cup and heated it in the microwave. He grabbed two plates from her cupboard. "How many pancakes?"

"Two, please."

"So, what time is your mom bringing Noah home?" he asked.

"After church gets out, usually around noon. Unless my parents take him for lunch after."

His gaze flicked toward the clock on the oven. "I guess I better hurry up and eat then. Sorry I slept so long, but like I said, your couch is comfortable."

"It's okay; it's not as if Noah hasn't met you before. He knows you're a friend." What the hell? Why was she saying it was okay, when five minutes ago she'd panicked seeing him still there?

"I imagine your parents will probably have a lot of questions if they find me here. You sure you want to deal with that?"

Just imagining her mom drilling him and her with questions was enough to turn her stomach.

"Never mind, just eat your pancakes. We'll save the parental inquisition about my intentions for another day," he said.

The two of them doctored their pancakes and ate in relative silence for several minutes. Dani studied him, wondering why he had really stayed. She didn't buy that it was late and he was tired. Had he been hoping she'd wake up and they'd get frisky?

"Why did you really stay over? I know you; it wasn't just because it was late and I asked you not to drive."

"Would you believe it was because I was worried and wanted to make sure you were safe?"

"I might. Is that the truth?"

A knock on the door interrupted his answer.

"I guess the end is nigh, huh?" he said.

Shit, her mom was early. Dani's heart threatened to pound right out of her chest. "If I asked you to hide, that would be immature and unreasonable, right?"

Around a mouthful of pancake, he said, "I can try, but the plate and second cup of coffee is a dead giveaway. I can, however, put my shirt on if you give me a second."

He was right. She would just have to deal with her mom like a mature, independent adult.

Dani waited until he was decent before she headed for the door, pulling it open with a bright smile for Noah. "Hey, buddy! Did you have fun?"

Noah flew into her arms, and she squeezed him hard, burying her face in the soft skin of his neck.

Suddenly, he was squirming to get away from her.

"Tywer!"

She released him, and he shot across the room to Tyler, who picked him up with ease. "What's up, Noah? Want some pancakes?"

A cleared throat turned Dani's attention from the scene, and she faced her mom, whose eyebrow was hiked up her forehead.

"Well, aren't you going to introduce me to your... friend?"

No avoiding it now, especially since her mom pushed right past her, stepping on her foot in the process.

"Sure, Mom, come on in. Tyler, this is my mom, Laura. Mom, Tyler. We met a while ago, when Tyler came in to evaluate some of the dogs at the shelter. He's a trainer for that military program I was telling you about, Alpha Dog?"

Her mom held her hand out to Tyler, who adjusted Noah on his hip to take it. "Nice to meet you, ma'am."

"It's nice to meet you, too, considering I've heard absolutely nothing about you."

Ouch, dig number one. Dani tried to convey an apology with just her eyes, but Tyler was focused on her mom.

"Well, we've known each other for over a month, but we just struck up a friendship recently."

"A friendship, really?"

"Mom, where's Dad?" Dani asked.

"He dropped us off and went to go fill the car up. You were saying, Tyler?"

"Well, ma'am, we were watching a movie, and both of us fell asleep. Because it was late, Dani offered to let me sleep on the couch, and I decided to return her kindness by making her breakfast."

Dani could tell her mom was studying the living room for signs that he spoke the truth and noticed the rumpled blanket on the couch.

"I see."

"Do you want some pancakes, Mom? They're really good, and Tyler made a huge stack." Finally catching Tyler's gaze, she mouthed *I am so sorry.*

He shrugged with a smile.

"No, I'm fine. Your father and I were going to take you to lunch, but I can see you already ate."

Tyler set Noah at the table with a stack of cut-up pancakes. He did it with such ease, as if it had happened a hundred times, and she could only imagine what her mom was thinking.

"Well, ladies, I should let you visit. I need to get Duke home anyway."

"I'll walk you out," Dani said.

Once she closed the door behind them, she leaned against it with a groan. "I am so sorry."

"Seriously, it's fine. My mom would have been the same way."

"You're just trying to make me feel better," she said.

"A little. Is it working?"

Putting her hands and her forehead on his chest, she breathed deep. "Thank you."

He laughed as his arms circled her waist. "Wow, the way you act, I feel like I should have more battle wounds."

Her arms wrapped around him. "How are you not running right now?"

"I don't know. Maybe I've got a good feeling about you," he said.

"Well, you'd better take that feeling and get the hell out of here before my dad shows up and then there are two of them."

He cupped her chin with one hand and brought her gaze up to meet his. As his lips dropped and covered hers, she hardly had time to worry about her breath before his mouth was moving over hers in a soft, loving kiss.

When he finally released her, she leaned back against the door in a daze.

"I'll call you."

"I bet you say that to all the girls," she said breathlessly.

Tyler's hand trailed over her cheek, an indiscernible expression on his handsome face. "But with you, I mean it."

Chapter Seventeen

TYLER WASN'T SURPRISED that Jeremiah was less than trusting of the trainers at Alpha Dog. Hell, most of the kids who came through those doors were leery of the staff, who tried to earn their trust with structure, understanding, and firmness when needed. But Jeremiah hadn't been a problem at all. Whereas most of the kids were harsh and angry or attention seeking, Jeremiah was soft-spoken and slightly awkward. Since he'd been at the program, he had hardly said anything, fading into the background. But Tyler hadn't forgotten about him.

"Jeremiah, why don't you show us how to put Lucky into a sit-stay?" he called.

Had Jeremiah's face actually paled? His light blue eyes were definitely wider than usual, but he stepped forward, his longish brown hair falling over his forehead as he stared at the ground upon approach.

Tyler frowned, concerned at the kid's timidity.

And then, just as Jeremiah reached the front of the group, Tyler heard a coughed word, loud enough for others to hear. Some of the boys started laughing, but Tyler's body stiffened with fury.

"Fag."

"Who the fuck said that?" The boys were dead silent, and Tyler stepped up to Jamie Platt, whose laughter died under Tyler's thunderous expression. "You think hate speech and slurs are funny? Huh, Platt?"

"No, sir!"

"Then why are you laughing?" he shouted.

The teenager didn't answer, visibly shaken, and Tyler stepped back. "Do I need to remind you that Alpha Dog has a zero-tolerance policy for bullying? That means that hate speech, racial and sexual slurs, and other derogatory violations of members of this group will not be tolerated. This is your one chance; whoever threw out that word better step in front of the group in the next ten seconds or it will get worse for you."

Tyler waited, knowing that the perpetrator wouldn't do it, but he wanted to give him the chance anyway. When nobody stepped forward, he shrugged.

"You wanna do this the hard way? Fine by me. Platt, Harlow, Meyers, Fredrickson, and Shields, hand your leashes off to a friend. And start running."

"Come on, Sergeant Best, we didn't do anything," Dwayne cried.

"That's where you're wrong. You're a team while you're in this program, and when one member is targeted, you should be defending him, not laughing at his expense.

Now, get moving. Every four laps, you get a five-minute water break, and you will keep going for the next hour, until someone confesses. At the end of that hour, if no one has stepped forward, then you five will be leaving the program. So, you better hope that whoever the comic was has some integrity."

Hank stepped forward. "Sarge, it was—"

"Unless you're about to confess, Hank, I suggest you keep your mouth shut. I don't want you to turn anyone in; I want that person to be a man and come talk to me. The rest of you are dismissed; take your dogs in and report to study hall. Except Jeremiah. You stay."

All the boys headed inside while the five others took off to run laps around the perimeter of the yard.

Once it was the two of them, Tyler nodded at the trembling teenager. "Now, show me that sit-stay."

Jeremiah did as he was asked, and Tyler timed him. A twenty-second sit-stay wasn't bad.

"Okay, go ahead and give him a treat." He walked closer to Jeremiah, who was squatting down in front of Lucky. The kid had been a good choice for the dog, and while Jeremiah rubbed Lucky's ears and told him what a good dog he was, Tyler crossed his arms over his chest as he stopped. "Is that the first time that's happened here? Someone calling you that?"

"No, sir."

Tyler placed his hand on the boy's shoulder. "I apologize for that. I want you to feel comfortable being able to tell one of us if you're being bullied. There is no excuse for it, not here."

"But calling them out is only going to make it worse," Jeremiah said.

"I have a hard time imagining they'll keep harassing you if the end result is them getting shipped back to juvie."

"They might stop in here, but what happens when we're out?"

Tyler had a suspicion that turned his stomach. "Whoever has been harassing you is someone you knew before?"

Jeremiah didn't need to answer; Tyler could see the answer in his expression. But the kid said it anyway. "You can't protect me from things like this."

Although Jeremiah had a point, the impotence of the situation pissed Tyler off. "You're right. You gotta decide how you're going to handle it, but that doesn't mean I'll have someone like that in this program. You might not feel safe anywhere else, but you will here. Go ahead and take Lucky inside and join the rest of the guys in study hall."

Jeremiah hesitated for half a second. "You didn't ask me."

"Ask you what?" Tyler said.

"If I was gay."

Tyler shrugged. "Gay or straight, it doesn't matter. He had no right to call you that."

The kid smiled brightly. "Thanks, Sergeant Best."

It blew Tyler away that Jeremiah was thanking him for stating the obvious. Then again, he'd been in the Corps with guys who hadn't thought twice about throwing around gay slurs, but Tyler never had.

He'd seen what his little brother had gone through the last few years after coming out. As much as the world was changing and evolving, there was still bigotry and hate.

Just not under Tyler's watch.

Tyler focused on the five boys running and already had an idea who had spoken, but he was determined to give him the benefit of the doubt. Not that he wouldn't be dealt with, but he wasn't a malicious boy. That was why singling Jeremiah out was so puzzling.

"Come on, you can run faster than that. Pick up the pace; as soon as you finish this lap, you can take a water break." As they came around another lap, Tyler glanced down at his phone for the time and saw a text message from Dani. They hadn't seen each other since Sunday, but he was hoping her text meant she was available for dinner. He was dying to get her alone.

"You have just over fifty minutes left! I hope you aren't getting tired," he said cruelly.

The boys ran to grab a drink at the fountain, and Harlow was the first to quench his thirst and start running again.

Sliding his finger over the phone screen, he read her message. *My babysitter is sick, and my mom and dad are out of town visiting my aunt. I'm homebound, I'm afraid.*

Damn, this whole keeping Noah and him separate was harder than he thought.

What if I bring pizza and a movie over after Noah goes to bed? Then we aren't breaking any rules, and if he wakes up, I can always hide in the closet.

Raised voices by the fountain pulled him away from his phone, and he looked up in time to see Platt push Meyers against the wall. The bigger boy was radiating anger even from a hundred yards away, but it was the shouting that made Tyler rush to intercede.

Tyler caught every word as he neared the fountain, confirming what he'd already known.

"I'm not running anymore for you, asshole! You're going to tell Sarge it was you talking shit, or you're going to have bigger problems."

Meyers might have been the smaller of the two, but he wasn't backing down. He shoved Platt back. "Fuck you, fat ass, what are you going to do, sit on me? Mind your business!"

Tyler sped up, hollering, "Hey, hey! Knock it off. Platt, get back to running."

Platt did as he was told, glaring at Meyers until he finally turned away.

Tyler held his hand up as Meyers started to take off, too. "You want to come clean now or keep torturing your friends?"

Meyers's face turned an ugly shade of red as he snarled, "They aren't my friends. I'm out of here in a few weeks anyway."

"That's true. You can spend that time getting shipped to juvie and losing all the goodwill you've earned from me and the rest of the instructors. That would be the easy way out of this. To just pretend that you didn't do anything wrong." He hoped his tone was conveying that was the wrong choice. "Or, you could show that you've actually learned something in your time here and deal with your mistake. Apologize to your team and especially to Jeremiah. I don't know what happened between the two of you before you got here, but I know you're better than this."

"I was just being funny, Sarge. Why do I need to apologize because the kid can't take a joke?"

"Because calling someone that isn't a joke. Words like that cut deep and can scar a person." Tyler's eyes bored into Meyers's until the kid's brown ones darted away. "You've been someone the other guys look up to and have earned their trust and respect. I'd hate to see you lose that."

"If I kiss that kid's ass, none of them will respect me."

"Now, I'm pretty sure you're wrong. Did you see Platt's face when you called him fat? That was hurt, which means he thinks you're friends. You shouldn't treat your friends like that."

Despite the kid's tough attitude, Tyler noticed Meyers's cheeks and ears were red with a blush. "I wasn't trying to start anything. I was just having a laugh."

"At other people's expense. How is making someone else feel like shit funny? Does that actually make you feel better?"

Meyers shrugged and answered honestly. "Sometimes."

"Then it sounds like you need to spend an hour a day with Dr. Stabler if you plan to stay. See if she can help you work through healthier ways to boost your self-esteem."

That seemed to be the kid's breaking point. "Oh, come on, I don't need a shrink!"

"Part of your probation, Meyers, if you accept my terms. You can talk to her and work out your shit or not—it's up to you—but you will show up to every appointment. And if anything else comes up, you're out of here."

Meyers stared mutinously at him, but Tyler wasn't going to cave, not on this. After everything his little brother had been through, with dick bags hassling him and calling him every shitty name in the book, it wasn't going to fly here.

"So, what's it going to be? Accept the consequences and apologize? Or do I need to make a phone call?" Tyler prodded.

Meyers's Adam's apple bobbed hard. "Okay."

"Good. First, you'll apologize to Platt and all of the other guys. Then, you're going to have extra cleanup duty this week after meals." Meyers nodded, not arguing. "And until you're discharged, I wanna hear that you're going to every counseling appointment. Are we clear?"

"Yes, sir, we're clear."

"Good. Hang out while I call your cohorts in." Cupping his hands over his mouth, he shouted, "All right, you're done. Get over here."

While they waited, Meyers said, "I know it's none of my business, Sarge, but I heard the black eye Sergeant Sparks has is from you. Why'd you hit him?"

Well, hell, the kid had him now.

"Honestly? He was being a dick."

Meyers laughed and with a definite twinkle in his eyes chided, "Now, you shouldn't hit your friends, sir."

Tyler grinned sheepishly. "You're right, I shouldn't have. I don't recommend throwing punches at your friends when they piss you off. It's something I gotta learn not to do, too. The point is, you need to learn from the mistakes of your elders and strive to be better. Which means we don't bully people just because we need to feel better about ourselves."

As the other boys gathered around, Platt shot Meyers a dark scowl. Meyers's jaw clenched, and for a second, Tyler wasn't sure Meyers would follow through, but he surprised him.

"I'm sorry I was a jerk, Platt. I didn't mean it; I was just pissed," Meyers said, relaxing.

Tyler thought Platt was going to draw it out, but instead he nodded, a small smile on his face as he held his hand out to Meyers. "All right, but the next time you try to dis all of this, I *am* going to sit on you."

The other boys laughed, and Meyers grinned as they shook hands.

"Let's go inside, and we'll find Jeremiah, who will receive an apology from each of you. No exceptions, got it?" No one argued. "After you."

Tyler fell into step behind them, pulling out his phone once more, and saw a new text from Dani.

Okay. You bring a pizza and movie, and I'll make cookies.

Here's hoping you get more than a cookie. The thought popped unbidden into his head, and he couldn't help laughing at himself. As much as he'd changed over the last few weeks, he still had a bit of the old Tyler in him.

The one who hadn't gotten laid in a while—had barely been kissed, actually—and he was starting to feel the withdrawal.

I wouldn't expect too much tonight. The last thing you want to do is be getting it on and have Noah walk in on you. Scar the kid for life.

But it wasn't just about the sex. They had hardly had time to figure out how they'd work without drama, parents, or friends getting in the way. Noah was one thing, he and Dani were a package deal, but it seemed like every time Dani and Tyler started to grow closer, something would put distance between them. It wasn't them; he had the feeling with no interruptions, they'd have a really good time together, as he'd experienced the few times they'd been alone.

Building something real was new territory, though, and he just hoped he wasn't going to royally fuck it up.

THAT NIGHT, JUST as Dani was closing the door to Noah's room, there was a knock at her front door. Bella and Shasta barked and howled, and she shushed them sternly as she ran past. She had been looking forward to going out with Tyler all week, and when she'd almost had to cancel, she'd been really disappointed. She hadn't wanted to be the one to ask him to come over, especially when she had been the one to suggest keeping him and Noah separate.

She hadn't needed to, though. And even if Noah woke up, she wasn't worried. Her son adored Tyler already, but as someone who introduced him to puppies, not as a potential dad.

No, it's you having all the fantasies about the three of you living happily ever after.

The thought wasn't completely off base. She had to admit, the big Marine holding her baby in his arms as he cut up a stack of pancakes for him was one of her favorite images. The ease with which Tyler fit in, even briefly, left her nearly floating with hope, and it was exhilarating but terrifying at the same time.

Especially since she was pretty sure she'd already fallen for him.

She opened the door without looking through the peephole, excitement radiating through her body as she expected to find Tyler and Duke on the other side.

Instead, Angel stood on her porch step, his red-rimmed, watery eyes looking back at her under the pale porch light.

Shasta stood behind her; she could tell by the dog's guttural growl.

"Hey, Dani. You miss me?" he asked.

"What are you doing here?" Panic made her voice squeakier than usual. "How did you get my address?"

"Oh, I got a buddy who can find just about anyone. Relax, why are you so tense?"

"Maybe because you're showing up at my house unannounced?" A thousand thoughts ran through her head, but the one that was truly alarming was that this wasn't the Angel she'd known three years ago. He'd been a jerk, no doubt, and had smoked a little weed and drank, but she'd never been afraid of him.

After recalling his explosion at the theater, though, she started inching the door shut.

He laid his hand against it, stalling her movement. Shasta's rumblings intensified, and Angel's gaze narrowed on the dog for a second before returning to her. "Now, why are you trying to close the door? I just want to have a talk with you."

"Fine, talk." Giving Shasta an "okay," she wasn't surprised that the dog quieted but refused to leave her post.

"Is my kid here? Can I meet him? Or her?" Angel was craning his neck to look past her, but she stepped back into his line of vision.

"No, he's at my parents' house," she lied smoothly. "They take him for me every other weekend."

"Him, huh? So I got a son? Well, that's really nice. You know, my mom has been so excited to meet him ever since I told her I saw you. Maybe sometime we could come over—"

"No, Angel, I don't want you coming back here. If you want visitation, you're going to have to go through legal channels to get it, because the way you are now…showing up here, obviously high, there's no way I'm letting you around my son."

His face screwed up in a menacing glare, and he pressed harder on the door, widening the opening. Shasta lunged past her legs, snarling and snapping at him until he stumbled back. She caught Shasta's collar just as Bella flew out the door, circling Angel with a series of high-pitched barks.

He kicked out at the fat pug, who was surprisingly fast for her size, and Dani, afraid he wouldn't miss again, snapped, "Bella, inside. Now."

The dog hesitated before bouncing back in. Probably not the brightest move in the world, Dani stepped outside and shut the door on both dogs. The last thing she wanted was Shasta to bite him while protecting Dani. She didn't need to give him any leverage against her, like saying that she owned a dangerous animal.

Angel, who'd seemed to get his bearings back, got in her face. "Who are you to judge me, huh? You were nothing but a little slut who was willing to spread her legs for anyone who'd buy you a drink. Yet you're going to stand there and preach to me? You're looking down your nose at me and telling me you're gonna keep me from what's mine?"

And like that, Dani's temper snapped in two, all common sense and fear fleeing with every insult, every dig. "You didn't want him! Don't you remember that?" She hissed the words angrily, stepping into him so he either needed to move or she'd run over him. "Don't you remember telling me to get rid of 'it'? That I shouldn't count on you to help because you were leaving? And I kept up my end. I never tried to find you. Never pressured you or sued you for child support. Nothing. Because I don't want your money, Angel. I want nothing from you."

"You've got a real brass set on you. Especially since you've all but admitted you're alone here."

"Except she's not alone." Tyler's deep, angry voice made them both jump, and she glanced toward the top of the driveway with relief. He seemed larger in the shadows, taking up the entire entrance to the walkway with his broad shoulders, and she watched Angel visibly swallow.

Whatever apprehension he'd felt was obviously fleeting, because the next second he sneered, "Well, if it isn't the hero."

Tyler had a pizza box in one hand with a plastic bag on top. Duke sat by his side calmly, watching the humans as if they were discussing tea and crumpets.

"It's Mr. Hero to you." Tyler's tone was devoid of his usual good-natured humor as he approached. Handing her the pizza box and movies with a kiss on her cheek, he whispered in her ear, "I want you to take this and Duke inside. I'll come in a few minutes."

Dani didn't like leaving Tyler alone with Angel. As she gripped Duke's leash, she warned, "Thirty seconds, and then I'm calling the cops."

As Tyler opened the door to let her back inside, Angel's cheerful good-bye sent a shiver down her spine. "I'll see you soon, sweet pea."

Please, Tyler, make those thirty seconds count.

Chapter Eighteen

TYLER TURNED TO face Dani's ex, trying to appear casual when all he wanted to do was pound the guy's head into the wall of the house. He'd parked at the end of the drive, noticing the Chevelle next to Dani's car, but he'd figured it was a friend or that the babysitter had come through after all. But when he'd heard Angel practically threaten her, he'd been about to drop everything, including Duke's leash, and tear the guy apart.

What really pissed him off was that the arrogant little fuck was either too high or too stupid to realize the danger he was in.

"Here's the deal. You're going to get into that piece of shit car, and you're going to drive away. And you aren't going to come back here ever again. You got it?"

Angel sniffed at him. "You think you can tell me what to do? She's got my kid, and I want to see him."

"Then I suggest you hire a lawyer. But if you show up here again, it's not going to end well for you."

"What, are you threatening me now? Ain't you a cop or something? You got that look that screams *pig*. I'll report you."

Tyler smiled coldly, and he knew it'd had the right effect on Angel when some of the puff went out of his chest. Stepping into the shorter man, Tyler said, "I'm not a cop. I'm a Marine."

The door swung open behind him.

"I said thirty seconds, and I gave you forty. I'm calling the cops."

Angel glared between the two of them a few times and finally turned away with a noise filled with anger. Tyler didn't take his eyes off his retreating form until he'd climbed into his car and started it up.

While Angel was backing out of the driveway, Tyler suddenly found his arms full of a trembling Dani.

"Oh my God, I have never been so glad to see anyone in my entire life."

Wrapping her up tight against him, he resisted the urge to shake her. "What the hell were you doing on the porch with him? Actually, why did you answer the door in the first place?"

"Because I thought he was you. I didn't even look out the peephole because I....I was so excited to see you."

Well, how could he be mad at that? "When I came up the walk and heard what he was saying, I wanted to pound him. But now, all I really want is to get you inside and give you a proper hello."

She looked up at him from the circle of his arms, and damn, nothing had ever seemed so right. "I like the sound of that."

Unable to wait, Tyler took her lips, coaxing them open with a slow sweep of his tongue. This had been what he'd been missing. Even if he'd kissed another girl, it wouldn't have been like this, sweetly fulfilling.

Because the only one who made him want like this was Dani.

"Mmm." She was the one to break away, taking hold of his hand from her waist and bringing it to her mouth. "Come on."

Tyler followed her in, and as she closed and locked the door, he asked, "Are you hungry?"

She turned to face him, her back against the door, dogs sniffing around her legs and feet.

"No. You?"

He didn't answer. Instead he stepped into her, moving the dogs out of the way and burying his fingers in her hair.

"I'm not much for pouring my feelings out, but this, what's happening with us, is something…" *Special.*

She leaned up on tiptoe, her mouth so close he could feel the warmth of her breath mingling with his. "I know exactly what you mean."

"Oh yeah?" His words were soft, pressing her to say more even though he couldn't find the words.

"Like you just…fit. It's effortless, like you belong with us, and I…shit." She pulled back a little, her eyes heavy with worry. "I shouldn't have said that. Now you're freaking out, afraid I'm thinking about marriage, and I swear I'm not. I just like spending time with you, and you're nice to my son and—"

"I'm not freaking out." And weirdly, he wasn't. Because ever since the day at the park, he'd been feeling the same way. They fit together, as if Dani and Noah had been placed on Earth just for him. They were his…his to protect and care for. What he had been waiting for; what he needed to make a change.

Although the hard-on in his jeans was proof he wasn't *completely* changed. With Dani so close, he could see the rise of her breasts beneath her shirt, the valley of her cleavage making his mouth water.

He might care about Dani, but he was still a man. A man who hadn't had sex in nearly six weeks, and with her staring up at him with those beautiful eyes shining, her lips swollen from his kisses, he wanted to mold her body to his.

"What *are* you thinking?" Her question broke into his thoughts, and this time, he was the one scared to answer, afraid she'd kick his ass out.

"How much I want you," he said honestly.

"Want me like…"

"I don't know if you can handle it."

The soft teasing did the trick. Her eyebrow rose, and her chin kicked up a notch.

"Why? Because you think I'm just a mom? That I don't think about *my* needs?"

He trailed a finger across her cleavage, and he heard her breath catch. "Tell me about what you want, what you need, and we'll see if we're on the same page."

"Why don't you go first?"

"Dani…" His voice came out as more of a growl.

"Okay." She held onto his shoulders, sliding her palms down his arms until the muscles were tight with tension. "I want these arms to stay around me, to never leave my body while you kiss me." He complied, his heart hammering against the wall of his chest as she stretched her body up against his. "I want to feel every part of you touching me, to know by the way you move that you want me."

"God, Dani, I—"

Her finger came up and rested against his lips. "I'm not quite finished yet."

Opening his mouth, he licked the tip. "I'm sorry; please continue."

"Thank you," she said huskily. "As I was saying, I don't want to talk or think…I just want to lose myself in you."

This time, the kiss they shared wasn't sweet in the least. It was explosive. Their lips and tongues played and danced, retreating and returning with a fervor. His hands slid down until they cupped her ass, bringing her up against his erection, rubbing her against him until it was almost painful.

She released a soft cry between kisses, and he wanted to rip her jeans off. To unbuckle his belt and drop everything to the floor. To nail her against the wall and plunge into her hot, wet passion until they were both spent.

Something vibrated between them, and Dani pulled her mouth away, her hands pushing against his chest. "My phone."

Taking a deep breath, he stepped away, flexing his fingers as he tried to pull himself under control.

Dani fumbled with her phone, her cheeks flushed pink as she pressed it to her ear. He had put that glow there, and he'd have been lying if he didn't admit how good it felt.

"Hello. What? No, I can't. I'm on vacation for another week. Is she okay?" Dani paused, her brow furrowed as she listened to the person on the other end. "That's awful. Can you call in Paula or Naomi?" More waiting. "You know I would do anything to help you guys out, but I don't even have a sitter."

Without thinking of what he was doing, he tapped her shoulder. "What's going on?"

"Hang on a second." Hitting mute on the call, she said, "My coworker was in a horrible accident on Eighty and is on her way to the hospital. They tried to call in one of the other techs, but they can't get ahold of anyone else."

Don't do it, man. What do you know about little kids?

"How long will you be?" he asked.

"If they can get ahold of someone else, a couple of hours, but if not, I won't get home until three or four in the morning," she said.

"Noah will sleep, right?" She nodded. "I can sit with him if you need to go."

She bit her lip, and he could read the uncertainty in her eyes. "I don't know…"

"I promise to keep him in one piece until you get home."

He could tell she was considering it. "It *is* double time because I'm on paid vacation. But what about us?"

He gave her a hard, fast kiss. "Oh, I intend to pick up right where we left off when you come home."

Laughing, she got back on the phone. "Okay, I'll be right in, but if you get ahold of one of the other techs, call me, please."

She ended the call and gave him a searching look. "Are you sure you're okay to sit with him? He probably won't wake up, but if he does, he might freak if I'm not here."

With more confidence than he actually felt, he assured her, "Trust me, I've got this covered. I can handle a sleeping kid for a couple of hours." His arms snaked around her waist, and he nibbled her neck. "Plus, I'm expecting an awesome reward for my selfless act."

"Okay, easy there, you're not volunteering to take my place in the Hunger Games." Kissing him quickly, she pulled away with an all-business expression. "Emergency numbers are on the fridge, including my cell, which you have. Fire extinguisher is over there"—she pointed to the wall next to the oven—"cookies are in the squirrel jar, and diapers are under the changing table. Sometimes, if he does wake up, warm milk in a sippy cup will help him go back to sleep, but not *too*—"

"Dani!" His loud whisper made her stop long enough for him to say, "He's a kid, not a bomb I need to defuse. We'll survive while you're gone, but if you don't get out of here, I'm going to have to find another way to quiet you down."

The way she pursed her mouth at him was just asking for him to do just that. "Fine, I'm going to change." She got halfway up the stairs and turned toward him with her mouth open—

"One more word, and I'm coming after you. And if I do, there is no way you're leaving tonight."

Her chin did that defiant little jut that drove him crazy. "I was just going to say that when I get home…it's your turn to tell me your needs."

His dick flexed painfully as he realized what she was saying.

Fuck, he was going to be counting down the hours.

TYLER YAWNED AND checked the time on his cell phone again. Dani had been gone several hours, having rushed out the door with a piece of pizza in one hand and a swift kiss for him. He'd actually thought for a second she was going to tease him into following through on keeping her home, but she'd left, giving him one more speech about what she'd do to him if anything happened to her baby.

Tyler had assured her again, and as soon as he'd made sure she was safely in her car, he'd closed and locked the door behind her. Since then, he'd watched several episodes of *Prison Break* as he munched on three slices and two cookies. He'd checked on Noah a few minutes ago, and he was still sound asleep.

Tyler had been tempted to lie down and get some sleep himself but was afraid he wouldn't hear Noah if he cried, so he'd been fighting it. Thinking about work and wondering how his guys were doing. Kline had them for the weekend, and Tyler had warned him to watch out for any bullying. So far, no calls, but then again, it was only Friday.

Then there were his friends. They'd been bugging him to go out this weekend, but he'd said he was busy. Although they'd seemed to accept that he was actually into Dani and this wasn't just a play, he wasn't ready to talk to them about her yet. And going for beers at Mick's would lead to just that.

Dani. He smiled just imagining Dani walking through the door and kissing him. How he'd pull her down over him on the couch and run his hands over her back lightly, learning the curves of her body…

He hadn't even realized he'd dozed before he sat straight up. Tyler heard a tiny voice crying, "Mama."

Tyler jumped up from the couch and went into Noah's room. Flipping on the light, he saw the tear tracks on Noah's flushed face.

"Hey, Noah, you okay?"

"Ma…Mama?" The kid was sucking in air as he spoke, and Tyler held his arms out to him.

"Mama had to run out for a minute, but I'm here. Did you have a nightmare?"

The toddler let him pick him up, and he felt something wet on his hand. Noah's sleeper was soaked through with pee.

"I think I know what the issue is. Your diaper exploded." Noah was still sniffling, and Tyler bounced him as he walked over to the blue dresser on the opposite wall. Opening the top drawer, he found a set of pajamas with bears on them. "How about these ones?"

Noah shook his head, stuffing his thumb into his mouth.

"No, huh?" Duke stood under them, pressing his nose into Noah's butt, and Tyler snapped, "Duke, get your nose out of there."

Tyler could have sworn he heard a giggle and saw the corners of Noah's mouth were lifted into a smile around the thumb.

"You think that's funny, huh? Well, how about a little less giggling and more pajama picking." Catching sight of blue feety pajamas with Mickey on them, he grabbed them. "How about these?"

Noah nodded enthusiastically.

"We have a winner." Carrying Noah over to what he hoped was the changing table, he laid him on his back on the boat-shaped mattress covered in soft blue terry cloth. Unsnapping his soiled pajamas, he gingerly removed them, and the diaper went with them.

"Okay, what do I use to wipe you down?" Spotting a pack of wipes on the edge of the table, he pulled out several and cleaned up Noah as best he could.

Now the diaper.

"Little man, you are going to have to bear with me, as this is my first diaper change. You've been through probably a million of these, right?"

Awkwardly, Tyler got it on, and when he had Noah set up in the Mickey pajamas, he went to lay him back down, but it occurred to him that the kid's bed might be wet. His bed felt surprisingly dry, though, so he attempted to put him back in the crib.

But Noah started screaming and hanging on to him.

"Shit, I mean, shoot. Don't ever say that, okay? What is it? Huh?" Lifting him back up, he felt the little boy's chubby arms circle his neck trustingly, and Tyler melted like a stick of butter in the sun.

"Wanna drink some milk and watch Mickey?" He felt Noah nod against his neck, and he shut off the light to his room as he exited. "Sounds good, man. Think your mom will be mad if we make it a party?"

"No," Noah said softly.

Tyler chuckled and decided the kid was gonna be trouble when he got older.

Chapter Nineteen

DANI WAS SEEING double on her drive home from the
veterinary hospital, she was so tired. They'd finally let
her go a little after two, when it had slowed down. So far
tonight, she'd assisted in three emergency surgeries and
nearly had her arm taken off by an injured St. Bernard
who hadn't liked having his temperature taken. All in all,
it wasn't bad for the money, but she wanted to get home
to her boys.

Her boys? It had a nice ring to it.

Tyler hadn't answered the text she'd sent him, but she
figured he'd probably fallen asleep. She wouldn't blame
him, as he'd already worked a full day.

When she finally reached the front door and unlocked
it, she treaded quietly despite the excited barks of Bella.
Shushing her, she put up with three dog noses sniffing
her all over as she took in the sweetest sight in the whole
word.

Tyler was lying on the couch on his back, snoring softly, and tucked against his side was Noah, his head on Tyler's chest. As she tiptoed closer, she saw Noah's tiny rosebud mouth was open, and there was a dark spot on Tyler's T-shirt, no doubt where her son's drool had puddled. The quilt from the back of the couch was draped over them, and the TV sported the bright red bubble asking if they wanted to continue watching the show.

She was loath to disturb them, especially since they seemed so content, but she didn't want Noah to wake up and wander around without her. He could climb out of his crib and often did when he heard her puttering around in the morning, but she could usually hear him on the baby monitor before that happened. She'd been meaning to convert his crib into a toddler bed but had wanted to wait until his second birthday in December.

Reaching under him to lift him off Tyler's chest, she felt the big man come awake with a start, his eyes flying open to catch hers.

"It's just me," she whispered.

A smile spread across his lips that had her heart kick up into overdrive. "We were waiting up for you."

"I can see that." Snuggling her son into her arms, she carried him back to his room. He didn't even stir as she laid him down in his crib and covered him with his fleece blanket.

She walked out to find Tyler examining the wet spot on his shirt.

"I think I need to change my shirt."

"Here." She held out her hand to him. "Take it off, and I'll throw it in with a load of laundry."

He did as she asked, but the grin he shot her gave her a better understanding of the word *devilish*. And with him standing there, bare chested with his muscles highlighted by the light from the TV, she wanted to be bad.

Very, very bad.

"I think you're just trying to get me out of my clothes," he said.

"Somehow, I don't think I'd have to try too hard."

She walked away, his chuckle following her down the hallway to the laundry room. Once she threw in his shirt, she stripped down to her bra and panties, wanting to get out of the blood-splattered scrubs. She would love to take a shower, especially considering that blood was the least disgusting thing on her scrubs, but her stomach was already fluttering just having Tyler half naked in her kitchen. If he made a naughty suggestion about a dirty shower?

There would be no resisting him.

I'm sorry, weren't you the one who'd suggested picking up where you two left off?

Except now she'd had a chance to think clearly, and they'd been about to hook up in the entryway before she got the phone call. Where Noah could have come out and found them. What the hell had she been thinking?

That you haven't had sex in over three years and you're horny as hell?

Grabbing her robe from the hook on the back of the laundry room door, she wrapped herself up in it. It was a simple red flannel her mom had gotten her for Christmas last year. Not the sexiest thing she owned, but maybe that was a good thing.

He was standing in the same spot, drinking a glass of water when she came out. The way his gaze traveled over her made her feel like she was wearing the world's sheerest negligee instead of just her house robe.

"I needed to wash my scrubs, too."

He set the glass of water down on the counter, his arm muscles flexing as he held onto the edge.

"So, what do we do while we wait?"

Dani had several ideas flash through her mind, but none of them were good with Noah in the house.

Still…

"We could go upstairs and try to get some sleep," she suggested.

Surprisingly, he didn't try to talk her out of it or even ask her if she was sure. He crossed the room in a few strides and took her hand. "I'm suddenly exhausted."

Laughing as he led her up the stairs quietly, she left the door open just in case. Turning the baby monitor on, she stood back and watched as Tyler lay down on top of her bed in just his socks and a pair of blue jeans. He took up quite a bit of the queen-size bed; she was definitely going to need to snuggle close.

"I should take a shower. You don't want to know what was on my scrubs."

"And yet, you picked up your son and got goo all over his clean pajamas?" he teased.

"It was dried. I just feel…icky."

With a sigh, he leaned back with his arms folded behind his head. "Fine, go shower. I'll just lie here imagining you naked under the running stream, your hands trailing soap over your skin, leaving bubbles along the way—"

Dani hit him in the face with a pillow, and he grabbed at it, spluttering, but she brought it down again.

"You are such a perv."

Laughing, she let him wrestle her down onto the bed, their chests pressing against each other rapidly as they caught their breath. Tyler had her hands in his, and she was pinned to the mattress as he hovered over her. She felt the chilly air on the skin of her chest and knew her robe had fallen open by the way Tyler's gaze dropped down.

His grip on her wrists loosened as his eyes came back up to meet hers. Lowering his body over hers with his weight on his forearms, he nuzzled his nose against the sensitive skin below her ear. A shiver shot along her skin, traveling down to the apex of her legs. Clenching them together, she sighed as his lips kissed her skin with feathery brushes.

"What did you call me?" he whispered, his breath rushing along the column of her throat.

"Hmm, I don't remember."

He nipped her skin with a growl. "I think you called me a perv. Impugned my honor. I must have satisfaction."

"What satisfaction canst thou have tonight?" she said with a giggle.

Tyler lifted his face from the crook of her neck with a puzzled expression. "What's that from?"

"Oh, come on! *Romeo and Juliet*? You can't tell me you never read the play in school."

"I probably did, but I can't quote it!"

"What can I say? I was the queen of drama class in high school."

"Well, to answer your question, my queen, I will not be satisfied until I kiss you."

She closed her eyes and pursed her lips playfully, startled when he didn't take her mouth. Instead, his lips pressed against the swell of her breast over her bra.

"Oh!"

"Hmm, not quite satisfied yet. Let's try the other one, shall we?" He sat up, using those rock hard abs to lift himself, and his hands got involved, pushing aside the cup of her bra so this time, his mouth covered her nipple. His tongue flicked across it, and she bucked off the bed.

God, had it always felt this good, or had it just been so long since she'd been touched that she'd forgotten?

Her hands slid up his arms until they hit his shoulders, kneading the muscles there as he tongued her. She felt his hand seeking between her legs, and his warm palm covered her, his finger teasing her through the cotton of her panties. She whimpered, her hips lifting off the bed as she silently begged for more. For him to strip her bare and put his mouth and hands all over her.

As if sensing what she wanted, he slipped his hand inside, and she moaned as he manipulated her slit, seeking something...

When he found her clit, she twisted and turned, wanting to move closer and further away from the sensations assaulting her. He had switched back to her other breast, sucking her as he rubbed her in fast circles. A steady throb increased between her legs as her orgasm built, her thighs tightening as she came, moaning quietly into her hands, muffling the cries as she flew higher and higher.

She came down slowly, jerking every time he brushed her swollen clit. She opened her eyes, the lids suddenly so heavy it felt like someone had attached weights to them.

"Still wanna shower?"

TYLER WANTED TO strip her down to nothing, to learn every curve and line of her body.

So, when he got up from the bed and lifted her into his arms, his plan was to do just that under a fall of hot water.

"What are you doing?" she asked.

"What do you think? I'm going to make sure you get all those nooks and crannies."

To his surprise, she didn't even put up a fight, just ran her hand along his jaw. "You, too."

He sat her on the counter while he turned on the hot water.

"Get out of those clothes."

She laughed while she pushed the robe down her arms, his eyes watching every move she made. When she reached behind and unsnapped her bra, he searched through the pockets of his jeans for his wallet. He kept his emergency condom in the money slot, but when he pulled it open, there was nothing but a few one-dollar bills.

"Shit!" His hungry gaze shot back up to her, her full breasts free of the confines of her bra and her blonde hair tumbling around her bare shoulders in beautiful abandon.

It was too cruel, too painful to even utter the words.

"I don't suppose you have any condoms floating around?"

Her face fell. "No. You don't have one?"

"I usually do in my wallet for emergencies, but I don't know what happened to it."

Suddenly, she looked furious with him and started yanking her robe up her body. "Maybe you used it and forgot about it."

"Hey." He went to stand between her legs, tipping her face up to his. "I swear, I haven't been with anyone. Not since that day at the park." His forehead pressed against hers, and he realized that she had no reason to believe him. He was a self-admitted man whore. Why would she?

"I don't want you going into this not trusting me." Damn, what the hell was happening to him? Mr. Sensitive and shit.

Her arms looped around his shoulders, her forehead still resting against his. "I'm sorry, I shouldn't have immediately gone there."

"It's okay. We've got time. And although it kills me to say it, maybe we should tap the brakes until you do trust me."

"I trust you, Tyler, obviously. I let you stay with my kid—"

"Hey, hey, you don't have to get defensive, I'm not mad. I'm just saying that I get you still have reservations, and I can wait." He tilted his head to kiss her, his mouth barely leaving hers to whisper, "You're worth waiting for."

And to his surprise, he meant every word.

She broke the kiss, her hands sliding down his chest and lower over his abdomen.

"You know, there are other things we can do while we wait." She peeked up at him from beneath her lashes, and his cock flexed at the heated look and suggestive tone.

"Yeah? Like what?"

Dani pushed him back and climbed off the counter. Before he could ask what she was doing she sank to her knees, her hands unlooping his belt.

"Oh, I think I'll just have to show you."

Chapter Twenty

TYLER WOKE UP with a start, confused for a second as he took in his surroundings. Finally, it sank in through his foggy brain that he'd stayed over at Dani's last night. Slept in her bed.

And he still hadn't gotten sex.

Well, okay, he couldn't say that exactly. Dani had taken care of him so well, his legs were still shaking ten minutes after he finished. Her breath warming his cock as her tongue slipped up and down his shaft, tightening his balls until she fully encased him in her wet mouth.

Shit, and now he had a boner tenting his boxers.

Climbing out of her bed, he picked his jeans up off the floor and pulled them on, careful of the hard-on as he zipped. He buttoned them as he started down the stairs, listening to the sound of Dani singing, high-pitched and a little off-key, but Noah's laughter joining in told Tyler Noah didn't mind that his mom was tone-deaf.

As he reached the landing, Tyler smiled at the sight that greeted him.

Dani, her hair pulled up in a messy bun, was holding Noah on her hip, letting him stir a bowl of batter. The two of them, with their heads bent close together, were the cutest thing he'd ever seen.

"Good morning," he said.

Dani's gaze jerked to his, her cheeks a bright, rosy pink. Noah squirmed in her arms. "Tywer!"

Dani let him down, and the little boy ran full speed out of the kitchen, Shasta trotting along beside him. Tyler picked him up and swung him into the air, making Noah squeal.

"What's up, little man?"

He started talking a mile a minute; most of it Tyler didn't catch, but he did recognize one word.

"You're making donuts with Mommy, huh?"

"Mini donuts," Dani said, holding up some kind of hot pink appliance.

"Awesome." Tyler carried Noah over to stand next to her, and he hesitated, wanting to kiss her so bad it hurt, but unsure. They'd already broken the rules by letting him around Noah and especially spending the night here, but would she shy away if he tried?

He decided to give her a back pat to be on the safe side, watching her ladle batter into the donut-shaped molds. Finally, she closed the lid and turned to face them with a grin. "And now, we wait. Do you like cinnamon sugar or chocolate dipped?"

"Chocolate!" Noah shouted in his ear, and he laughed.

"I'm with him."

"Okay, I'll melt the chocolate. Why don't you two go watch TV or play?"

Tyler's lips twitched. "Yes, Mom."

She gave him a playful glare as Tyler carried Noah to the couch. "What do you think we should watch?"

"Mickey!"

"Don't you like anything besides Mickey?" Tyler asked.

Noah shook his head, his thumb going into his mouth.

"All right, cool, we can watch Mickey." Tyler clicked through, searching for the cartoon mouse in the queue, but it wasn't there. He went to search. Typing the word in, he found the cover but saw that it read *unavailable*.

"Sorry, buddy, but it looks like they don't have it anymore."

It was like a volcano erupted in the form of a screaming toddler. Big tears ran from Noah's eyes as his mouth hung open, spittle oozing down his chin.

Tyler put his hands up as Dani came running in. "I didn't mean to!"

"What happened?" she asked.

"They got rid of Mickey on streaming, and when I told him, he detonated."

Dani seemed amused by his discomfort, if the little smirk on her full lips was any indication. Kneeling in front of her son, she took his hands in hers.

"Noah, stop crying. We've got Mickey on DVD, remember? Why don't you grab whatever one you want to watch, and I'll put it on for you?"

Noah still whimpered and sniffled as he got up from the couch and went over to the DVDs, proceeding to pull all of them off the shelf.

For some reason, Tyler felt like apologizing. "I didn't mean to upset him; I was just telling him. I didn't expect that reaction."

"Yeah, sometimes he just has a giant meltdown, usually when he's tired. Don't worry about it, seriously."

Tyler had a hard time relaxing after that, worried about saying the wrong thing and setting off another tantrum. He was just starting to think he'd gotten the hang of dealing with little kids, and now he was back to square one. With his confidence a little shaken, he pulled out his phone and saw a text from his mom.

Hey, honey! Just wanted to make sure you're going to be here by five. Your dad is pretty upset about having veggie burgers instead of the real thing, so he's grumpy, but I just keep reminding him about what the doctor said. Looking forward to seeing you!

Shit. He'd forgotten about his dad's birthday. Not totally, he had a gift and everything, but he forgot the party was today…in South San Francisco.

He looked over at Noah curled up on the edge of the couch and sucking his thumb as he stared at the TV. And Dani, who was dipping the donuts in melted chocolate and placing them on a plate. For a second, he imagined that this was his life, spending his weekends watching cartoons and playing with Noah and his nights making love to Dani.

Even with the unnerving tantrums and the druggie ex, it sounded pretty good to him.

He got off the couch and went into the kitchen, leaning against the counter and watching Dani work. "So, I've been thinking…"

"A dangerous pastime," she sang.

"What?"

A pink blush stole up her cheeks. "Sorry, too many hours watching Disney movies. What were you going to say?"

"Okay. Today is my dad's birthday. I was thinking maybe I could take Noah and you to the San Francisco Zoo, and then afterward, we could head to my parents' house for the party. If you're ready for that."

Tyler wasn't quite sure what her expression meant. The wide green eyes and almost slack-jawed look was definitely surprise, but was that a good thing?

"I…I mean, we would love to. That sounds like a lot of fun, but are you sure?"

Without worrying about the appropriateness this time, he reached out and pulled her to him, hugging her against him. She didn't tense or try to disengage. In fact, she slid her arms around his waist and laid her head on his chest.

The trust in the gesture made his heart do a flip in his chest. "Absolutely."

SEVEN HOURS LATER, Dani walked on the other side of Noah, smiling as Tyler squatted down next to him, pointing out some kind of exotic bird. Dani was hardly paying attention to what he was saying, she was too distracted by the giddy, happy feeling bubbling up her throat.

Okay, so it was stupid, and she'd sworn she wouldn't get like this, but the day had been amazing so far. They'd gotten dressed while Tyler went home to get changed and drop Duke off at his friend's place. When he'd picked them up, she'd had the diaper bag packed, Noah in a cute polo and cargo pants, and she was wearing a simple green dress, black leggings, and boots. She'd walked out the door carrying Noah, and the way Tyler had looked at her right before he'd leaned over and kissed her lips sweetly...

Well, it had set the tone for the whole trip, during which Noah slept soundly in his car seat while Tyler and Dani talked about everything from music to his family. She knew he had two half siblings that were twelve and ten years younger than him, and from the way he talked about his stepdad, she could tell they were close. The closer it got to three thirty, the more nervous she became. Tyler had wanted to be at his parents' house early, and now that she was out of time, she kept wondering whether or not his family would have a problem with her. If they wouldn't like her or would think she wasn't right for Tyler.

"What do you think?" Tyler asked, pulling her out of her fretful thoughts.

"About what?"

"Ice cream before we take off. Noah's for it."

Her son was dancing and jumping around them awkwardly, yelling, "Ice cream! Ice cream."

She smirked. "I can see that. Fine with me."

Noah took first her hand and then sweetly reached out for Tyler's. Within a few seconds, he was swinging between them until he was squealing and Dani's arm burned in protest.

"Okay, sweetie, no more. Mama's arm is going to fall off."

When Noah kept trying, Tyler swung him up and put him up on his shoulders. "Hang on tight, buddy."

Dani opened her mouth to protest, seeing her small son so far off the ground. Noah held onto the top of Tyler's head, skewing Tyler's baseball cap a little. She noticed Tyler's hands circling Noah's ankles and took a deep breath. Her dad used to do the same thing to her when she was a kid, and she'd lived. In fact, she'd loved the view from the top of her dad's shoulders, something Noah had never had.

She did walk a little behind them, prepared to catch Noah if he started to fall back, but that didn't happen.

They stopped at the ice cream vendor, and Tyler swung Noah down. When Dani saw him reaching for his wallet, she covered his hand with hers. "You paid for lunch and admission. I can get the ice cream."

He shook his head. "I asked you two out on a date; I'm paying."

A date?

Dani's vision blurred a little, and she discreetly wiped at her eyes. Would this man never stop getting to her? He surprised her at every turn. Just when she thought he'd call it and run, he would offer to babysit or hold a couple of mini donuts over his eyes and do a monster voice at breakfast…

Or call a day trip to the zoo for the three of them a date.

Without thinking of why she should keep the public displays to a minimum, she raised up on tiptoe and kissed him. She could tell she'd surprised him, but she just cupped his stubbled cheek as she pulled away.

Before she could say anything, the ice cream vendor cleared his throat. "Do you still need a minute?"

Dani broke the contact with Tyler and smiled at the man. "Sorry, yeah."

He nodded and stepped back. Noah tried to peek up into the glass case, but he was too short, so Dani lifted him up. "What do you think? Vanilla?"

" 'Nilla," Noah said.

"Can we get two small vanilla cones?" She turned to Tyler, watching him peruse the different flavors, absently thinking about how sexy he looked in that hat. Maybe he'd leave it on when they finally did it.

Heat burned her cheeks at her train of thought.

"I'm just gonna do two scoops of strawberry in a waffle cone."

After they got their cones, they sat down at one of the benches, Noah sitting between them. Soon, Tyler stretched his arm across the back of the bench and squeezed her shoulder. She glanced over at him, and the happy grin on his face seriously made her heart stutter to a standstill.

The splat of something hitting the ground had them both looking down, and Dani saw Noah's whole face crumble. His scoop of ice cream lay on the concrete.

"Oh, Noah, it's okay, I'll get you a scoop in a cup this time."

She got up and went back over to the ice cream shack before Tyler could protest. She didn't want him buying her son endless ice cream cones. She got the ice cream in a cup with a spoon and walked back over in time to see Noah take a lick from Tyler's strawberry ice cream.

"No, he can't have that!"

Tyler jerked at her shout, and Noah started crying, reaching out for Tyler's ice cream.

Running over to where the diaper bag sat on the bench, she set Noah's cup down and started rummaging through the pockets, looking for the children's Benadryl and wipes.

"He's allergic to strawberries. Even synthetic flavors, they make him break out, and if the juice gets on his skin, he gets a rash."

"Oh, my God, I'm sorry. Is he gonna be okay?"

She finally found what she was looking for and started mopping away any traces of the pink ice cream from Noah's face. "You really should have asked before giving him any."

The minute the words were out, she wished she could call them back. Not that she was wrong, he should have made sure it was okay, but she didn't have to sound so sharp about it.

"I should have asked, you're right."

She gave Noah the chewable allergy tablet and looked up at Tyler. His normally tan skin had a definite pallor to it, and his blue eyes were locked on Noah, teeming with worry.

The flash of irritation she'd felt toward him melted away, and she put her hand on his knee. "I'm sorry I snapped at you. It's not serious, more of a mild irritation. Really."

The skin on the sides of Noah's mouth were already red and swollen slightly, but it didn't stop him from picking up the dish of vanilla and going to town.

"No, you have every right to be pissed at me. It was stupid." He tossed the rest of his cone in the trash, and Dani wished she had mentioned Noah's allergy when he'd ordered.

How could you know he would have been cool sharing his food with Noah? Most people wouldn't have done that.

No one except Tyler, who hadn't thought about sharing germs with her son. They sat in silence as Noah finished his ice cream.

Finally, when they were walking out of the zoo, Tyler said, "If you want to skip the party and get Noah home, I understand."

"No, he's fine, really. See, his face already looks better." She swallowed hard, dread settling in the pit of her stomach. "Unless you'd rather just take us home."

"If you're good with it, then so am I."

The words weren't said with a lot of enthusiasm, but Dani didn't know what else to say.

Chapter Twenty-One

TYLER, DANI, AND Noah stood on the porch of his parents' house, already an hour late to the party after the ice cream kerfuffle, and without knocking, he opened the door and ushered them in.

"We're here." He actually hadn't mentioned bringing Dani and Noah, mostly because he'd wanted to see the shock on his mom's face. He knew it wouldn't be a problem—usually he brought one or more of the guys with him for company on the drive, and his mom had always been a more-the-merrier type.

However, he wished that things weren't so tense and weird between Dani and him. The drive south they'd said very little, and he'd turned on Disney children's radio for Noah, so there hadn't been anything for him to sing along to for a distraction.

So many niggles of self-doubt chewed through his brain right now. He should have known better than to give Noah a bite of his ice cream, so why had he done it? Just because the kid had looked so sad and dejected, and he'd felt bad? No matter how much he cared about Dani and Noah, he wasn't the kid's dad. Which meant he had no business making any decisions about his well-being without asking Dani first.

"Who's we?" his dad called gruffly.

As they rounded the corner into the family room, his dad looked over at them and did a wide-eyed double take. The big burly man climbed to his feet and came over, clapping Tyler in a tight hug. Several back slaps were exchanged before Gareth Best pulled back and grinned at Dani and Noah, holding his hand out.

"Hey there, I'm Gareth Best, this knucklehead's dad."

"Dad, this is Dani Hill and her son, Noah," Tyler said.

Dani took his dad's hand with a smile, balancing Noah on the opposite hip. "It's very nice to meet you. I've heard a lot about you."

"Really? Well, to be honest, sweetheart, you are a welcome surprise." His dad held his hand up to Noah. "How are you, kiddo? Can you give me a high five?"

Noah hesitated, ducking his head shyly, but with a little coaxing from Dani, he slapped Gareth's hand.

"All right!"

"Where is everyone?" Tyler asked. The house was unusually quiet except for the sound of the TV.

"Everyone is out back except your brother, who is playing video games with Chris and those hooligan nephews of mine."

Tyler laughed at his dad's description of his cousins; he always called the twins, Kent and Kyle, hooligans because of their love of practical jokes. The twins were both twenty-one, and his aunt swore they would be the death of her.

"Why are you hiding out in here?" Tyler asked.

"Because your sister, mother, and the rest of the hens are clucking away out back. Your uncles abandoned me to go get more ice, and I was feeling a bit outnumbered."

"Well, we'll head out and say hi," Tyler said.

"You watch your mother and make sure she doesn't try to steal that child. Three of you were enough for me!"

To Tyler's relief, Dani laughed at his dad's joke.

"Just so you know, my dad has three sisters and my mom has two, so there are going to be a lot of people asking you questions. If you need a safe word for when you need rescuing, we could probably use something like 'Mickey.' "

For the first time since the strawberry fiasco, she placed her hand in his. "Tyler, I'll be fine, I promise. Besides, you've met my mom. If I can handle her, I can handle anyone."

Tyler kept ahold of her hand as he opened the sliding back door. It was a nice sunny day, just around sixty but not a cloud in the sky. As they stepped out, the women surrounding several outdoor tables turned toward them.

"Tyler!" His fifteen-year-old sister, Zoe, flew out of her chair and hurled herself into his arms.

"Hey, Pita, good to see you, too."

She pulled away from him, making a face. "Are you kidding me with the Pita? Still?" Zoe's gaze went past him to Dani, and her green eyes widened. "You brought a *girl*?"

Tyler rolled his eyes at his sister's loud whisper. "Like I said, still a pain in the—"

"You watch your mouth, Tyler. You're not too old for me to get a bar of soap." His mother came up and practically shoved Zoe out of the way to hug him before turning her attention to Dani. "I apologize for my children's appalling behavior. I blame their father."

"No, it's fine. Really. It's very nice to meet you, Mrs. Best. I'm Dani, and this is Noah."

"You call me Gloria." She scooted closer to Noah, smiling as she held her arms out to him. "Hello, Noah. Wanna come see me? We have all kinds of finger foods, a fruit and veggie tray—"

"He's allergic to strawberries," Tyler blurted.

His mom's eyebrow rose at his outburst, but otherwise, she just waited for Noah. The toddler sucked his thumb, eyeing her seriously and then looking at Dani.

"It's okay," she said encouragingly.

"You know what, why don't you two come sit by me, and then he'll get used to me." Gloria took Dani's hand and gave Tyler an expectant look. "You don't mind if we steal your...friend, do you?"

Tyler shook his head. "No, that's fine. She knows to yell the safe word."

Dani gave him a dirty look.

Tyler greeted each of his aunts, who were hardly paying him any mind, their maternal focus on Noah and how adorable his curls were. He finally escaped with Zoe hot on his heels.

"Dude, is that your kid?" she asked bluntly.

"No, dummy."

"I'm just asking. You're the one who showed up without telling anyone you were bringing a girl. I mean, I don't even think I've seen you with a girl!"

"Who brought a girl?" Dereck asked from the kitchen doorway, his boyfriend, Chris, standing behind him. Like Tyler, Dereck had their mother's blue eyes, but his hair was dark like Gareth's. He was shorter than Tyler by a few inches but stockier. Chris was African American with a shaved head and glasses, exactly Dereck's height but wiry.

"Our brother brought home a girl," Zoe said, bringing Tyler out of his head.

"No shit?" Dereck went to the back window, and his jaw dropped. "Is that her kid?"

"That's her son, Noah," Tyler growled.

Chris hovered over Dereck's shoulder. "She's pretty."

"How long have you been dating?" Zoe asked.

"A couple of weeks."

"Really?" Dereck dragged the word out, and Tyler was grateful when Chris elbowed him. "What?"

"Give your brother a break, or he might not bring her back."

"Chris, you in the kitchen?" Gareth yelled.

"Yeah, Pop."

"Grab me a beer, will ya?"

Chris went over to the fridge. Dereck was giving him a look that appeared to be a mix of humor and exasperation.

"You know you don't have to do that. He can get his own beer."

"Stop it, it's his birthday." He gave Dereck a kiss on the cheek as he walked by. "Besides, I love your dad."

When Chris walked out of the room, Tyler chuckled. "Dad lets him call him Pop?"

Dereck shook his head. "Yeah, believe it or not. Sometimes I think Dad likes Chris more than me."

"Shut it with your poor middle-child whine," Zoe said.

"Yeah, if you don't want to be replaced, you shouldn't date people Dad likes," Tyler teased.

"Enough about me, tell us about her," Dereck said.

Kent and Kyle made their grand appearance, and when they saw Tyler, they whooped with excitement.

"What up, bro?" Kent said.

After a lot of back slapping, Tyler said, "Nothing, just got here a little bit ago."

"Holy shit, who's the hot blonde with Aunt Gloria?"

"That's Tyler's new girlfriend, Dani," Zoe said.

"Let me see!" Kent raced over to the window and whistled. "Damn, she is smoking. Whoa, wait, is that her little boy?"

"Yes, that's Noah," Tyler growled, already exhausted by his family.

"Now, why can't I meet a girl who looks like her?" Kyle lamented.

Tyler walked over and grabbed both of his cousins in a headlock. "Stop ogling her, or I'm gonna kick your asses."

He was only half joking, and both of them wiggled out of his grip, their nearly identical faces wearing mischievous grins.

The front door opened and shut, and several loud male voices argued, drawing closer.

"Oh, I can't wait to tell Uncle Troy about Dani," Zoe said, talking about the twins' dad.

Tyler decided that there was a good chance he was going to murder his baby sister before the night was over.

Chapter Twenty-Two

DANI KEPT LEANING over so she could watch Noah in the backyard as she helped Tyler's mother with the dishes. Her son was running as fast as his chubby legs would take him, trying to get ahold of the soccer ball Tyler's cousins and siblings were gently kicking around, playing a mild game of keep-away with the toddler. The aunts still sat at the tables, watching and occasionally shouting something she couldn't hear, but Dani wasn't really worried. This family, with their big, loud voices and welcoming words, had put her completely at ease.

"You know, you're so sweet to offer, but if you want to go outside and play with them, I'm fine finishing," Gloria said.

Dani shook her head and turned back to her task. "I'm happy to help. I appreciate you allowing us to crash the party."

"Oh please, you aren't crashing anything. We are all just so excited to meet you. And Noah, that boy is just the sweetest thing, letting us pass him around and snuggle him. That says he knows he's safe and loved, and that tells me all I need to know about you."

Dani blinked back the sting in her eyes. "Thank you."

"Mom, are you seriously making Dani do the dishes?"

Tyler's voice made Dani jump, and she almost dropped the plate she was setting into the dishwasher. They had hardly talked since they arrived, with him visiting with all of his family and her caught up with the barrage of questions everyone had for her.

"Here, I'll take over that. You're a guest. Go relax."

Forgetting his mother was there, she bristled. "How about you don't boss me around?"

Gloria cackled and reached up to first pinch, then pat Tyler's sheepish face. "I like her. She doesn't put up with any of your shit."

"No, she certainly does not," Tyler murmured.

Dani blushed as he pulled her toward him. "Dani, can I please take over helping mom with the dishes?"

Knowing he was teasing her, she gave in. "Fine. Where's the bathroom?"

"Go down the hall, and it's the first door on the right."

She left the room and headed for the bathroom, sticking her tongue out at him as she left.

Dani caught his mother's smile just before the swinging door closed.

"Have I mentioned how much I like her?"

"Several times, Mom."

"So, ARE YOU going to tell me what's on your mind?" his mother asked, tearing his gaze away from where Dani had disappeared.

"What makes you think I want to talk? Maybe I was just looking to do something nice."

"Because I raised you. I couldn't get you to do a dish unless you wanted something."

"Gee, thanks, Mom."

His mother wiped her hands on the towel hanging from the cabinet door and turned to face him. "Talk to me."

Unsure exactly what he wanted to say, he set the plate in the dishwasher, stalling. Finally, he listened for the sound of footsteps or anyone lingering, and when he heard nothing, he said, "When you and Dad were dating, how long were you together before I met him?"

"Well, I think we'd gone out three or four times, but I knew he was what I wanted after date number one."

"Did he ever make a mistake, or did you ever have doubts about him being a good father?"

A light came into his mother's blue eyes, and she smiled gently. "Ah, baby, what did you do?"

"What makes you think I did something?"

"Because I remember that look. That worried I'm-not-sure-I-can-do-this look."

"On Dad?" he asked.

"No, when I looked in the mirror."

Tyler couldn't have been more shocked if she'd told him she had walked on the moon. "What? When?"

"Pretty much from the moment I brought you home. I was only seventeen when I had you, and my parents had kicked me out. I was living with my grandmother, who was brisk and cold. I never did understand why she took me in, but I remember this one time, I had you in your Moses basket on the bed while I folded laundry. I left the room for just a second, and when I came back, the basket was on its side and you were on the floor, screaming. I ran you up to the emergency room, which I couldn't afford, and after the doctor assured me you were fine, I called my mother crying. She came, and we left my car in the parking lot. She drove us to the nearest Denny's, and as I cried into my short stack, blubbering about what had happened, she reached across and squeezed my hand."

His mother drew in a shaky voice, and he saw tears in her eyes as she continued. "And she said, 'Gloria, as a mother, you're going to screw up and make bad decisions. Things you regret, and at some point, you're going to think you can't do anything right. But as long as you do your best and love your son, everything is gonna be okay.'"

She wiped at her eyes, and he pulled his mom in for a hug, always hating the sight of her crying. She patted his chest and pulled away with a chuckle. "Anyway, after that, she drove me back to my grandma's, where she helped me pack up all my stuff and brought me home. When my dad started bellowing and telling her to take me back, she told him if he wanted to leave, he knew where the door was. Otherwise, he needed to get his fat ass up and drive over to pick the rest of my stuff up from Grandma's. And eventually, he did. It took a while for us to forgive each other, but he loved you."

She slapped his arm lightly. "So, I'm gonna ask you one more time, what did you do?"

He looked away and stared out the window at the adorable little boy he'd grown to care for way too much. "I gave Noah a bite of my ice cream without knowing he was allergic to it. I was just trying to keep him from having a meltdown because his ice cream fell and Dani went to get him another scoop. But she got upset with me, and I don't blame her, but it got me thinking... What if I'm just not cut out for this? What if I'm not the guy?"

His mother pinched him in the side, and he jumped to the side as she laid into him. "Tyler Wyatt Best, that is just stupid. You made a mistake, and you'll learn from it. Jesus, I nearly killed Gareth the first time he took you dirt biking in the foothills, and you broke your arm. I came into that ER madder than a hornet, hollering at him about how he'd better never do anything like that with *my* son again. We'd only been married a few months, and when he left the hospital and I walked into the room you were in, you were crying, so worried that Dad was going to leave us. And I realized that in my fear, I hadn't just lashed out at him, but I'd hurt you. When he came back, I could tell he'd been crying, and I'll never forget that relieved look on your face.

"But Dani doesn't seem upset with you, and that boy's face lights up every time he sees you, so I'm sure it's not as bad as all that." His mother laced him with a stern look.

"But if you're really not sure about a future with that girl and her son, then you need to break it off now."

Tyler leaned back against the counter and shook his head. "I know, Mom, but I care about her, and I adore that kid. When it's just us, I feel like they're...as if they belong with me. Like they were meant to be mine, but I'm afraid that's crazy."

"Absolutely not. Your dad said almost the exact thing to me when he proposed, that it was as if we'd been waiting for him." His mom took his hand and squeezed. "I am so happy for you, baby."

"I'm not a baby, Mom."

"You'll always be my baby."

DANI STOOD OUTSIDE the kitchen, her heart hammering as she listened to mother and son talk. She didn't mean to eavesdrop, but when she'd heard her name, she couldn't help pausing to catch what Tyler was saying.

She couldn't even describe her elation and joy when Tyler had said that Noah and she felt like his.

Because she had been thinking the exact same thing about him and was afraid she'd ruined it today.

Tyler's mother told him to go outside and play with the kids, and Dani soon heard the back glass door slide open and close.

"You can come in now, Dani," Gloria called.

Dani nearly banged her head against the door with a groan, but with no other choice, she pushed through. "I am so sorry; I shouldn't have listened in on your conversation."

"I always listen in on interesting conversations. It's how I learn the things my children don't want me to know about." She waved her hand to the square table in the dining room off the kitchen. "Come have a seat, and we can talk as the kids play."

Dani did as she requested, her hands sweating buckets.

"Now, it's none of my business, and you can tell me to butt out, but as a mother, I need to know." Leveling Dani with the same deep blue eyes her son had, she asked, "What are your intentions with my boy?"

Dani choked on a laugh. "My intentions?"

"Yes. Are you serious about him?"

"Very."

The older woman's face softened. "So, you're not upset with him?"

"No. Well, I was a little irritated that he didn't ask, but then I just couldn't stop thinking about how for a guy who is constantly saying he isn't good with children, he had no problem sharing his ice cream with Noah. He's just so comfortable and good with Noah. He's constantly surprising me."

"Don't let him fool you; he has always had a way with kids. He was ten and twelve when his brother and sister were born, and he used to love playing with them. Feeding them. He probably doesn't even remember begging to learn how to change a diaper."

"No way!" Dani laughed.

"Oh yes, he loved being a big brother...up until he discovered girls, that is. To be honest, I was a little worried about him. I know he's only twenty-eight but he never seemed to have any desire to get serious. Until you."

Dani's cheeks warmed with pleasure as she looked out the window. Tyler had Noah in his arms and was chasing after one of his cousins. His hat was turned backward, so nothing was obscuring his wide smile.

"You know, Gloria, if you don't mind, I think I'd like to go play with the kids."

Gloria patted her hand and stood up. "And I'm going to make sure that my husband hasn't conned poor Chris into getting him another beer. He knows he needs to lay off the alcohol and red meat, but Chris adores Gareth and will do anything for him."

Dani stood up and went outside just as Tyler set Noah down. Her son took off after Dereck, who ran backward at a slow pace, laughing.

"Man, this kid is fast. I think he's going to be a sprinter someday," Dereck said.

Dani wrapped her arms around Tyler's waist, and she felt him start.

"Hey, I didn't even hear you come out."

"You were having too much fun," she teased.

"Yeah, Noah's a big hit. I've got six other cousins who are living out of state, but other than that, Zoe is the last baby we've had around here." His arms went around her, and he whispered in her hair, "About what happened with the ice cream…"

"No, it's okay. I love that you didn't give a second thought about sharing with Noah. I just had a mommy meltdown moment."

"I've heard of those. Do they happen often?"

"Probably, but I'll try to keep them at a minimum," she said, snuggling against his chest.

"Hey, can I get a hug?" one of the twins called.

Dani looked up in time to catch Tyler's murderous glare. "No."

"Ah, come on, cuz," the other chimed in.

"You're both asking to get your dicks knocked in the dirt."

"Whoa, little ears!" Zoe protested, covering Noah's ears and removing her hands with a laugh. "Earmuffs, Noah!"

Suddenly, Dani was picked up from behind and pulled away from Tyler. She squealed as Dereck spun her away and then dumped her over his shoulder. "Wanna play keep-away, big brother?"

He took off at a run, and Dani's full stomach protested as she bumped along on his shoulder. "I'm gonna puke on you!"

Dereck set her down in a hurry, but before she could get her bearings, one of the twins swung her up, cradling her with an evil laugh as he ran. She glanced over his shoulder at Tyler, who was shaking his head with a scowl.

"Toss her to me, Kyle!" Kent called from a few feet away.

"Wait, don't throw me—" She was laughing too hard to say more as Kyle tossed her up. Luckily, Kent caught her before she hit the ground, and, finally catching her breath, she shouted, "Okay, that is enough! I am not a toy!"

Kent released her when Tyler came up behind him and grabbed him by the back of the neck.

"Ow! Ow...ow...ow..."

"You heard her. Down, now."

Dani escaped over to where Zoe and Chris were trying not to laugh.

"Now, Noah, don't ever try to be like Kent, Kyle, and Dereck. They are naughty," Zoe said.

Dani held her arms out for her son, who flew into them. She turned around to watch as Tyler flipped Dereck over his shoulder and took down Kyle next.

Kent, who she'd now figured out was wearing the green shirt while Kyle was in red, lay on his back, his chest rising and falling rapidly. As he climbed to his feet, he called, "It's not fair. You have all that ninja training. Even with the gimpy knee, you're still—"

"Shut up, Kent!" Dereck snapped.

Everyone in the yard stiffened, and Dani had no idea what had happened to change the mood of the play, but as Tyler climbed to his feet, she noticed a definite limp in his step.

As he neared her, she stepped forward with Noah. "Are you okay?"

"Yeah, we just probably should start heading back. It's getting late."

"Tyler, I'm sorry," Kent called.

Tyler didn't say anything, but as they opened the glass door, she heard Zoe hiss, "You are such a fucking asshole, Kent."

TYLER WAS READY to get out of the car. He was stiff, and his knee was aching, despite the Tylenol his mother had given him.

The only good thing about the long drive was getting to hold Dani's hand the whole way home.

"What did Kent mean?" she asked finally. Tyler was surprised it had taken her so long to bring it up.

"You know how I told you I was shot?" He saw her nod out of the corner of his eye. "Well, it was actually a sniper bullet that went through my dog and my knee. Tore up the cartilage pretty good."

"Your dog? Oh God, Tyler."

He chuckled bitterly. "Yeah, I never knew something could hurt so bad, and Rex…Well, I couldn't leave him. I lay there on the ground, holding my dead dog in my arms instead of trying to crawl. Trying to get myself to safety. Luckily, some of the guys from my squad heard my distress call and came for me. They put me on a chopper, and after several surgeries, they sent me here to recover. Physical therapy and group counseling. I guess I was too valuable as a military dog trainer for them to give me a medical discharge, but they'll never send me back into the field again."

Her hands covered his and she squeezed. "Do you want to go back?"

"Hell no. Sparks did, until he met Violet, and I get he had his own reasons, but I was done. I still remember the sound and smell and Rex's blood on my hands…" Dani gave a soft whimper, and he cursed. "I'm sorry, you don't need to hear this shit."

"No, I'm just picturing the whole thing, and it makes me ache for you." She brought his hand up to her cheek, turning to press her lips to his palm.

Needing to lighten the mood a bit, he joked, "If you really want to make me feel better, you should use my hand to cup something else."

She smacked him in the chest.

"Ow, don't abuse the driver."

"Then stop being a pervert."

Tyler got off the freeway and headed straight for Dani's place. It was a little after ten, and he was exhausted. He still needed to pick up Duke, and he had switched with Bryce tomorrow so he needed to be at the program at nine in the morning.

He parked the car in her driveway and got to the back door first. "I'll get him. You get the door."

She nodded and went to go unlock it. Tyler ducked into the backseat and unbuckled Noah, who snored on softly. He lifted the toddler out and held him with his head against his shoulder. They'd changed him into pajamas before they'd made the drive back, and considering how out the little guy was, Tyler was glad Dani wouldn't have to wrestle pajamas onto him.

Dani pushed the door open and went first, shooing and shushing her two dogs as they barked excitedly. Shasta stood up on her hind legs and tried to sniff Noah, and Tyler patted her head.

Tyler laid Noah down in his crib and ran a hand over his curls gently.

"Night, buddy."

He pulled the fleece blanket over him and left the room, closing the door with a soft click. Dani was standing in the kitchen, holding her phone to her ear with a frown.

"What's up?" he whispered.

She held the phone out to him. "Press play."

Tyler did as she said and listened.

"Hello, Danielle, this is Camila Ramirez, Angel's mother. I would like to talk to you regarding my grandchild. Please call me at 916-555-0923. Thank you."

Tyler's body pulsed with anger. God, Angel was a fucking pussy. "Nothing like sending his mommy to do his dirty work. Are you going to call her?"

"I think I should talk to a lawyer first. See what my options are. I just...I only met his mother a few times, but I know she hated me." With a heavy sigh, she took her phone back and set it on the counter. "I just don't get why he's even interested in Noah, you know? He was the one who said he wanted nothing to do with either of us. Now I've got not just him, but his mother contacting me."

"How did they get your number?" he asked.

"I've had the same number for years. I've never changed it."

"Might want to think about doing that," Tyler said.

"Yeah, I might, depending on what the lawyer says, but they already know where I live. Unless I want to move, too, not sure how helpful that will be."

Suddenly, Tyler wasn't so sure about going back to his place tonight. Maybe he should get Duke and his uniform and come back. Tyler cupped her face in his hands and peered down at her. "I don't like you being here alone. What if he's watching the house?"

"Okay, now you're just being paranoid. We're fine, and even if he was watching the house, I can't imagine he'd try anything. Plus, there is no way he is getting past a locked door and two ferocious guard dogs."

Tyler glanced down at pudgy, snorting Bella and Shasta, whose tail thumped against the carpet.

"Not sure about the ferociousness."

"You didn't see Shasta when he came to the house. She almost launched herself at him. I would have been scared of her if she hadn't been my dog."

"Speaking of dogs…" He kissed her, rubbing his thumb across her cheek. "I gotta go get Duke."

"So go," she whispered back.

"I will. But we had a long day that included our first real fight, and we didn't properly make up."

"I told you, it's fine. What do we need to make up for?"

Tyler kissed her again, deeper this time, his hips pressing her back into the counter. He pulled his mouth away long enough to say, "Fun?"

Dani reached around and gripped his ass through his jeans in response, and he groaned. Dropping his hands from her face, he picked her up by her rear end and lifted her onto the counter. "Lie back."

She did as he asked, her chest rising and falling rapidly as he shoved her dress up, revealing the black leggings keeping him from what he wanted most.

He buried his head between her legs and pressed his mouth against her through the soft cotton. After turning his cap backward so the bill wasn't in the way, he hooked his fingers into the sides of her leggings and pulled them, along with her underwear, down to her knees.

With the kitchen light shining over them, he saw that she'd shaved, and his excitement grew until his cock was practically pulsating with hunger. Lifting her legs and ducking his head between them, he let them fall so her boot heels hit him in the middle of his back.

He spread her lips with his thumbs and swept his tongue over the hard nub of her clit, listening to the hiss of her breath with pure male pride. Foreplay was something he'd done on occasion, but with Dani, it wasn't a chore to get to the final act; in fact, Tyler realized he liked it. The anticipation, her sounds of ecstasy as he licked, sucked, and fingered her until she was smothering cries of joy, her muscles squeezing his fingers as she came. It was almost better than sex.

Giving her slit one last long lick that left her shuddering, he lifted her legs over his head and redressed her lovingly.

Taking her hands, he pulled her up into a sitting position, his hand stroking her cheek. "I better go."

"Wait, now?"

"I still need to get my dog, and when we do it, I'm going to want to spend the whole night with you after."

Her hands trailed over his chest and abdomen until they were cupping his dick through his jeans. "But that doesn't mean you need to leave without being satisfied."

"It's not necessary..." he began, sucking in his breath when she pushed him back.

"I think it is." She hopped down from the counter and stalked toward him.

DANI SLIPPED TYLER'S belt from the buckle, her tongue sliding inside his mouth. He tasted of mint and her, and she was rabid with wanting him. The need to make him feel as good as she did, to give him more pleasure than he could handle so he wouldn't...

Wouldn't go to someone else?

God, why did that thought keep creeping though her mind? He'd brought her home to meet his parents, had shown her in every way that he cherished her and Noah.

Pushing all the negative thoughts from her mind, she proceeded to get swept up in what she was doing now. It had been a long time since she'd given head, until last night with Tyler. She'd been afraid that it would be awful, that she'd be so bad he'd walk out with a *thanks anyway.*

Instead, she'd looked up at him, at the look of pure bliss on his handsome face, and instinct had taken over.

And she wanted that feeling again. To be responsible for Tyler losing control, to hear her name on his lips as he came.

Leading him to the couch, she unbuttoned his pants on the way, sliding the zipper down to expose his boxer briefs.

"It's your turn to lie back. On the couch."

Tyler kicked off his shoes and pushed his jeans and underwear all the way off. When he was naked from the waist down, she licked her lips.

He reached up to pull off his hat, and she stopped him. "No. The shirt can go, but the hat stays on."

He raised a brow but didn't argue. Stripping so the only thing he wore was a hat and a smile, he lay back on the couch.

"I'm all yours."

Yes, you are.

Her possessive thought escaped before she could catch it. She kicked off her boots and leaned over the couch until she was settled on her knees between his legs.

"Scoot up a bit."

He did as she asked, and, twisting her hair into a knot on top of her head, she leaned over him, her hands cupping his balls before circling the base of his cock. Her tongue swirled around the tip and then dipped into the tiny hole there, catching the first drop of excitement that had gathered.

As she slid her mouth over him, pressing down until her lips met her hands, she started to pump and suck, swirling her tongue, massaging his balls, her breasts tightening as he started talking.

"Fuck, God, yes. Holy shit, just like that. Dani…"

She fought a smile as she stepped up the speed, his groans becoming a beat to music only she could hear. She was sweating, and her jaw was starting to ache, but she pushed through it, keeping up the pressure until she felt his cock jerk in her mouth.

His hand tangled in her hair, freeing the strands from the makeshift knot, and as the curtain of her blonde hair shrouded her, she swallowed his pleasure. He shouted her name this time as he came, and when she was sure he was done, she licked up his shaft one more time, similar to what he'd done to her.

Flipping her hair off her face, she smiled up at him. "So…are you satisfied?"

"Fuck, yeah."

She kissed over his abdomen, his six-pack muscles jumping under her mouth as she climbed up his body, tucking her knees along both sides of his hips as she straddled him.

"Good." She started to lift herself off him, but he reached up and grabbed her hips. "You don't have to move."

Stretching out on top of him, she laid her cheek on his bare chest. "Okay, but I thought you had to go get Duke."

"I do, but shit, Dani, I don't want to leave you."

His chest rumbled with every heavenly word coming out of his mouth, and she lifted her head, folding her hands on his chest.

"So, how about next weekend I come over to your place? Noah will be at my parents', and I could make you dinner."

His thumb brushed across her lower lip.

"Will you be cooking naked?"

"If you want me to," she said.

"You are such a tease. Now I'm gonna think about you standing in my kitchen naked with a wooden spoon...Fuck, I'm going to have blue balls all week!"

"Hey, you were the one who brought it up. I was just being accommodating."

"I think you like knowing you drive me wild."

Her fingers played across his pecs. "I like knowing that you want me."

Tyler's hand tangled in her hair, cupping the back of her head. "Oh, I want you, all right. I want you more than I've ever wanted anything."

His words sent her stomach somersaulting, and she leaned up to kiss him, softly and sweetly.

"What was that for?" he asked.

Because I might just love you.

Chapter Twenty-Four

TYLER TOOK HIS squad out to the off-site team-building course Alpha Dog had been working on during the summer months. Dr. Stabler had suggested that if the boys did some team-building exercises together, it might help Meyers and Jeremiah come to a resolution.

Only the mud from the rain that had been pouring down all week made the course harder than usual.

"All right, here's the deal. We'll break up into two teams for the day, of my choosing. The losing team will do the winning team's chores for a week, and as long as your schoolwork is done, the winning team will get a movie night every night for a week. Sound good?"

The boys hollered and whooped.

"Then here we go. Meyers, Walton, Harlow, Platt, Locke, and Benton Team One! The rest of you are Team Two."

Meyers and Walton eyed each other warily.

"Team One, you're with me. Team Two, you're with Sergeant Kline."

Once Kline had led the kids over to the London Bridge, Tyler waved Team One over to him. "First up is the spider web." Tyler indicated the ropes in the shape of a giant web. "You need to get every member through those holes without waking the spider. If you vibrate her ropes too many times and she drops, you have to start over. So, come up with a strategy, and let's go."

Tyler had to admit, the six teenagers acted as though there had never been a conflict as they came up with a strategy. Three on each side, they would put one guy through right to left and the next, left to right. Platt was the only one putting up a stink about the other guys not being able to lift him, but to Tyler's surprise, Jeremiah Walton was the one to shut him up.

"Dude, stop it! I know what you're doing, but we need you to suck it up and trust us. We can get you through the hole and win this."

"What is it I'm doing?" Platt asked.

"You're calling yourself fat before someone else does it. I do the same thing."

"How is that? You're not fat."

"No, but with my long hair and being a twig, people call me shit all the time. I figured for a long time it was just better to make fun of myself before they did or ignore them. But that's not good for either one of us. We're your teammates, and it's our job to build you up and make sure you get to the other side."

"Better listen to him, Platt. He makes sense."

Tyler wanted to throw his fist in the air as Meyers backed up Walton. This was what he'd been looking for, and he would have to remember to send Dr. Stabler a fruit basket for working with Meyers.

By the time they finished the course, Team One beat out Team Two by fifteen seconds. There was a chorus of good-natured groans and razzing, but otherwise, they all shook hands and climbed into the van without issue.

On the way back to Alpha Dog, they stopped off to grab Taco Bell, and when the boys started making jokes about the cafeteria food, Blake threatened to tell their head cook. Tyler grinned as he drove, chalking today in the win column.

He parked in front and got out to open the door. The boys filed out, and he just happened to glance down the sidewalk.

And into the hate-filled stare of Carlos Mendez.

Tyler pushed through the boys when he saw the gun and said, "All of you get down."

Tyler put his hands up, hoping to make himself a big enough target so Carlos wouldn't think about the other boys. A cold sweat covered his whole body as he looked down the barrel of that gun, the pain and panic coming back to him like a flash flood.

"What now, motherfucker? You thought you could disrespect me and I would just go down like a little bitch?"

"No, I didn't think that. But I also didn't expect you to show up at a military-run building with a firearm."

"Shows what you know, huh, *puta*? You think you're so bad, but looks like I got you pissing your pants. What you got to say now?"

Tyler took a step toward him, and Carlos told him to back up. Faces flashed through Tyler's head as he tried to stall. His parents, Zoe and Dereck, his aunts, uncles, and cousins...

Dani and Noah.

But he couldn't think about that. Not when there were a dozen kids in his care, boys he was supposed to protect.

"Look, you want me, you got me. But let everyone else go inside."

"You mean those other shitheads that laughed at me? Nah, I think they'll stay. I got an extra clip just for them."

"You haven't hurt anyone yet, Carlos. You can walk. You're only sixteen. Your whole life ahead of you. I'll speak to the judge about leniency—"

"Sure, you want to talk now that I got you by the balls. Go ahead, talk. Not going to save you."

"Except this is murder. If you do this, you'll have taken fourteen lives. You'll get life or worse, the death penalty. Do you really want that? Don't you want to open that custom car shop with your little brother?"

Tyler thanked God he'd read Carlos's file several times. Carlos had had dreams and aspirations. It was why they'd picked him for the program in the first place.

Only Carlos's dark gaze didn't hold anything except emptiness.

"Enrique bit it last night. Got shot by the cops last night when he pulled a piece. Stupid fucker tried to boost a car by himself." Tyler could hear the pain in his voice, even if he couldn't see it.

"Carlos, I'm sorry, but you don't want this—"

"Don't tell me what I want!" he screamed, spittle flying. "Maybe I'm planning on ending this today. What do you think about that? No jail, no death penalty. Just me going down and taking you assholes with me."

If that was his plan, Tyler had a choice. He could rush him and try to tackle him before he got a shot off, or he could try to keep him talking and hope help would show up.

The decision was made for him when someone raced from the other side of the van toward Carlos.

Jeremiah Walton.

The kid was fast, but he wasn't as fast as a bullet.

Just as Carlos turned toward Jeremiah, Tyler rushed him, ignoring the pain in his knee every time his feet hit the pavement. It seemed as though he was running in slow motion, and his gut wrenched as Carlos took a shot at Jeremiah. It must have gone wide, because the thin kid kept going, plowing into Carlos. The two of them were grappling for the gun, and then a loud pop echoed around them.

Tyler reached them just as Carlos pushed Jeremiah off him, his hands covered in red.

Tyler wasn't thinking as he clocked Carlos across the jaw and snatched the gun. He threw it across the lawn.

"Blake, get him!"

Tyler knelt next to Jeremiah, putting pressure on the wound. Blood oozed up between his fingers, and his hands shook as he chanted.

"Please. Please. Please."

The sound of sirens in the distance broke through the adrenaline pounding in his ears, and he whispered, "Hang in there, Jeremiah. They're coming."

TYLER SAT IN the hospital waiting area alone. He'd called Jeremiah's mom on the way to the hospital and gotten her voicemail. That was hours ago, and Jeremiah was still in surgery. The bullet had gone through the right side of his chest, but they were worried about a collapsed lung.

God, while he'd been waiting to make his move, he'd been saved by a fourteen-year-old kid. One who had already been through the seven circles of hell in his short life.

Holding his face in his hands, he tried to concentrate on just breathing and drawing deep, calming breaths.

"Sergeant Best?"

Tyler's head swung up, and the surgeon who had taken Jeremiah up stood in the doorway. She was a short Asian woman with a blank expression that scared the hell out of him.

"Is he all right?" he asked.

"Is his mother here yet?"

"No, not yet. Please, can you just tell me—"

"He was very lucky. We were able to repair the damage to his lung, and barring any further complications, he should make a full recovery. He needs to rest, but if you would like to check on him tomorrow, that should be fine."

Tyler held his hand out, and the doctor took it with a smile.

"Thank you so much. The kid is a hero."

"So I heard. I'm sure his mother will be proud."

Just at the mention of the woman who had chosen a man over her own kid, Tyler's vision blurred with a red fog. He didn't even remember driving to the Walton family home until he was standing on their doorstep, pounding on the front door.

A barrel-chested man answered the door, and the scent of pot wafted out, hitting Tyler full in the face.

"I need to speak with Virginia Walton."

"Who the fuck are you?"

"I'm the man who has no problem kicking the shit out of a woman-beating dickhead. Get Virginia. Now."

"Maybe I'll just call the cops—"

"Who is it, Neil?" a woman's voice called from inside the house.

"Some army dick who thinks he can tell me what to do in my own home."

Suddenly, a pale, heavyset woman pushed into the doorway. "Jeremiah?"

"Your son is at Sutter Memorial. He was shot today and just got out of surgery about an hour ago."

"Oh God." Her eyes filled with tears, and Tyler's attitude toward her softened a bit.

"I called your cell phone and left a voicemail."

"It…it's broken." Her gaze shifted toward Neil, and Tyler had a feeling Jeremiah's absence hadn't made it easier for her.

"How'd the little queer get himself shot, anyway?" Neil asked, unaware of how close Tyler was to beating the ever-loving shit out of him.

Tyler grabbed Neil by his throat and squeezed until the man's face turned red.

"Don't call him that ever again."

"You're hurting him," Virginia whimpered.

Just as Neil was starting to turn purple, Tyler pushed him away. The fat man stumbled back and fell into a table before he hit the floor.

Tyler spared Virginia one last disgusted look. "Your son was a hero today. He saved over a dozen lives…and you picked that piece of shit over him."

That seemed to wake her up, and fury blazed through her dark eyes. "Get out of here!"

He let her slam the door in his face, shaking all over as the events of the day finally sank in. He got in his car and drove back to Alpha Dog to grab Duke.

As he walked through the door, everyone stared at him. It wasn't until he got to his office that he realized why.

His shirt and pants were painted dark with Jeremiah's blood.

Tyler grabbed his spare fatigues from his desk drawer and was in the middle of stripping off his T-shirt when someone knocked.

"Who is it?"

"Sparks."

"Hang on, I'm changing." He finished changing his pants and called out, "Enter."

Sparks's face was a mask of concern. "How's Jeremiah?"

"He'll live. Not as if his family gives a shit."

Sparks searched his face and then pinched the bridge of his nose. "Do I need to spin any kind of damage control?"

"I barely choked the douche bag."

"Well, I'm on orders from General Reynolds to put you on medical leave for a week. You'll need to go see a psychiatrist and have them clear you to come back."

"I'm fine, Sparks. Just pissed off."

It was true, he was, but not at Carlos or Jeremiah. Hell, not even at that dick, Neal.

Tyler was angry with himself. He should have acted sooner, taken out Carlos so Jeremiah hadn't tried.

"Regardless, you're on leave. We'll shift things around to handle your squad. And don't forget to set up the appointment—"

"Sparks, get the fuck out of my office."

Sparks didn't argue, just started to leave.

As an afterthought, Tyler asked, "Hey, how're Blake and the other kids? Are they okay?"

"Yeah, Blake is shaken up, and given his history, I can't blame him. The boys have just been asking about Jeremiah. Might be nice if you went out and gave them an update."

Jesus, he could barely keep it together now, but to go out there and talk to the guys?

He pulled up his big-boy pants and went into the study hall, where the guys sat doing their schoolwork. The minute they saw him, they all stood up and started talking at once.

"Is Jeremiah okay? Did you see him? Is Carlos going to prison?"

He held up his hands, and they quieted. "Jeremiah is going to be okay. He had a collapsed lung, but the doctors have repaired it, and barring further complications, he should be fine. I'm going to stop by and check on him tomorrow."

"Can I go, too, Sarge?" Meyers asked.

"Well, I can't take all of you, but if it's okay with everyone else, you can represent the squad. Maybe you guys can do something for Jeremiah. I know you like to think you're big tough guys, but it would go a long way to helping Jeremiah recover."

Tyler took a deep breath before moving onto the next order of business. "Now, if you haven't heard already, Sergeant Sparks has put me on medical leave for a week. This means one of the other instructors is going to take over for me, and if I hear one thing about you giving them a bad time, I will be back here and making you do updowns until you're blue in the face. Is that clear?"

"Sir, yes, sir!" they all chorused.

"Good."

"Hey, Sarge, did you get hurt? Is that why you're on leave?" Hank asked.

"No, I'm on leave so I can get my head shrunk. They just want to make sure I'm not going to lose my shit."

"Are you? Going to lose your shit?" Harlow asked.

Good question.

"Of course not. I'm gonna be fine."

Chapter Twenty-Five

DANI PUT THE finishing touches on the romantic meal she'd planned all week. Tyler had left her a spare key to get in, and as soon as her mother had picked up Noah, Dani had started getting ready. Hair and makeup, check. Sexy negligée, done. Mood lighting.

She heard the key turn in the lock and fiddled with her hair as she tried posing seductively by the table.

But when Tyler's gaze met hers, she stiffened, caught off guard by the raw pain in his face.

"Tyler, are you okay?"

He unclipped Duke's leash and let him amble toward her to say hi. He'd gotten his cast off this week, and when he shoved his snout right between her legs, she jumped back with a laugh.

"Gross, go away, Duke."

She focused on Tyler once more, and her smile died. His shoulders were stiff as he threw his cap across the room. He washed his hands at the sink, still not saying a word, and she folded her arms over her chest.

Why wasn't he saying anything?

"I made chicken, garlic mashed potatoes, and green beans, and for dessert, I grabbed a cheesecake, fresh cut strawberries, and whipped cream." He didn't comment on the whipped cream, not even a lecherous grin about her attire. She took a few steps toward him and placed her hand on his arm.

He turned on her so swiftly she didn't have a chance to react before his mouth claimed hers roughly. Tyler had always treated her with passionate sweetness, but this was different.

This was raw, painful need in every sweep of his tongue. Every nip of his teeth and press of his lips. His arms wrapped around her in a vicelike embrace, and she put her hands against his chest.

"Tyler, please talk to me."

"I don't want to talk," he said, trying to kiss her again.

This time she pressed him more forcefully. "Well, I do."

He released her swiftly and threw a glass across the room, startling Duke and her. The shattering ting of the glass scattering across the floor was the only other sound besides their heavy breathing.

He released a shaky breath. "I'm sorry. You should go."

She was tempted, ready to grab her stuff and take off. After all, he was acting bizarre, scaring the crap out of her.

But on the other hand, she could hear the tremble in his voice, tell he was trying to keep it together until she left.

Well, she wasn't going to go. Not until he told her what was going on.

She found his broom and dustpan in the closet and, flipping the lights back on, went to work sweeping up all the glass off the wood floor.

"What are you doing? Just leave it, I'll pick it up later."

"I'm almost done, just stay there," she said.

"God damn it, Dani, can't you tell when someone just wants to be alone?"

Dumping the glass into his wastebasket, she put the broom back, ignoring his question.

"Just get out!" he shouted.

Dani slammed the closet door, her desire to find out what was wrong disintegrating.

"I don't know why you're treating me like this, but you're being a real asshole." Grabbing her coat off the back of the chair, she shrugged into it. "Don't call unless you've got one big fat fucking apology for me."

Her hand was on the knob when she heard a thunk behind her. "I thought of you today." She looked at him over her shoulder and was surprised to find his strong, handsome face tear-streaked. "When I thought I was going to die, I thought of you and Noah."

Dropping the knob, she went to him and slid to the floor next to him, her back against the cupboards. "What do you mean, when you thought you were going to die?"

"I mean when I had an angry kid pointing a gun at me, telling me that he was going to murder me in cold blood, you were among the people I loved and would be leaving behind."

Dani's body went cold as his words sank in, and without another thought about how mad she was, she wrapped her arms around him. "Tyler…"

His arms held onto her, his face buried in her chest. "I stood there, trying to figure out how to protect Blake and the kids behind me, how to make it so he only hit me, and then out of nowhere, Jeremiah comes running and knocks the guy with the gun down. Only then did I move, and it was already too late."

She stroked his hair, shoulders, and back, rocking him as she felt the warmth of his tears on her chest.

"Do you mean he…Is he dead?"

"No, but he spent hours in surgery for a collapsed lung, and it was my fault."

"How can you say that? You didn't shoot him!"

"No, but the kid who did was there for me. He was there because I kicked him out of the program. He was ready to kill a dozen people and then himself, just to get revenge on me."

"Stop that. You can't blame yourself for the evil others do. I know you. You're not malicious or unfair. If you kicked him out of the program, then he deserved it, and if this isn't proof enough, I don't know what is." Dani cupped his face, her voice harsh with a thousand terrifying emotions. Fear that she'd almost lost him, anger at the faceless teenager who had threatened him, and gratefulness because he was still here.

She kissed him. "I can't imagine what you're feeling or how much you're hurting, but I want to help any way I can. If you'll let me, that is."

This time when their lips met, Tyler wasn't harsh or aggressive, but gentle once more. His hand cradled the back of her neck, and when they broke apart, he laid his forehead against hers. "I am so sorry."

"It's okay. I understand." She climbed to her feet slowly and reached down for his hand. "Come on, let's go lie down."

"What about your dinner?" he asked.

"I think as long as Duke is with us, it will be safe," she said.

She led him by the hand behind her while he whistled for Duke, pausing to blow out the dinner candles. Once they were in his bedroom, he shut the door behind them, and Dani just held him, leaning her cheek against his chest, listening to the steady thump of his heart.

"Tyler..."

"Yeah?"

"You can talk to me, always. I will listen; you just have to use your words."

His chest vibrated as he laughed. "Did you seriously just tell me to use my words?"

"It made you laugh, didn't it?"

She felt his lips brush the top of her head. "Yes, it did."

"Come lie down with me."

He didn't argue, just stripped down to his boxer briefs and climbed into the bed. She shrugged out of her jacket and the lingerie, crawling under the covers with him and fitting her body next to his, their bodies a tangle of arms and limbs. She stroked her hands over his shoulders and down his arms until she heard the soft, even sound of his breathing and knew he was asleep.

Her mind strayed back to his words. *"You were among the people I loved..."*

And today, she could have lost him. Before she'd been able to tell him she loved him, too.

THE GUN WAS *like a gaping black hole, endless darkness waiting to swallow him up.*

He stood in front of Carlos Mendez, a human shield, protecting the people behind him. Suddenly, the soft sound of a crying child and woman reached his ears, and he glanced over his shoulder.

Dani and Noah were huddled on the ground, trembling with fear, and Tyler yelled, running for them instead of Carlos. Just before he reached them, two loud pops sounded, and red blossomed on their chests.

"Tyler..." Dani moaned, but little Noah was completely limp in his arms as he cradled them to him.

And then searing pain shot through his back as one last bullet tore through him.

Hands gripped his shoulders, shaking him out of the dream with an insistent voice. "Tyler, it's just a nightmare. Come back to me."

Tyler opened his eyes and saw Dani's worried face in the moonlight shining through his window.

"Are you okay?" she asked. "You called out my name."

He realized his hand was trembling as he reached up to touch her face and let it flop back to bed.

"You were shot...you and Noah."

"Oh, baby." She took his hand and put it over her heart, the steady beat thumping against his palm.

Suddenly, he realized he wanted more than just the pace of her heart in his hand. He wanted her body and soul, to lose himself in her and let his love for her chase the fear away.

Flexing his fingers, he slipped them over the mound of her breast, his gaze locked on hers as she sucked in a breath. Her nipple puckered against his skin, and he reached up to squeeze both full mounds at once.

She threw her head back, her eyes closed and mouth open in a little O.

And surprisingly, he was no longer worrying about losing her, but whether or not he would be able to last long enough to finally feel her around him.

Rolling her beneath him, he reached past her to the drawer next to the bed. He pulled out a foil condom wrapper and kissed her lips hungrily as she helped him out of his boxer briefs.

Tyler yanked on her lacy thong, unapologetic when he heard the skimpy fabric rip. He dipped his head to suckle first one nipple then the other, loving the way she arched her back against his mouth, pushing more of her flesh between his lips.

Finally, he pulled away to rip the condom wrapper open and slid the latex over his painfully erect dick.

He didn't ask permission or wonder if they should wait this time. Just kissed her as his hand sought her entrance, and her arousal soaked his fingers. There was no more foreplay, no more playful prepping.

He needed all of her, and he needed her now.

Tyler pushed into her with one smooth thrust as Dani's thighs hugged his hips, a heavy sigh escaping her lips. He didn't even pause, too caught up in the warm stretch of her body encasing him as he rocked against her, short deep thrusts that had her crying out softly every time he pressed forward.

His movements became harder, jerking slightly as he held himself above her, watching her face. Her eyes were closed, her mouth open slightly, and he could see a hint of flush on her cheeks.

"Dani, I'm close. So close, baby. I'm going to need you to come, because, fuck, you feel so fucking good. Come on, sweetheart."

Beads of sweat broke out on his forehead as he concentrated on her satisfaction as he increased his tempo. Finally, she broke around him, her hand gripping his bicep as she screamed his name, her channel spasming around his cock, squeezing him until he couldn't hold out any longer. He came so hard it bordered on pain, his hips still moving after he was spent.

Falling to his side off her, he pulled her back against him with a sigh. "That was definitely worth the wait."

Dani released a breathless laugh as he stood up to go clean up.

When he climbed back in behind her, he thought she might already be asleep.

Until she wiggled that sweet little ass back against his cock.

"See, now you're just asking for it," he murmured against the side of her neck.

"Maybe I am. Is that a problem?"

"Not at all." His hand spread over her naked stomach, traveling down to cup her. "Although, it might take me a while to recover."

"That's fine, I can wait."

His finger dipped between her folds, and he placed his mouth against her ear. "I want to hear you scream again. You're always so careful to be quiet, to not wake Noah." He pressed her clit and started rubbing it in slow circles. "I want you to let go and shout my name so loud the roof shakes. I want to feel you soak my hand as you come."

"You're awfully demanding," she said huskily, her hips rotating in a circular motion. Her breath hitched every so often, and he soon waited for it, speeding up his motions until there were no longer breaks in her cries.

When her orgasm overtook her, she did scream his name, and he didn't need any more recovery time. Covering his cock with another condom, he pushed inside her as they lay on their sides, her back to him. He cupped her breasts, squeezing and testing their weight as he thrust inside her slower, using more control this time. He trailed kisses over her neck and shoulder, unable to stop talking dirty against her ear, his tongue running along the delicate shell.

"Do you like it when I fuck you? When I slide my cock into you and take you slow and deep?"

"Yes, yes." She was panting, pressing back into him, and he pulled out, but he was enjoying himself, enjoying her.

"Because your body tells me you want it faster, rougher, harder." To demonstrate, he slammed into her, and she gasped loudly. "Well?"

"Yes."

"Yes, what?"

"Yes to everything."

Chapter Twenty-Six

THE MORNING LIGHT swirled into the room, and Dani lifted her arms over her head, stretching. Her muscles ached, and she was sore in the best possible way.

Turning over to look at Tyler, she was surprised to find his eyes wide open.

"Morning." His dark, raspy voice sent a shiver down her spine as she recalled all the naughty things he'd whispered when he'd taken her that last time on all fours, rocking the bed until it squeaked in protest.

"Good morning. How are you feeling?" she asked.

"Better, especially with you here."

His words warmed her from her stomach to her chest, joy spreading out to the tips of her fingers.

"I left my bag downstairs, and I kind of want to brush my teeth," she said out of the blue.

Tyler propped his head up on his arm, his expression puzzled. "Okay, so?"

"Well, I'm a little…embarrassed to prance around naked in front of you."

"If you're going to prance, I need to see this."

"Stop it," she said, pushing at his chest. He caught her hand, holding it against his skin, his eyes locked with hers.

"If you want me to turn around so you can grab your bag, I will, but you don't have anything that you need to hide from me. I love everything about you."

There was that word again. *Love.* All night they'd made love, cuddled, and talked, yet neither of them had said the words. Not in their simplest form, at least. They'd alluded to it, but they hadn't strung the words together.

What was she waiting for?

"Fine, I'll grab it." Sitting up with her back to him, she tried to take the sheet with her and wrap it around her body, but he wrestled it away from her.

"You suck," she hissed.

Standing straight as she came around the edge of the bed, fighting the blush that seemed to be covering her from head to toe, she stopped dead in her tracks when she caught sight of what Duke had in his mouth. The sides of her frilly pink thong hung from either side of his massive lips, and the crotch covered his lower jaw like a bandit's bandana.

"You dog is chewing on my underwear."

Tyler crawled to the edge of the bed, laughing. "At least he has good taste."

"Not funny, those were expensive." She marched over and reached down to pull the underwear out of his mouth. "Duke, drop it."

Instead, the massive dog scrambled to his feet and, taking advantage of his newly cast-less state, took off down the hall as fast as his long legs would carry him.

"Damn it." She took off after him and rounded the corner in time to see the dog actually toss her thong in the air as if it was a toy, catching it again with surprising accuracy.

"Tyler, your dog is playing keep away with my panties!"

"Do you want me to get the video camera?" he called.

"Har har, you are not funny." Heading toward Duke with purpose, she pointed to the ground. "Duke, drop those panties, or it won't go well for you."

The dog dropped down onto his front paws with his butt in the air, his thin tail whipping back and forth as she neared. Just as she was inches away from snatching the pink scrap from his jowls, he was off, racing back to the bedroom.

"Oh, come on." She picked up her backpack from the ground and headed back to Tyler's room, giving the underwear up as a lost cause.

Tyler sat at the edge of the bed, swinging her thong around his finger while Duke whimpered and whined in front of him, his intent gaze never leaving the object of his desire.

"You and that dog are perfect for each other." She tried to grab them, but he held them away from her. As she fell across his lap, he held her there, amusement lending an unholy twinkle to his blue eyes.

"I'll give you back your underwear in exchange for a loving kiss."

"I told you I wanted to brush my teeth first."

"Then you won't mind if I hang onto these."

"Evil." Sitting up, she wrapped her arms around his shoulders and kissed him, tongue and all. When she pulled back, he seemed a little dazed. "There."

He gave her the thong, and she noted several large holes that weren't there before.

"You owe me new underwear."

"Whatever you want," he said absently.

She started to climb off his lap, but he held her there.

"Was there something else?" she asked.

"Yeah." This time, when he kissed her, she was the one left a little light-headed. "I love you."

Dani's throat closed up, and she didn't think she would be able to speak past the lump of happiness lodged in her throat. Even though it really wasn't that long, it felt as though she'd been waiting forever for those words.

"I love you, too."

He gathered her to him, and she laid her head on his shoulder, taking in the strength of his arms, and basked in the warmth his words sent rushing over her.

"So, what does this mean for our relationship?" he said, his tone light, teasing.

Trying to hold her joyful tears at bay, she laughed wetly. "Are we seriously about to have the talk? You do know your mom asked my intentions, right?"

"She did? What did you say?"

"I don't know, something about thinking you were great. That I might keep you."

"Sounds good to me."

TYLER SAID GOOD-BYE to Dani a few hours later, after a lot of stalling and kissing, and headed out to visit Jeremiah. He picked up Meyers at Alpha Dog, and they drove down to the hospital. They were given visitor stickers at the front desk, and they made their way up to the recovery wing with a card the guys had made and a gift card from all the instructors, organized by Blake. Tyler wasn't sure what kind of gift card you gave a kid who risked his life for others, but he'd still added a hundred bucks to the pool.

They were directed to his room and knocked on the closed door. Tyler put his hand on the knob just as it swung open, and he came face-to-face with Virginia Walton.

"What are you doing here?" she asked. Her tone wasn't hostile, more hollow, and he wondered why she wasn't screaming at him to leave after what he'd done.

"The boys in Jeremiah's squad made him a get-well card, and all the instructors got him something."

She hesitated before they heard a croaked voice call out, "Let them in, please."

Virginia stepped back, and they passed by her. Tyler got his first good look at Jeremiah since he'd been bleeding out in his arms. He was sheet-white with oxygen tubes in his nose and electrodes coming out from under his blanket in every direction. He looked like hell, but he smiled shyly at them.

"Thanks for coming by," he said.

"Maybe you shouldn't talk. You sound like shit, dude," Meyers said, earning a smack to the back of his head from Tyler. "I was trying to be helpful, Sarge!"

"How 'bout you give him the card and be less helpful?" Tyler said.

Meyers handed Jeremiah the eight-by-eleven handmade card with *Get Well Soon* in large block letters colored in with green, black, and brown. "We all signed it. And I just wanted to tell you that all the guys are sorry we were such assholes, me especially. You're a total badass."

"Thanks, this is really cool."

Tyler handed Jeremiah the envelope with the storebought card and gift card. "And this is from the staff at Alpha Dog. We all want to thank you for what you did and hope that you recover quickly."

Jeremiah opened the card, and when he glanced at the gift card amount, his eyes widened. "Wow, seriously, Sergeant Best?"

"Yep, we all pitched in. And I have a pretty good feeling that the dozen or more letters Judge Garrison receives today and tomorrow are going to sway his decision to overturn your conviction."

"So, I'm not coming back to Alpha Dog?" Jeremiah said, frowning.

"Doesn't look like it." Tyler caught Jeremiah's crestfallen expression. "Hey, what's up, kid? I thought you'd be happy to be going home."

"Not if *he's* there," Jeremiah muttered.

Tyler turned to glance at the boy's mother over his shoulder, noting her red face and downcast eyes.

"Well, if you want to stay at the program, I guess we could just tell the judge you don't think you've learned your lesson."

"I think you should leave now," Virginia snapped.

Meyers turned to Jeremiah's mother, and before Tyler could stop him, the teenager said, "Your son shouldn't be scared of his own house."

"It's not like that, and besides, it's none of your business."

"It's exactly like that, Mom," Jeremiah said. "You chose him over me. You do it every time, no matter how many times he hits us. You just let him stay to do it again, and it's enough. I'd rather go into the system than go back to you."

All the color leeched from Virginia's face. "You don't mean that."

"I do. If you aren't going to leave him, then I'd rather go from Alpha Dog to a group home. At least then I wouldn't have to watch you take his abuse."

"You're just agitated and exhausted. We'll talk about this later." She glared pointedly at Tyler. "I want to speak to my son, alone."

Tyler took the pen on the side table and wrote down his cell on the back of the envelope, handing it to Jeremiah. "If you need anything, you call me. No matter what time it is or what it's about. And I'll be back tomorrow."

"Thanks, Sarge."

Meyers glared at Virginia as they passed, and Tyler didn't even bother to scold him. The woman deserved every bit of it; he didn't care if she was a victim, too. The difference between her and Jeremiah was that she chose to stay, while Jeremiah had no choice.

Except maybe he could help give him one.

DANI WAS GETTING ready to go back to work that night when someone knocked, sending Bella and Shasta into a fit of excited barking. She didn't have any plans with Tyler, and at six thirty on a Saturday, she was definitely checking the peephole this time.

On her step was an older Hispanic woman with dark hair that was threaded with silver and pulled back severely from her deeply lined face.

Angel's mother.

Camila Ramirez looked much older than she had the last time they'd met just two years ago, but she would recognize her anywhere. Her cold, calculating eyes stared directly into the peephole, as if she could see Dani on the other side.

Dani pulled open the door enough to keep the dogs inside and tried to smile. "Mrs. Ramirez, good to see you."

"*Hola*, Danielle. I called you a week ago, and you never returned my call."

"I know, and I apologize, but like I told Angel, if you would like visitation, you need to go through the proper legal channels."

Camila's lips thinned into a hard line. "You know as well as I do that my son will not receive visitation the way that he is."

It was hard for Dani to feel bad about that when her son had threatened Dani. "Then I would get him the help he needs, because I'm not letting him near my child the way he is."

"And me? Would you allow me to see him? He is, after all, my grandson."

Dani's gut churned, screaming at her to slam the door in her face. There was something about Camila's demeanor that was almost frightening, and if she had her way, the woman would never see Noah.

"No, I'm sorry. If you want to have a relationship with my son, then I suggest you help your son get his act together and go through legal channels. And if you or your son show up at my home again, I'll file a restraining order against you both."

Shutting the door and locking it with a rapidly beating heart, she could hear Camila cursing her in Spanish as she walked away.

Did she really think that Dani was going to be okay with her just showing up here, asking for visitation for her druggie son?

With shaky hands, she dialed Tyler on her phone. She knew he had the next week off, and when she'd told him she was heading back to work tonight, he'd decided to go out with his friends.

Was it clingy if she called him now? Would he think she was checking up on him, even though she was just calling for a little comfort?

He picked up on the second ring. "Miss me already?"

"I sure do," she said.

"Hey, what's wrong? Your voice sounds funny."

"It's nothing, really…"

"Dani, just tell me, or I'm going to drive over there and tickle it out of you."

Dani smiled at his silly threat. "I'm no longer ticklish. Totally immune."

"Then I'll kiss you until you're so complacent, you won't even realize what you've done." His teasing tone disappeared as her laughter died, and he said, "Please just tell me, or I'm going to worry."

"Angel's mother showed up here, asking for me to reconsider letting Angel see Noah. When I said no, he needed to go through the proper channels, she asked if she could see Noah. I said no."

"Understandably. These people need to stop harassing you. I think you should go down to the police station and report it, maybe file a restraining order."

"I told her I would if either of them showed up again."

"Do you want me to come over and follow you to work?" he asked.

"No, you have fun with your friends. If I get the heebie-jeebies, I'll just take Shasta to work with me."

"All right, well, if you need me, I'll have my phone on. I love you."

A chorus of male voices saying "Ooooh" blasted through the phone, and Dani's whole face heated.

"Shut the fuck up, you idiots," Tyler snapped.

"I didn't realize the guys were all there."

"Yeah, we're gonna grab some food and head over to Mick's. If you aren't too tired and you want to come over after work, you're more than welcome."

"I'll call you if I do. I love you, too, by the way."

"Oh, good, for a minute there, I thought you were going to leave me hanging."

She laughed. "Nope, I love telling you. Almost as much as I like hearing it."

"Same goes. Good night," he said.

"Night." She pressed the red button to end the call and stared off into space. She thought about Tyler's concern, that maybe she should report their visits to the cops so there was a record, but finally dismissed it. She'd told them both to stay away and was pretty sure they'd gotten the message.

Chapter Twenty-Seven

TYLER SLIPPED HIS cell phone into his pocket and gave his friends a dark scowl. "You're a giant bag of sweaty ball sacks."

"Oh, I think we embarrassed him in front of his girlfriend!" Martinez crowed.

"I think it's awesome to finally see you happy, man," Blake said.

"I appreciate that." Tyler pointed toward Blake, who was kicking back in his recliner. "See, he is a true friend."

"Please, we've all earned the right to torment you...God knows you've given us enough shit."

Sparks had a point, but Tyler wasn't going to admit that out loud.

Besides, he was distracted, thinking about the Ramirez family. They definitely had a steel set, showing up at Dani's place not once, but twice. He couldn't figure out what they hoped to gain, but Tyler wasn't sure they'd gotten the message.

"Hey, before we grab food, would you guys be up for taking a ride with me?"

"What are you thinking?" Blake asked.

"Dani's ex came back, but he's all strung out. He and his mother have shown up at her house asking to see Noah, and she told them if they want visitation, they need to go through proper channels. I just want to make sure they understand that means they stay the hell away from them."

Sparks stood up before he even finished. "Hell, you had my back when Violet's sister was being stalked by that punk ex of hers. You know I'm down."

"I've got your six," Blake said.

They all turned to look at Martinez, who let out a string of curses. "Fine, but if we get arrested, Eve is going to kill me. Her father barely tolerates me as it is."

A quick Google search later, they had the Ramirezes' address off of Arden. They all piled into Blake's Charger and followed the GPS until they parked in front of a run-down blue house. Tyler recognized Angel's piece of shit car in the drive and got out. He headed up the walk and rang the doorbell. When no chime sounded, he knocked loudly.

A woman inside shouted, "Get the door!" Tyler then heard the dead bolt turn.

Angel opened the door, looking and smelling as greasy as ever, and he stared out at him blankly. "What?"

"You don't remember me?" Tyler asked.

Angel seemed to be having trouble focusing on him and swayed a bit. Finally, his eyes narrowed. "You're Dani's dick boyfriend. What the fuck you doing at my house?"

"Yeah, funny how *you* don't like when people show up unannounced at your place."

Angel spit at Tyler's feet and started to shut the door, but Tyler grabbed him by his grimy white T-shirt and yanked him outside.

"Listen up, asshole. You want to see your kid? Get yourself straight and get a lawyer. This is your last warning. You show up at her house, her work, her parents'—if you even bump into her at the store, I will call the cops and have your ass arrested for stalking. And I guarantee when they search your car and your house, they're gonna find your stash. Now, if you're actually interested in getting to know your kid, then man up. Don't send your mom over to do your dirty work."

"I didn't, man, I swear, she did that all on her own. All I did was mention Dani and the kid, and she kept pestering me about it. Wants me to let her see him. I told her that Dani said not without a court order, but she won't let up."

Tyler let him go. "So, you don't want anything to do with your son? This is all to make your mother happy?"

"What the fuck would I want a kid for? If Dani had just gotten the abortion like I told her to, my mom wouldn't be on my ass now."

Just the idea that Dani might have listened to this piece of garbage made Tyler clench his fists.

"From now on, you're gonna keep your mom in check and leave Dani alone. Right?"

"Yeah, sure, whatever."

"Angel, who is out there?" Mrs. Ramirez came to stand in the doorway, glaring out the door at him. "What are you doing with my son?"

"He was just telling me that both of you are going to leave Dani Hill and her son alone."

Rage made the woman's face contort into a monstrous mask. "That little slut stole my grandchild from me!"

Tyler had to remind himself he couldn't hit a sixty-year-old woman. "Your son told Dani to get an abortion, and he doesn't want anything to do with his son."

"He doesn't know what he wants. That girl tricked him. She doesn't deserve to raise my grandson!"

The old woman was screaming now, her eyes popping out of her head. People around them were turning on their porch lights and peeking out the door.

"Then I suggest you get a lawyer, ma'am. Because the next time, it will be the cops banging on your door."

She hurled some colorful Spanish words at his back as he walked away, and he could hear Angel trying to calm her down. As he climbed into the car with the guys, Tyler said, "Hey, Martinez, what did she just say to me?"

"You do not want to know, my friend."

Tyler figured he was probably right, but a nagging concern followed him around the whole night. The woman had come off as a little unhinged, and Tyler was more resolved than ever to get Dani to go down to the police station. He wanted a record of them harassing her, so if things escalated, the cops had the whole story.

"Why so serious?" Blake asked, lining up his pool shot.

Tyler laughed, shaking off his unease. "Nothing, just thinking about how long it will take to kick your ass."

"You're a funny guy."

"So, now that you two are at the 'I love you' stage, what's next?" Sparks asked.

"Next? There's a next? I thought we'd just stay here in this stage for a while. Give me time to adjust to all this relationship shit."

"That's fucking romantic," Martinez said. "Don't let her hear you call it 'relationship shit.' First tip, women don't like that."

"Fine, but I just want to savor this."

"Savor away, no one's stopping you," Blake said.

Tyler lined up another shot, shaking his head when he missed it. "Damn it!"

"Woo, looks like Best lost all those mad skills."

Tyler's phone chimed with a new message. He pulled it out of his pocket and clicked on the text folder.

Wanna come over?

He didn't recognize the number, and it wasn't assigned to anyone in his phone. *Who is this?*

Cammie. We hooked up a couple months ago? Maybe this will help jog your memory.

His phone dinged again, and a pair of large breasts popped up on his cell phone screen.

"Who are you texting?" Martinez asked.

"No one, some girl I hooked up with texted me, and I'm telling her I'm not interested."

His fingers flew over the pad. *Sorry, I've got a girlfriend.*

"There we go. Used the *g* word. Shut it down."

His phone beeped, and the guys crowded close, trying to peek over his shoulder.

She doesn't have to know.

"Shit, did she send you a titty pic?" Blake asked.

"Fuck off."

No thanks, lose this number.

Tyler deleted the thread and, after placing his phone back in his pocket, picked up his cue. "Well, are we gonna play some pool or sit around gossiping like a bunch of chicks?"

AROUND NOON SUNDAY, Dani sat in a booth at IHOP with her mother and Noah. Her mom had asked her to lunch after church, since her dad was sick and hadn't attended.

"What's wrong with Dad?" Dani asked.

"Football-itis," her mom grumbled.

"Yeah, I heard that's going around."

"Enough about your father's obsession. I want to know about this man you're seeing. You've hardly said a word about him since I dropped Noah off two weeks ago. Are you still seeing him?"

"Yes, I'm still seeing him."

When she didn't offer anything more, her mother waved her hand. "Well, you're going to have to give me more than that! He's in the military, right? Have you met his parents?"

"Yes, he took Noah and me to the San Francisco Zoo last Saturday. Afterward, we went to his parents' home in South San Francisco for his dad's birthday."

"Well, that's nice." Her tone said the exact opposite. "And why haven't you brought him by so we can get to know him better?"

"Because I want to continue dating him?" she joked.

Her mom sniffed. "I see. You think we'll embarrass you."

"No, although, yes, I know you will, but that isn't it. We're just taking things as they come, and I haven't been ready yet."

"Have you slept with him yet?"

Dani choked on her water, wheezing as her gaze shot to Noah. "Mom!"

"What, he doesn't even know what that means."

"But it's none of your business."

"I'm going to interpret that as a yes."

"You can interpret that any way you want, but I am still not answering that question."

"Well, I want you to bring him to Thanksgiving," her mom said as their food arrived.

Noah tried reaching for his pancakes, but she got there first and began cutting them up into bite-size pieces. "Come on, Mom, he probably has plans to go to his parents' or something."

"Well, the least you can do is ask, Danielle. Sometimes I don't know why you make things so much more complicated than they need to be."

"Fine, I'll ask him."

"Call him now."

Dani slid the plate of pancakes in front of Noah and scoffed. "I'm not calling him in the middle of a crowded restaurant with my mom listening in."

"Thanksgiving is on Thursday, and I need to know how many people to plan for."

Giving up on actually getting to eat her own stack of pancakes, Dani climbed out of the booth. "I'm going outside to call him." When her mom started to protest, Dani held her hand up. "One argument from you, and I will sit back down and never let you get your claws into him."

"You're not very nice to your mother," she said.

"I'm too nice to you, which is why I allow you to still boss me around."

Dani escaped before her mom could respond and walked outside, standing on the sidewalk as she dug her phone out of her purse. She scrolled through, wishing she hadn't been such a pushover as she pressed the little green phone next to Tyler's name.

When he picked up, the smile in his voice was obvious.

"Hey, beautiful, I was just thinking of you."

God, would the sappy things he said always make her grin like an idiot?

"Hi, funny, I was thinking of you, too. And so was my mom."

"Um, that's a little weird," he said.

"Well, we were having lunch, and she started asking about you and whether we are serious or not, and well, one thing led to another, and she…She wants you to come to our house for Thanksgiving dinner."

"Huh, a family holiday? Turkey? Mashed potatoes? Awkwardly watching football with your dad?"

"That's the one. I told her you probably had plans with your family, so I completely understand if you can't—"

"Actually, I was going to say yes, unless you don't want me to come."

Stuttering with surprise, she said, "No, that's great. I just…I…great!"

"Say it one more time, and I'll really believe you," he said.

"Shut your face." Listening to his deep chuckle for a few seconds, she finally added, "Okay, well I better get back inside and tell Mom. She's going to be over the moon that she can interrogate you all she wants."

"Looking forward to it."

"Okay, love you."

"Love you, too."

Chapter Twenty-Eight

As soon as he got back to work, Tyler had called Virginia into his office, armed with options for Jeremiah once he left Alpha Dog. The only thing to do now was get Jeremiah's mother to understand where her son was coming from.

Someone knocked on his door.

"Come in."

Sparks led Virginia inside and came around to stand at the side of Tyler's desk.

"Please have a seat, Mrs. Walton."

She did, her wide face a mask of suspicion. "Why am I here? I thought that my son had already decided to finish his sentence here."

"He has, ma'am, but we wanted to talk to you, to prepare you for some of the concerns Jeremiah has expressed to me," Tyler said.

"I don't want to hear anything you have to say. You assaulted my husband."

"And I'm very sorry about that, Mrs. Walton. It was an emotional moment for me, with Jeremiah being shot, and I lost my temper. But that doesn't change the fact that Jeremiah doesn't want to come home to you. He is terrified of your husband—and for you."

Virginia winced. "Things are going to be different this time. Neil promised."

"Mrs. Walton," Sparks said, "Neil has said that several times, and Jeremiah doesn't believe or trust him. He is such a good kid; you have raised an amazingly brave, kind young man."

"But it's our job to make sure that when Jeremiah leaves Alpha Dog, he doesn't backslide," Tyler said firmly. He was definitely playing bad cop today. "Which is why I'm going to recommend a temporary placement for Jeremiah until he feels comfortable moving back into your home."

Virginia's face turned molten red. "You're trying to steal my son from me!"

"Not at all, Mrs. Walton. It was actually Jeremiah who voiced the concerns and requested more information on other options for him after he leaves the program," Sparks said.

"He wanted to look into emancipation, but I didn't think a fourteen-year-old should be on his own," Tyler said.

"No, he belongs with his mother," she snapped.

"Not if his mother continues to make him live in a dangerous and toxic environment," Tyler said.

"Okay, this is getting out of hand," Sparks said. "Tyler, why don't you go ahead and take off for the day? I'd like to speak to Mrs. Walton alone."

Tyler left the building and drove to Sutter Memorial to talk to Jeremiah, his folder of information on the seat beside him. He'd called a couple he'd known forever, both of them veterinarians, whose children were all grown. One of Alpha Dog's other program graduates, Liam, was staying with them as a foster placement, and when he'd talked to them about Jeremiah's situation, they'd been the ones to offer their home to him.

Tyler took his hospital visitor pass and headed up to Jeremiah's room. As he came off the elevator and rounded the hallway, he heard shouting. Taking off at a jog, he reached Jeremiah's room in time to watch Neil shove a nurse who was standing between him and a bedridden Jeremiah.

"You little fuck, you're going to stop upsetting your mother with this whiny crybaby crap and come home. No more trouble or talk of me hurting you. You're just a selfish little shit—"

"That's enough, Neil," Tyler said, stepping into the room. He didn't trust himself to touch Neil, not when he was already clenching his fists at the guy's bravado. Coming in here and yelling like an idiot... He'd be lucky if the nurse didn't accuse him of assault.

Neil paled as he recognized Tyler but tried to bluster. "You don't tell me what to do with my family."

"I'm not your family," Jeremiah said loudly.

Neil started toward the bed, but Tyler was quicker. Grabbing Neil by the back of his shirt collar, he dragged him around to face him, getting the full force of bitter beer and bong breath in his face.

"Security is going to be up here any minute, and when they walk through that door, I'm going to tell them you assaulted this nurse. Then the cops will be called, and you'll have another arrest and pending charge on your record. Plus, I'm gonna go out on a limb and guess you drove here, and by the smell of you, I think you're going to find a nice little DUI tacked on."

Neil twisted out of his grasp, and Tyler let go of him. Neil's face was contorted with rage, his skin an ugly shade of violet.

"You think you're such a hero, but I've got you figured out. You're one of those boy-loving pedo—"

Self-control could only take him so far. Putting all his weight behind the right hook, he wasn't surprised when Neil crashed to the ground. His mouth hung open, and his eyes were closed, and for a second, Tyler thought he might have hit him harder than he meant to.

Security walked through the door just as Neil started snoring.

"What happened here?" asked the security guard with the shiny cue ball for a head.

"He passed out," the nurse said swiftly.

"Yeah, he was drunk and raving and then he just fell over," Jeremiah added.

Tyler was going to come clean, but with the little dark-haired nurse grinning at Jeremiah conspiratorially, who was he to disagree?

The security guards lifted Neil up and carried him out, Cue Ball commenting that he stunk while Tyler shook his head.

"He's gonna wake up and start yelling about me assaulting him."

"Please, no one will believe that idiot, nor would they blame you," the nurse said. "Besides, it was a good thing you came in, 'cause I was just about to sing for him."

"Huh?" Tyler and Jeremiah said at once.

"Solar plexus, instep, nose, groin. Damn, haven't you ever seen *Miss Congeniality*?"

"No," they said together.

The nurse muttered something about men and left the room. "So, I stopped by to tell you that Sergeant Sparks is in a meeting with your mom, discussing other options for you after you're released from the hospital."

"What kind of things?" Jeremiah asked.

"Well, for starters, if you really aren't ready to leave Alpha Dog, you can stay and finish the remainder of your sentence. We'd be happy to have you."

"And after?" Jeremiah asked.

"Well, you could still go home with your mom and stepdad—"

"I'd rather live on the street than go back there." Jeremiah's pointed chin jutted out stubbornly, as if he was afraid Tyler would make him go back.

"Relax, no need for it to come to that. If you're open to it, there's a couple I know who are really good people. They're both veterinarians and have a small ranch just outside of Folsom. Their kids are grown, and they're fostering another boy from the program but offered you their third bedroom, if you want it. Sparks is discussing them taking over temporary guardianship of you until you either turn eighteen or decide being with your mom would be safe for you again. It's up to you."

Jeremiah sat thoughtfully playing with the hospital blanket. "Can I still see my mom, even if they're my guardians?"

"Absolutely, but we can get a restraining order against Neil. After the stunt he pulled today, I don't want him showing up when you're alone."

"Even if I said yes, my mom is never going to go for it."

"Which is why I think you should write a letter telling her everything you want and need and the future you see for yourself…and why that won't happen if you move back in with her and Neil."

"Do you think that will really work?" Jeremiah asked.

"I don't know, but it's worth a shot."

DANI, TYLER, AND Noah stood outside her parents' home the next day, and Dani swallowed down the nervous bile rising up in her throat. She really wanted her parents to like Tyler, but considering her dad had never liked any of her boyfriends in the past, she wasn't holding out a lot of hope.

"Hey, it's gonna be okay," Tyler said, squeezing her hand.

"I know. I'm good. I'm ready." She caught his smile, which clearly said *sure you are.* "I am."

"Okay then, I'm ringing the doorbell."

The chimes erupted inside the house, and Dani took another breath. Thanksgiving with her parents. It wouldn't be so bad sitting around all day while her dad watched football and her mom asked Tyler if he liked every dish on the table.

"Okay, real fast, don't talk politics and who's your favorite football team?"

"The Raiders," he said.

"Shit!"

Before she could tell him *not* to mention that to her dad, the door swung in, and her mom, dressed in a brown sweater with a giant beaded turkey on the front, said, "Finally! I told you that dinner would be ready by three!"

"Which is why we're here at one, Mom," Dani said.

Tyler held up the grocery sack in his other hand, a large bouquet of flowers poking out the top. "Hello, Mrs. Hill. I grabbed the crescent rolls you requested and a bottle of wine. I hope you like red."

"Please call me Laura," she said, reaching her arms out to Noah, who stood next to Dani, holding her other hand. "Wanna come see all the goodies Mapa is making?"

Noah launched himself into her arms, and the two sauntered off, leaving Dani and Tyler alone on the step.

Dani pulled him along behind her. "Later on, when you're gazing at the door longingly, looking for a means of escape, I want you to remember that you chose this."

Tyler leaned over and kissed her sweetly. "Shut up, it will be fine. I swear, I'll make them love me."

"YOU'RE A RAIDERS fan?" George Hill spat out, as if it was a dirty word. Tyler was a little surprised he didn't spit on the floor in disgust. They'd been sitting in the living room watching football while Dani and Laura were in the kitchen. Noah was sitting in the middle of the living room, playing with huge Legos.

So much for getting on her dad's good side.

"Yeah, I always have been. My dad's a 49ers fan."

George grunted. "I like your dad already."

Unlike Tyler, whose unpopular football team choice had just given him a big black check.

"Hey, what are you guys talking about in here?" Dani asked as she came in. Stopping alongside Tyler's chair, she set her hand on his shoulder and gave him an *are you okay?* look.

"We were just talking football. Apparently, your dad and I are mortal enemies on the field."

"Can't believe you're dating a Raiders fan," her dad grumbled, but Tyler was pretty sure his eyes twinkled. That was a good sign, right?

"Oh no, you actually told him that? I told you not to!" She shook his shoulder, and he could tell she was trying not to laugh. "Football is serious business in the Hill house."

"Hey, I told him my dad likes the 49ers. I'm just the black sheep of the Best family."

"Should have listened to your dad. He has some taste."

"Okay, how about we not talk about football anymore and change the subject?" Dani suggested.

Tyler squeezed her hand and shot her a mischievous look. "So, George, are you a Democrat or a Republican?"

"Politics? Really? That's a better subject for you?" Dani asked.

"I'm an Independent," George said.

"Okay, on that note, I'm going to go back to the kitchen," Dani said.

Tyler turned around and watched her leave the room. She was wearing a pretty floral dress that hit her just below the knees and swished when she walked.

He loved that dress. The minute she'd put it on this morning, he'd been dreaming of the moment later tonight when he'd be under it, listening to the sounds of her screams…

"Hey, now I asked you a question. Stop looking at my daughter's ass and answer."

Tyler chuckled, getting the feeling that George Hill enjoyed being obnoxious and making other people feel uncomfortable.

But if he thought he could get one over on Best, he didn't know who he was messing with.

DANI BREATHED A sigh of relief as they left her parents, who had insisted on keeping Noah overnight.

"My parents loved you, even my dad. And even after you told him who your football team was."

"Your dad has a low tolerance for bullshit, which I appreciate."

"So, you never told me who the extra plate was for," she said, indicating the foil-covered plate.

"The kid at the hospital, the one who risked his life for the rest of us? Well, I'm pretty sure his mom won't even visit him today, so I thought we'd drop it by on the way home, before the visiting hours are over."

Dani's heart swelled with love for this kind, generous man. "Of course, I'd love to meet him."

Tyler held onto her hand as they drove to Sutter Memorial and didn't release it, even as they entered Jeremiah's room at the hospital.

And found Jeremiah's bed surrounded by Blake and a handful of other teenaged boys. Dani glanced at Tyler, who seemed pretty surprised to see them.

"Hey, what are you all doing here?" Tyler asked.

"Having Thanksgiving with this kid," Blake said.

"And you brought these troublemakers? I bet the nurses are thrilled," Tyler said, setting the plate they brought down on the counter. "This is from us. We've even got a separate container of dessert for you."

"Thanks, Sarge," the boy in the bed—obviously Jeremiah—said.

Dani took a few steps forward, releasing her hand from Tyler's and holding it out to Jeremiah with a wide smile. "It's nice to meet you, Jeremiah. I've heard so much about you."

"This is my girlfriend, Dani," Tyler offered from behind her.

Jeremiah took her hand shyly. "Nice to meet you. Thanks for the food."

"We already brought the goods, Sarge. Cook made us a whole meal to bring over and eat with Jeremiah, so he wouldn't be alone," one of the other boys said to Tyler, and Dani could see the admiration on their faces.

"Dani, you know Blake, but these pains in the asses are Dwayne Harlow, Olsen Myers, Jamie Platt, and Hank Osbourne."

"Nice to meet you, ma'am," they all chorused.

"So nice to finally meet you. Tyler talks about you guys a lot."

They all shot him a look, as if wondering what he said, so she added, "All good things, I promise."

The boys relaxed.

"She's lying; I complain about you constantly."

Dani rolled her eyes. "Sure, you never tell me how fast Dwayne is or how hard Jamie works with his dog. Or that Hank is really smart and Olsen is a born leader. Nope, he never says anything nice about you."

All the boys were beaming now, and Olsen said, "I like you. If the Sarge ever breaks up with you, just wait for me."

"I saw her first," Jeremiah said, surprisingly, a wide grin on his face.

Dani's cheeks burned, and Tyler came up behind her, placing his hands on her shoulders. "Both of you are shit out of luck. She's all mine."

And as all the boys started chattering, each vying for Tyler's attention, Dani leaned back into him and just enjoyed being his.

Chapter Twenty-Nine

THE EARLY DECEMBER air nipped at them as they climbed the steps to Eve and Oliver's place for their holiday party, their hands interlaced as Tyler pressed the button.

Dani should have been used to Tyler's friends after nearly six weeks together, but they still seemed to stare at her as if she was some kind of exotic creature. As if they still couldn't believe Tyler hadn't dumped her for a bar wench.

Eve threw open the door. "Hey, come on in, guys. Everyone is just meandering. Can I get you anything to drink? Wine? Beer? Eggnog and brandy?"

"We'll get it ourselves, Eve, thanks," Tyler said.

"Sure. Feel free to make yourselves at home."

"Hey, Best." Kline clapped him on the back, and Dani noticed he wobbled a little.

"What's up, buddy? Started the party early, I see." Tyler was frowning at his friend, and Dani wondered if Blake didn't usually drink.

"I just needed a little pick-me-up. You know how it is around the holidays. They suck balls."

Dani and Tyler laughed a little awkwardly.

"Well, looks like I need another glass of holiday cheer. What an oxymoron, right?"

As he stumbled away, Dani leaned close to ask, "Is he okay?"

"I'm not sure. He lost his wife a few years ago, and after the shooting last month, he hasn't really been himself."

"Poor guy."

"Yo, Best, you're under the mistletoe! Better give that girl a smooch," Martinez called from across the room.

Tyler reached out to bring her close, but their new law enforcement trainer, Zack Dalton, came up behind Dani and kissed her cheek.

He backed up too quickly for Tyler to catch him, moonwalking backward as he taunted Tyler. "Oh, yeah, Best, I kissed your girl."

"I'll fuck you up, Dalton."

Dani reached up and pulled him down for a real kiss, ignoring the catcalls from the room. When they pulled away slowly, Tyler whispered, "Ready to go yet?"

She laughed and took his hand, leading him over to where Megan Bryce was making a cookie that looked suspiciously as if it had a giant penis.

"Hey, guys," she said warmly.

"That looks tasty, Bryce," Tyler said. "Never knew you were a big balls kinda girl."

"Well, they gotta be bigger than mine." Her attempt at a joke fell a little flat, and she cleared her throat. "You know, I'm gonna go talk to Eve."

Once she was out of earshot, Dani asked, "Is it just me or is everyone acting weird tonight?"

"Don't ask me; I wanted to stay in and do it under the tree. You were the one who saw the invitation and said, 'Oh, this sounds like fun.' " His high, screechy imitation of her made her scowl.

"I don't have a tree yet."

He pressed his lips to the side of her neck. "We could have rectified that with a trip to Home Depot."

"Not without Noah, we couldn't!"

"I'm teasing, babe," he said, wrapping his arms around her waist from behind. "Wanna make a cookie together? I bet if we worked together, it would be epic."

She laughed and leaned back against him as he took her hands in his, manipulating them to spread frosting over the sugar cookie.

Have I ever been this happy before?

The answer was definitely no.

TYLER STOOD WITH his friends several hours later, drinking beer and bullshitting. They'd decorated cookies, done an ornament exchange, and even sung Christmas carols. Tyler was definitely ready to go, but it was the first time he'd seen Dani relax around his social group, and he was loath to pull her away.

"So, Blake, any thoughts to getting back out there?" Martinez asked.

"Nah," he said, nursing his beer.

"I still can't get over how Best landed a woman like Dani," Sparks said.

"You guys are a bunch of assholes, you know that, right?"

"Hell, Best has it good. He's so fucking pretty, even when he blows women off, they still send him naked titty shots." Blake's words carried across the room, and everyone stiffened.

Tyler's gaze found Dani's, her face sheet-white.

"Dani—"

She got up from the couch with a mumbled "excuse me," and he pushed past his friends to follow her outside.

"Dani, it's not what you think, I swear."

She stood at the bottom of the steps, her arms wrapped around herself.

"So, women haven't been sending you naked pictures?"

"Yes, one girl, and I told her I had a girlfriend and to lose my number."

She spun around, her hand held out to him. "Let me see."

"I deleted the thread. It happened weeks ago."

Her laughter had a bitter edge he hated. "Erased it, huh? That's convenient."

Tyler recoiled as if she'd slapped him. "Have I ever given you any reason not to trust me?"

"None, except your track record and the reaction of everyone who knows you. I actually started to think that I had everything, that my life was pretty fucking perfect, but that's the problem with trying to convince yourself people can change."

"So, that's it? You assume I'm guilty of something because you can't believe I want to be with you?"

"Whoa, that is not what I said. I said that you like sex and women, and I was crazy to think that would stop."

"It did stop. It fucking stopped the minute I saw you sitting next to Noah in that hospital room. I didn't know why, but I couldn't get you out of my head."

"And yet"—before he could stop her, she snatched his phone out of his hand—"Alison, Alicia, Amy, Andrea, April…Wow, we haven't even made it to the Bs yet."

He jerked his phone out of her hand, his body shaking with hurt and rage. "Stop this. I love you. I wouldn't hurt you, and I haven't cheated on you."

She sniffled, and he saw the tears rolling down her cheeks. He was dying to reach out and brush them from her cheeks.

"I really want to believe that. I want to believe that you love me and you're committed to me, but you didn't delete them from your phone, Tyler. You kept other women's numbers. Women you've slept with. And that tells me that even if it's just on a subconscious level, you're keeping your options open."

He opened his mouth, wanting to tell her that he hadn't thought about it because his mind had been taken over with thoughts of her, but what was the point? She didn't trust him, didn't believe him.

"I'm gonna grab my coat and see if Megan will give me a ride," Dani said.

"I can drive you home."

"Not right now." She climbed up the stairs past him, closing the door behind him, and he wanted to yell. Scream and rail at his idiot friend, call out to Dani that he hadn't thought about the numbers or how she might interpret it.

The door opened again, and Sparks came out with a drunken Blake hanging on him.

"Best, hey, I'm sorry for what I said. I hope Dani isn't mad at you, bro."

Tyler wanted to hit him, and it took everything he had not to knock Blake off his feet and pound him.

"You need to get some help, man," was all Tyler said, turning his back on his two friends and heading for his car.

Chapter Thirty

DANI CHECKED ON Noah again the next afternoon, and when she saw he was still out, she went into the living room to find something to watch. Preferably nothing romantic or funny. She wasn't in the mood to laugh.

In fact, she'd spent most of last night neck-deep in tissues. In the fresh light of day, she had a feeling she'd overreacted. Tyler had never given her a reason to be suspicious of him, and holding his past against him wasn't fair. He could do the same thing to her, and she definitely wouldn't come out smelling like a rose.

She needed to call him but wasn't even sure what to say. *I'm sorry for being such a judgmental bitch? For not trusting you? Thinking the worst of you?*

All of it was bred of her own insecurities. That good guys, men who were honest, trustworthy, and kind, could care about her.

Because you're a young mother?

Yes, in a way, but not totally. More that she had made so many bad calls, it was hard to trust her gut.

Someone knocked on the door, and Dani went to peek through the hole. Blake Kline stood on her porch.

She pulled open the door and noted he looked like hell. His hazel eyes were bloodshot, and his skin looked a little green.

"Blake, what are you doing here? I didn't even know you knew where I lived."

"Your address is listed online," he croaked.

"Well, I'll have to change that." Okay, so she wasn't being very nice to the guy, but to be fair, he'd started shit by bringing up titty pics in the middle of a Christmas party. "What can I do for you?"

"I wanted to apologize for my behavior. I was in a bad place, and I shouldn't have said what I did about the text messages. Best did get one while we were at the bar, but he told the girl he was taken. I saw the message myself."

Confirming what she'd already figured out for herself—that Tyler was telling the truth—she nodded. "I appreciate you coming by and telling me."

"Yeah, sorry for just showing up, I just…Best isn't talking to me, and I feel like a real asshole, you know?"

Dani softened a little toward him. "We've all gone through bad times. It happens. Besides, no matter what you said, I was the one who didn't believe him. So he's probably not talking to me, either."

"He really loves you, Dani. If you call him and tell him that, he'll forgive you. Believe me, love makes you do stupid shit, but when it's real, it can overcome a lot."

"Thank you, Blake."

"Well, I'll let you get back to whatever you're doing. Just wanted to come by and say how sorry I was."

"Thanks again."

She closed the door on him and leaned against the solid wood. God, she hated apologizing. It always made her feel weak and at the mercy of the receiver, who was usually her mother.

But she wanted Tyler more than anything, and he deserved to know she believed him.

Dani picked up her cell and dialed his cell, but it went straight to voicemail.

"This is Sergeant Tyler Best. Leave me a message, and I'll get back to you."

The phone beeped, and she said, "Hi, Tyler, it's Dani. I need to talk to you, so if you could please call me back, that would be great."

She hung up without saying I love you, not sure if she had the right anymore. What if he was avoiding her calls? Her eyes stung with tears, and she chided herself for imagining the worst.

She heard Noah calling for her, and she went into his nursery with a smile, wiping at her wet eyes. "Hey, sweetie."

"Tywer here?"

He must have heard her on the phone. "No, honey, he's not here right now. Do you wanna go see him?"

Noah nodded emphatically.

"Okay, let's get you changed, and we'll go."

Fifteen minutes later, she set Noah down next to her outside as she shut the door on an excited Shasta and Bella. "Sorry, babies, you can't come this time."

She heard an answering whine and scratch as she picked Noah up and carried him to the car. She buckled him into the car seat and pulled out of the backseat.

Blinding pain exploded in the back of her head, and she slammed into the side of the car before sliding to the cement. Her vision blurry, she rolled over and tried to climb to her hands and knees, but something hit her stomach with enough force to knock the breath from her.

Dani lay on her back, blinking against the painful sunlight. She could hear Noah screaming and tried to say his name.

Someone blocked the sun, standing over her. She couldn't make out the features, and she didn't recognize the terrifying voice.

"Say good night, bitch."

And everything went black.

TYLER WAS AT the park playing basketball with Jeremiah. He seemed to be doing better, especially living with Sue and Martin Grayson. Tyler had gotten a call from Jeremiah after Thanksgiving, and Jeremiah had told him that his mom was willing to sign the guardianship papers. Apparently, they'd had a long talk after Neil's visit, and after some hard truths, Jeremiah had convinced his mom that she needed to do what was best for him. Tyler wished he knew what Jeremiah had actually said, but he'd never pressed.

Despite the cold air outside, sweat dripped down Tyler's forehead as he chased after the teenager, and he finally gave up after the kid did a perfect jump shot. He grabbed his knees and took several gulping breaths as the ball arched in the air and swooshed through the net beautifully.

"Wanna take a water break, Sarge? You look a little winded."

"Smart-ass kid," Tyler muttered, though he took him up on it. Last night, after he'd left the party, he might have gone home and finished off a couple glasses of whiskey, and he was definitely paying for it today.

He took a long pull from his water bottle and saw his phone light blinking. Sliding his thumb over the screen, he saw a missed call from Dani.

He walked away from Jeremiah to listen to the voice-mail. *"Hi, Tyler, it's Dani. I need to talk to you, so if you could please call me back, that would be great."*

Very formal. No *love you* at the end like usual.

Maybe she's calling to dump your ass.

If that was the case, no sense in putting it off, although a hard knot twisted his stomach painfully.

He hit the call button and waited.

"Hello, this is Officer Coleson Ricks with the Sacramento Police Department. To whom am I speaking?"

Tyler's heart stopped. Why the hell did the police department have Dani's phone?

"This is Tyler Best. I'm trying to get ahold of my girl-friend, Danielle Hill."

"Mr. Best, Ms. Hill is on her way to Sutter Memorial—"

"Why? What happened? Is Noah okay?"

"Noah?" the officer repeated.

"Yeah, her son, he's almost two. Is he okay?"

"Mr. Best, Ms. Hill was found outside her home near her car, unconscious. She appeared to have been assaulted."

Assaulted.

"Her mom. Did you call her mom?" Tyler asked.

"No, but, Mr. Best—"

Tyler hung up the phone and dialed Dani's parents' house.

"Hello?" Laura answered.

"Laura, it's Tyler. Is Noah with you?"

"Noah? No, Dani picked him up this morning. Why?"

"I don't have the details yet, but Dani's been attacked. She's on her way to Sutter Memorial Hospital, but Noah wasn't at the scene."

"Oh, my God! George!" He could hear Laura screaming for her husband, but Tyler didn't have time for hysterics.

"Laura, I need you to listen. Go to the hospital and tell Dani I'm going to find him, okay? I am pretty sure I know who has him, and I'm bringing him back to her."

He hung up the phone. "Come on, Jeremiah, I'm dropping you at home."

"What's going on—"

"Just move your ass!" Tyler barked, sprinting for the car.

TYLER JUMPED OUT of the passenger side of Sparks's truck and didn't even wait for his friends to catch up.

He tried the front door of the Ramirez home, and it was unlocked.

He burst through, and Angel scrambled up off the floor, his meth pipe falling to the floor as he stared at Tyler, his eyes wide in terror.

"I don't know nothing!"

"Yeah, you don't know nothing, you piece of shit?" Tyler hauled Angel up by his throat, running on nothing but adrenaline. "Where is Noah?"

"I swear, I didn't take him—"

Tyler squeezed, and Angel clawed at his hands. "Maybe not, but you know where he is. And if you want to ever be able to walk again, you're gonna tell me."

"Might want to ease up on him so he can talk, Best. He's turning blue," Martinez said.

Tyler dropped him onto the torn-up couch, and Angel coughed and sucked in air.

"Clear the house."

His friends did as he asked, while Sparks stood at his back.

"You can't...do this," Angel wheezed.

Tyler squatted down. "Like I told you before, I'm not a cop. And if you think for one minute I'm above putting you through the worst kind of hell imaginable to find that little boy, you're wrong."

Tyler's tone was cold and deadly, and Angel appeared on the verge of passing out with fear.

And then a bit of the bravado the guy seemed to have in spades shone through. "Whatever, you'll never find him. My mother is on her way to Mexico with him right now."

Cold fingers of fear gripped Tyler's heart as he imagined Noah terrified and calling for his mom. If this was the kind of cockroach Camila raised, what would Noah become in her charge?

And Dani? How would he look her in the eye if he couldn't bring her son home?

Tyler pulled out his large, serrated knife, and, calling Angel's bluff, he trailed it over the outside of the other man's pant leg. "If you don't tell me where they are, I'm going to start with your Achilles tendon. It won't kill you, but you'll be in so much pain you'll wish I had."

"You crazy motherfucker!"

Tyler knew he wouldn't do it, but he needed Angel to believe he would.

"Hold him down," Tyler said and felt his friend move forward.

"All right, all right! Shit, she wanted him, okay, and she wouldn't stop bitching at me about it. So I had my cousins go get him and take him to their place!"

"Write down the address. And it'd better be right."

Angel wrote down an address and handed him the paper with shaky hands.

Tyler pulled out his phone and typed the address into his GPS. Twenty minutes away.

Hauling Angel to his feet, he placed his face within a millimeter of his. "If you breathe a word about our visit to anyone or tip off your mother or cousins, we'll be back."

THEY PARKED DOWN the street from the house, and Tyler scoped out the two-story, a plan forming.

"How long is it going to take for the cops to get here?" Martinez asked.

"About five minutes out."

"Man, you do realize this is going to fuck us if shit goes south?" Sparks said.

"If you want to back out, I get it. You can wait for the cops, but these people have already had Noah for almost two hours, and if Angel's right, Camila is getting ready to take him out of the country." Opening the car door, he hopped out. "I'm going in."

"I've got your six," Kline said, following him.

Tyler nodded. He still owed Kline a shot to the jaw, but when he'd called for backup, he hadn't hesitated.

"Shit, I'm coming." Sparks climbed out of the passenger side and Martinez followed him out of the back.

They shut the doors silently and formed a tight triangle, Tyler taking point.

They rounded the back and went through the unlocked door.

"People really should learn to lock their doors," Blake joked softly.

The sound of a TV blared from the front of the house, and they came through the living room.

Two men on the couch jumped up, and Tyler held his finger to his lips. They didn't move a muscle; apparently having three large strangers break into the house was enough to freak them out.

"Where is Noah Hill?" Tyler asked quietly.

The man on the left sniffed at him, obviously thinking they weren't armed. "Man, I don't know what the fuck you're talking about, but if you don't get out of my house, I'm gonna call the cops."

"Cops will be here in a few minutes anyway. Really hope there's nothing in here you don't want them to find," Tyler said.

The one on the right looked like he was gonna piss his pants.

"But if you want us to let you leave this room so you can flush whatever you've got stashed, you'd better tell me where Camila Ramirez and Noah are."

Scared dude on the right caved pretty quickly. "The kid's upstairs with his grandmother."

"Fuck, José, shut your mouth," the other man said.

"I'm not going to prison for your bitch aunt, *ese*. I'm getting the fuck out of here."

"You were right there with me, bro. If I go down, you're coming with me, mother—"

"Don't let them leave," Tyler said to his friends.

The men on the couch protested, but Tyler was already gone. He raced up the stairs and went for the shut door at the end of the hallway. When he tried the knob, it was locked, and he pounded on the door. "Noah!"

"Get out of this house!" Camila screamed from the other side.

Tyler kicked in the door and found himself facing down a trembling Camila pointing a gun right at his chest.

"I will shoot you if you take another step." Her shrill, irrational voice pierced his ears, and he held his hands up, trying to appear nonthreatening. Tyler saw Noah's still form on the queen-size bed, a blanket pulled over him. He could see the blanket moving in deep, even breaths. Tyler's gaze missed nothing as he scoped out the room, spotting the clear medicine bottle half full of red liquid on the nightstand.

"Noah?" he called loudly, but the toddler didn't stir. The crazy witch must have drugged him. Tyler focused his attention back on Camila, his mouth set in a grim line.

"How much did you give him?"

"I told you to get out!"

"I need to know what you gave him and how much. He could be overdosing as we speak." Tyler stared down the woman, noting her wide, wild eyes and the overstuffed suitcase on the bed. "You don't want him to die, do you? You went through all the trouble to steal him; there must be a part of you who cares."

"He's fine," she snapped. "I used to give it to Angel when he wouldn't calm down. I would worry more about your safety right now."

"That's really nice, drugging your own kid and repeating it with your grandson. No wonder your son is a fucking addict."

Camila took several steps forward, waving the gun around angrily, and a cold sweat broke out over Tyler's skin as he prayed it wouldn't go off.

"You shut your mouth. I was a good mother. I did everything for him. If I'm guilty of anything, it is indulging him. But now, I have a second chance."

"A second chance? You stole a child from his mother. If you think you're getting out of this city with him, you're out of your damn mind."

Tyler was already convinced she was off her rocker, but the last thing he wanted was for her to accidentally shoot Noah. Or him.

"José! Pablo!" she yelled.

"Sorry, my friends have got them a little tied up right now."

The gun went off, whizzing by Tyler's arm and hitting somewhere behind him.

"I have five bullets left. Next time, I won't miss," she said.

"I'm not leaving this house without Noah," he said.

"You're going to leave in a body bag if you don't get out of this house."

"Then you can add murder to the list of felonies that California is going to charge you with. Either way, Noah will be back where he belongs." He shook his head, keeping his hands up so she didn't shoot. "Why in the hell are you doing this? You could have gotten a lawyer for visitation."

"He is my son's child, and I have every right to see him! I won't let that little slut keep me from him."

The sound of sirens in the distance reached him, and he smiled. "You won't have to worry about Dani keeping Noah away from you. A judge and a jail cell will."

To his surprise, Camila unzipped the front pocket of the suitcase and crammed the gun in. As she was slipping it under the bed, Tyler took the moment to run to the other side of the bed, opposite Camila.

Tyler's heart hammered, as he expected Camila to snatch Noah before he could, but she didn't make a move. As Tyler picked Noah up, cradling the tiny child against his chest, he breathed in Noah's sweet scent and almost sighed aloud in relief. His eyes pricked as he realized how scared he'd been that he'd never hold Noah again. He hadn't just tracked Noah down for Dani.

He couldn't imagine his life without the kid.

"I've got you now, buddy. You're safe."

Watching Camila suspiciously, he edged toward the open doorway, but she didn't move, just watched him like a hawk.

He climbed down the stairs two at a time as he heard the front door burst open. "Sacramento Police Department!"

"Don't shoot," Tyler yelled from the last step. "I'm Sergeant Tyler Best, United States Marine Corps, and I have Noah Hill."

Several officers stepped into view, their weapons drawn.

"I think he's been drugged," Tyler said.

"Help me!" Camila screamed behind him. "That man is kidnapping my grandson! He threatened me!"

Tyler gritted his teeth as the officers tensed at her accusation. When Camila came into view, he could see their gazes turning suspicious as they looked between him and Camila, the hysterically crying woman.

"Put the child down slowly and move away," one of the officers ordered.

Tyler caught Camila's triumphant smile and had to hand it to the manipulative bitch. She was very convincing.

"I'm not kidnapping him," Tyler said, holding onto Noah more tightly. "I called you guys. Noah was taken from his mother two hours ago after she was attacked in front of their home. This woman has no legal rights to him."

Officer Zack Dalton, the newest trainer at Alpha Dog, stepped past the others. "It's cool, I know him."

Coming up behind him, he patted Tyler down. "Got any weapons, Best?"

"A knife on my right calf. You got an ambulance out there?"

"We do."

Once Tyler was completely disarmed, Dalton held out his arms. "Why don't you hand him over to me. I'll run him out to the ambo."

"Don't let her anywhere near him," Tyler said.

Dalton nodded.

Tyler handed Noah off reluctantly, tears pricking his eyes as the child whispered softly, "Tywer."

"On your knees," another officer said, stepping forward with cuffs in his hand.

Tyler dropped and put his hands behind his head, watching Dalton carry Noah out the door and out of sight.

Chapter Thirty-One

DANI WOKE UP to the sensation of tap-dancing elves stomping on her brain. She could barely open her eyes, as a white light burned every time she tried.

"Can someone"—God, why was she so thirsty?—"get the light?"

"Oh, she's awake. George! She's awake."

Dani opened her eyes this time and was able to take in her surroundings groggily. "What happened?"

"You were attacked. You have a concussion and a few broken ribs, but the doctors told us you're going to be fine."

Flashes of memory came back to her. Pain…a hateful voice…Noah's crying.

"Noah…Where's Noah?"

"He's in the pediatric ward. He's fine. Your friend Megan is with him."

Dani tried to sit up and winced.

"Honey, don't move. You're pretty banged up," her dad said.

"But I want to see my son."

"You will, as soon as he wakes up," said her dad, patting her shoulder.

Relaxing slightly, she asked, "Where's Tyler? Why isn't he here?"

She might have been out of it, but she didn't miss the look that passed between her parents.

"Mom?" she prodded.

"Tyler's at the police station, baby."

"What—" she started coughing and moaned, as her whole body ached—"what happened?"

"He's the one who found Noah, but the police are holding him and his friends for questioning."

"Why? What are they questioning him for if he saved Noah?"

"From what Blake said, the police are just trying to sort everything out, and he should be released soon."

"Where's Blake? Is he with him?" Dani asked.

"Not anymore. They released him, but Tyler was armed and coming down the stairs with Noah in his arms when that woman started making all kinds of accusations. Blake said they arrested him at first, thinking he was the kidnapper—"

"He did not kidnap Noah!" she cried.

"No, but from what an Officer Dalton told us, it shouldn't take them much longer to release Tyler." Her father's lips pinched into a grim line. "Although, Blake told me that the little weasel, Angel, is claiming Tyler threatened to torture him after breaking into his house. Tyler's friends are saying all they did was talk to him."

Dani stared at her parents, shock rolling through her. Tyler had gone on a full-on rescue mission to get Noah back. Noah was safe because of Tyler.

Suddenly, Dani was laughing and crying at the same time.

"Danielle, are you all right?" her mom asked.

She nodded wordlessly, trying to catch her breath to speak. "I just...I love him so much."

Her mom seemed at a loss, while her dad just stood up and said, "I'm gonna get some coffee."

"Dad, can you stop by and ask Megan to find out if Tyler's parents know where he is?"

"Sure, sweetheart."

Dani started to scoot forward, ignoring the pain. She needed to get out of there and see Noah. To help Tyler.

"Wait, what are you doing? The doctor said you needed to rest."

"I am going to see my son, and then I am going to find a way to get Tyler released."

"Danielle, you get back in that bed right—"

"*Mom!*" Dani tried to stand, but she ended up gripping the side of the bed when the world tilted. "I am leaving this room, even if I have to crawl out of here. So, are you going to help me or not?"

Her mom huffed at her. "I'll go get a wheelchair."

"Thank you." Dani sat back down on the bed, taking a painful breath. Once she held her baby and knew he was going to fine, she could work on getting to Tyler.

TYLER SAT IN the holding cell, staring straight ahead. It was nearly seven in the morning, and he had already been interviewed twice. He'd called his parents first, then the hospital to check on Noah and Dani. Her father had told Tyler they were both fine, but Tyler couldn't wait to find out for himself.

He wondered if Dani was awake yet and if she knew where he was.

If they did believe Angel, he could be looking at obstruction and maybe even assault with a deadly weapon, though he hadn't hurt the little turd. His friends had all been released already, but he was the last one. He'd told the felony assaults detective everything, except the threat of torture, and explained that all he needed the detective to do was talk to Dani.

Tyler couldn't regret his current situation. If he had to do it over, he wasn't sure he'd change anything. Even if the cops had traced the kidnapping to Camila, Angel might never have told the cops where his mother was, and if he had, it might have been too late. Camila would have been gone with Noah, and Dani would have been devastated.

Tyler would have been devastated.

Noah was safe, and he couldn't regret that. Even if it meant he lost everything, it was worth it.

"Tyler Best," an officer called from the edge of the cage. "Stand up. The rest of you, turn and face the wall."

Tyler got up and went over to the cell door. As the officer let him out, he asked, "What's going on?"

"No charges are being filed."

Tyler followed behind the officer, shocked. As he gathered up his personal effects—except for his knife—he was escorted out to the lobby, where Martinez and Sparks stood waiting for him.

"Come on, dude. There's a lot of people waiting for you," Sparks said.

Tyler followed behind them as they walked outside and climbed into Sparks's truck.

"Yeah, a whole crowd looking to welcome back the conquering hero," Martinez said.

Tyler shook his head in the backseat. "I'm nobody's hero, man."

"I don't know. You rescued that little boy, and the people responsible were arrested today. Makes you a hero to me," Martinez said.

"Plus, I know at least two people who think so, too." Sparks got on the freeway and headed east.

"Where are you going? I want to go to the hospital and check on Dani and Noah."

"They aren't at the hospital. They're waiting for you at your place," Sparks said.

Tyler had never heard sweeter words in his life.

DANI STOOD OUTSIDE of Tyler's house with Noah in her arms, surrounded by Tyler's friends and family. Some of the kids who had gone through the Alpha Dog Program, including Jeremiah Walton, stood in a group with banners and signs. Most had trickled in overnight, and had been waiting for word on when Tyler would be released. Noah had been up for an hour, and Dani hadn't slept at all since she'd woken up in the hospital a little before midnight.

Megan stood next to Dani—well, hovered over her was more accurate.

"Why don't you let me hold Noah?" Megan asked for the tenth time.

"Because I'm not ready to give him up yet." Dani kissed her son's forehead, more than aware of how close she'd come to losing him today.

"Then at least sit in the chair before you both fall down."

Dani sank into the folding chair with a sigh. "I'm fine, Megan."

"Yeah, so you keep saying. Don't make me get your mother."

Her mom was standing off to the side with Gloria Best, gushing about Tyler, and the two women kept hugging and holding hands as if they'd been friends forever. Gareth and her dad stood with Blake, talking intently, and Dani could only imagine football was the topic.

"Here they come," one of the boys hollered as the truck rounded the corner.

Dani started to get up again, and a hard hand on her shoulder pressed her back down. She glared up at Megan.

"It will take a minute, so you might as well keep your ass in that chair."

Noah lifted his head and grinned up at Megan. "Ass."

"Way to go. You're never babysitting," Dani said, not even bothering to correct Noah now.

Dani couldn't see over the group as it surged forward. The truck pulled into the driveway, and ignoring Megan, she stood up with Noah.

"Tywer!" Noah shouted when he saw him.

Dani waited for him to find her with that deep blue gaze, and once he did, she wanted to run. Wanted to vault over the crowd and into his arms.

But he was already pushing past everyone and rushing toward them.

His arms closed around the two of them, and she ignored the pain in her ribs as Tyler's mouth found hers, his kiss filled with desperation.

He pulled back and stared into her eyes intently. "Are you all right?"

"Yes, sore and my head is killing me, but I'm good. Better now."

Tyler took Noah from her without asking, and she watched his eyes close as he hugged her son until tears blurred her vision.

"And how about you, Noah? You okay?"

"Okay," Noah said.

"Thanks to you," Dani whispered.

It didn't even feel like there was anyone else, just them in their little bubble.

"Come on, everyone, let's move the party inside and let these two have a proper reunion," Sparks said, leading the way inside.

As the crowd trickled past, Dani held Tyler's free hand to her cheek. "I am so sorry about last night. I called you and was headed to your place when—"

"I know. Blake already told me he talked to you—"

"But I knew before he showed up—"

"Baby, I don't care. I don't care about one stupid misunderstanding in the grand scheme of things. Today, I could have lost you. We could have lost Noah."

She loved the way he said *we*. "And Noah and I could have lost you. I still can't believe you were crazy enough to go all *Die Hard* on Angel and his cousins."

"It wasn't like that. They weren't exactly hardened criminals," he said.

"Still, things could have gone really bad today."

"Instead we're all here. All together." Caressing her check, he continued, "I used to think that fate was a bunch of bullshit, but I'm beginning to believe there's got to be something higher guiding us. Leading us to where we're supposed to be." Kissing her again, he pulled back enough to whisper against her lips. "My place is with you and Noah. You're my everything."

She wrapped her arms around Tyler's waist and leaned her head onto his chest, looking up into Noah's smiling face.

"Are you two gonna be much longer? There's a celebration in your honor, you know!" Dereck yelled from the front of the house.

"So much for enjoying the moment," Tyler groused.

Dani pulled away. "That's okay. I have a feeling we're gonna have plenty of moments."

Epilogue

TYLER BEST WATCHED his eight-year-old son, Noah Best, kick a soccer ball to Jeremiah Walton across the park. It was Noah's birthday, and they had invited all of their friends and family to the park to celebrate. Tyler couldn't help smiling at the relationship between Jeremiah and Noah, who were twelve years apart but as close as two brothers. When Jeremiah's mom had moved out of state with his stepfather, Jeremiah had split his time between his guardians' home and Tyler and Dani's place until he'd accepted a scholarship to run track for Arizona State two years ago. Now, when he came home, he usually crashed on their hide-a-bed if the Graysons had a full house.

Olsen Meyers and Dwayne Harlow were swinging Tyler and Dani's second son, Gareth, between them as they walked. The two-year-old's laughter reminded Tyler so much of Noah when he was that age.

There were a few other graduates from Alpha Dog standing around, talking with the other instructors, and of course, Dani's and his families were spread out. His dad was manning the barbeque while George, Dani's dad, told him everything he was doing wrong. Tyler laughed, just imagining how things would go in a few minutes, when his dad would start shouting at him. It was all done in good spirits. It was actually a little weird how easily the Bests and the Hills had meshed, even sharing holidays so their kids wouldn't have to split their time between them.

Which had been really helpful when Dani was pregnant with their daughter, Felicity, and so uncomfortable and crabby that no one could make her happy. Now that Felicity was four months old, Dani was back to her old self.

Her old, completely tone-deaf self, who was currently singing to their daughter as she rocked her in her arms.

"What's that you're singing?" he asked.

She looked up from the baby, her eyes twinkling. "Usually, you call it wailing."

"I'm being nice today."

"Ah, well, in that case, I'm singing 'Baby of Mine.' "

"Oh, yeah? How come you don't ever sing me to sleep?" he asked.

"Um, did I not mention that you mock me?"

He kissed her forehead. "Come on, show me you love me."

"I show you I love you every morning." Her tone was hushed and intimate, and he started looking around the park for somewhere to make out with his wife.

"I know what you're doing, pervert."

He laughed, now considering the name an endearment.

"Tyler, you're going to have to show me again how to make Cookie stay when I tell her to!" his mother-in-law yelled, wagging her finger at her new golden retriever puppy. He'd started giving private obedience training, and it had expanded into a side business that had allowed Dani to drop down to part time at the emergency clinic.

Although it could be a little more frustrating dealing with actual owners instead of just the dogs…especially when it was family who'd hired him.

"I'll be right there, Laura."

Noah came running up, his hazel eyes bright. "Is it time for cake yet, Dad?"

Tyler's chest swelled with pride, the same way it had the first time Noah had said the word. "Not yet. Go torment your cousins and tell them it's from me."

With a grin so much like his mother's, Noah took off in search of Kyle and Kent, who still hadn't managed to mature, much to their mother's chagrin.

Dani laid Felicity into her playpen and while she was bent over, he came up behind her. Wrapping his arms around her waist and pulling her back against him, he asked, "Are you sure you don't want to sneak off with me?"

"We'd be missed. Tonight, though"—she turned in his arms and ran her hand over his cheek—"I'm all yours."

"Unless one of the kids needs something."

"Hey, you knew what you were getting into the first time you bought me coffee."

Bending to drop a long, lingering kiss on her lips, he ignored the catcalls and whistles from their family. "And I wouldn't change a thing."

"Good answer."

Acknowledgments

FIRST AND FOREMOST, I want to thank my amazing husband and children for being so understanding while my deadlines were so crazy. I love you. My fabulous agent, Sarah Younger, for making this series happen and to my editor, Rebecca, and the entire marketing, publicity, and creative team at Avon for working with me again. To my sister from another mister, Tina, for being there whenever I need to talk. Thank you to the rest of my family for being so supportive with every release. To my Rockers; I love your guts. And thank you to all of my readers who have followed me through the ups and downs of this crazy journey. You are beyond awesome.

About the Author

An obsessive bookworm, CORI CARY likes to write sexy contemporary romances with humor, grand gestures, and blush-worthy moments. When she's not writing, she can be found reading her favorite authors, squealing over her must-watch shows, and playing with her children. She lives in Idaho with her family.

To keep up with new releases, contests, and more, sign up for Cori's Newsletter at http://www.corigary.com/books-commnewsletter.html

Give in to your Impulses . . .
Continue reading for excerpts from
our newest Avon Impulse books.
Available now wherever ebooks are sold.

THE VIRGIN AND THE VISCOUNT
A BACHELOR LORDS OF LONDON NOVEL
by Charis Michaels

LOVE ON MY MIND
by Tracey Livesay

HERE AND NOW
AN AMERICAN VALOR NOVEL
by Cheryl Etchison

An Excerpt from

THE VIRGIN AND THE VISCOUNT
A Bachelor Lords of London Novel

By Charis Michaels

Lady Elisabeth Hamilton-Baythes has a painful secret. At fifteen, she was abducted by highwaymen and sold to a brothel. But two days later, she was rescued by a young lord, a man she's never forgotten. Now, she's devoted herself to save other innocents from a similar fate.

Bryson Courtland, Viscount Rainsleigh, never breaks the rules. Well, once, but that was a long time ago. He's finally escaped his unhappy past to become one of the wealthiest noblemen in Britain. The last thing he needs to complete his ideal life? A perfectly proper wife.

Bryse.

He had introduced himself as Bryson that night, so long ago, and despite her residual horror, she had clung to the sweet intimacy of that introduction. She'd devoted years of foolish fantasies to guessing whether those close to him referred to him as Bryson or Bryse or perhaps Court . . .

She looked up at him. *Bryse.* And now she knew. Now she was being invited to become one of those people close to him.

Cowardice compelled her to back away and retake her seat. "Forgive me, my lord." She spoke to her knees. "I don't know what to say, and that is a rare circumstance, indeed."

"I would also speak to your aunt," he assured her. "It felt appropriate to suggest the idea of a courtship to you first."

She laughed, in spite of herself. "I'd say so. Unless you wish to court my aunt."

"I wish for you," he said abruptly, and Elisabeth's head shot up. It was almost as if he knew she needed to hear it again, and again, and again.

I wish for you.

He crouched before her chair, spreading his arms, putting

one hand on either side of her chair, caging her in. "How old are you, Elisabeth?" he asked.

"How old do you think I am?" A whisper.

"Twenty-six?" he guessed.

She shook her head. "No. I am the ripe old age of thirty. Far too old to be called upon by a bachelor viscount, rolling in money."

"Or"—he arched an eyebrow—"exactly the right age."

She laughed and finally looked away. And she thought he'd been handsome at nineteen. Her stomach dropped into a dip. She reminded herself to breathe.

"Why me?" she asked, looking out the window. "Why pay attention to *me*?"

His voice was so low she could barely discern the words. "Because I think you'd make an ideal viscountess."

An ideal what? Hope became a living, pulsing thing in her chest. It became her very heart. She fell back in her seat and closed her eyes, but the room still swam before her.

He went on, "You are mature, and intelligent, and poised. And devoted to your charity, whatever it is."

A thread of the old conversation. She sat up, determined to seize it before he could say another thing. "I've just told you what the charity is."

"You spoke in vague generalities that could mean a great many things. I let it go because I hope for more opportunities to learn."

Elisabeth breathed in and out, in and out. She bit her bottom lip again. She watched his gaze hone in on her mouth.

She closed her eyes. "My lord." She took a deep breath.

"Rainsleigh . . . Bryson." She opened her eyes. "If your far-reaching goal is to earn an esteemed spot in London society, you're going about it entirely the wrong way. My charity is . . . unpopular, and no one has ever asked to court me before. It's really not done."

"Why is that?"

Because I have been waiting for you.

The thought floated, fully formed, in her brain, and she had to work to keep her hands from her cheeks, to keep from closing her eyes again, from squinting them shut against his beautiful face, just inches from her own, his low voice, his boldness.

"I'm very busy," she said instead.

"Then I will make haste."

"Is this because of last night? When I . . . challenged your dreadful neighbor?"

The corner of his mouth hitched up. "It did not hurt."

"It's very difficult for me to stand idly by when I hear a person misrepresented."

"And to think I was under the impression that you could barely abide my company. Your defense came as a great surprise."

"Oh . . . I am full of surprises."

"Is that so?" His words were a whisper. He leaned in.

She had the fleeting thought: *Dear God. He's going to kiss me . . .*

An Excerpt from

LOVE ON MY MIND
By Tracey Livesay

Tracey Livesay makes her Avon Impulse debut with a sparkling and sexy novel about a woman who will do anything to fulfill her dreams . . . but discovers that even the best laid plans can fail when love gets in the way.

Chelsea Grant couldn't tear her gaze away from the train wreck on the screen.

She followed press conferences like most Americans followed sports. The spectacle thrilled her, watching speakers deftly deflect questions, state narrow political positions, or, in rare instances, exhibit honest emotions. The message might be scripted but the reactions were pure reality. If executed well, a press conference could be as engaging and dynamic as any athletic game.

But watching this one was akin to lions in the amphitheater, not tight ends on the football field. Her throat ached, impacting her ability to swallow. She squinted, hoping the action would lessen her visual absorption of the man's public relations disaster.

He'd folded his arms across his chest, the gesture causing the gray cardigan he wore to pull across his broad shoulders. The collar of the black-and-blue plaid shirt he wore beneath it brushed the underside of his stubbled jaw.

When he'd first stepped onto the platform, she'd thought he was going for "geek chic." All he'd lacked were black square frames and a leather cross-body satchel. Now she understood he wasn't playing dress-up. These were his everyday clothes, and as such, they were inappropriate for a press conference, unless he was a lumberjack who'd just won the lottery.

Had someone advised him on how to handle a press conference? No, she didn't think so. *Any* coaching would have helped with his demeanor. The man stared straight ahead. He didn't look at the reporters seated before him. He didn't look into the lenses. He appeared to look over the cameras, like there was someplace else he'd rather be. His discomfort crossed the media plane, and her fingers twitched where they rested next to her iPad on the acrylic conference table.

A female reporter from an entertainment news cable channel raised her hand. "Mr. Bennett?"

The man turned his head, and his gaze zeroed in on the reporter and narrowed into a glare. Chelsea inhaled audibly and leaned forward in her chair. His eyes were thickly lashed and dark, although she couldn't determine their exact color. Brown? Black? He dropped his arms, and his long, slender fingers gripped the podium tightly. The bank of microphones jiggled and a loud piercing sound ripped through the air. He winced.

"How does it feel to be handed the title by David James?" the reporter asked, her voice louder as it came on the tail end of the noise feedback.

The camera zoomed in and caught his pinched expression. "Right now, I feel annoyed," he responded sharply.

"Annoyed? Aren't you honored?"

"Why should I be honored?"

"Because *People Magazine* has never named a non-actor as their sexiest man alive."

"An award based on facial characteristics is not an honor. Especially since I have no control over the symmetry of my features. The National Medal of Technology. The Faraday Medal. The granting of those awards would be a true honor."

The camera zoomed out, and hands holding phones with a smaller version of the man's frustrated image filled the screen. Flashes flickered on the periphery, and he rubbed his brow, like Aladdin begging the genie for the power to disappear.

"How does one celebrate being deemed the most desirable man on the planet?" another reporter asked.

"One doesn't." His lips tightened into a white slash on his face.

"Is there a secret scientific formula for dating Victoria's Secret models? Didn't you used to be engaged to one?" A male reporter exchanged knowing looks with the colleagues around him. A smattering of chuckles followed his question.

"Didn't she leave you for another model six weeks before the wedding?"

"So you're single? Who's your type?"

"What's your perfect first date?"

"Can you create a sexbot?"

Questions pelted the poor man. The reporters had found his weakness: his inability or unwillingness to play the game. Now they would try to get a sound bite for their story teaser or a quote to increase their site's click-through rate. The man drove his fingers through his black hair, a move so quick and natural she knew it was a gesture he repeated often. That, and not hair putty, probably explained the spikiness of the dark strands that were longer on the top, shorter on the sides.

"This has nothing to do with my project," he snapped, then scowled at someone off-camera.

Chelsea glanced heavenward, grateful she wasn't the recipient of that withering look.

An Excerpt from

HERE AND NOW
An American Valor Novel
By Cheryl Etchison

Former Ranger Medic Lucky James feels right
at home working long night shifts in the ER, but
less so during the day, when his college classes are
filled with flirtatious co-eds. When his 19-year-
old chem lab partner shows up at his work with
dinner for "her Lucky," he quickly enlists the
help of Rachel Dellinger, a nurse and fellow third
shift "vampire." From there a friendship is born
between two people just trying to make it through
the night. Neither are living in the past or planning
for the future—until one day changes everything.

When the phone kept ringing non-stop and the desk clerk asked her to take a set of scrubs to exam room seven, Rachel didn't think much of it. It was, after all, an ER and she assumed they were for a patient whose clothes were ruined and was in need of something to wear home. She gave a light tap to the exam room door and pushed it opened further, expecting to find someone at least sitting on the exam table and requiring assistance. What she did not expect was to see a fine physical specimen, upright and most certainly able-bodied, whipping his shirt off over his head in one swift, fluid motion. Nor did she expect to be greeted by strong shoulders, a broad muscular back, and narrowed hips.

Holy moly.

This guy was by far the best looking man she'd seen in the flesh in a very long time. Maybe ever. And she hadn't even seen his face.

She clutched the scrubs to her chest and stood silent and tongue-tied, watching, appreciating, as the muscles in his back and arms flexed and strained as he unfastened the leather belt around his waist and released the button. All those finely sculpted muscles worked in unison to create a stunning physical display of power and strength as he shoved his pants to the floor.

Wearing only white crew socks and gray boxer briefs, he turned to face her and she nearly forgot how to breathe. She thought the back was nice? The chest. The abs. The dark trail of hair that began just below his navel and disappeared beneath the waistband of his briefs.

"You could've dropped them on the table and left instead of just standing there."

Her gaze shot upward to see one corner of his mouth lifted in a half smile and as dark brown eyes stared back at her she was immediately struck by the feeling she knew this guy. There was something so familiar about him, but she couldn't quite put her finger on it.

She swallowed hard in an effort to unstick her tongue from the roof of her mouth. "You knew I was standing here?"

Instead of answering, he simply held out his hand, his eyes flicking to the scrubs she held in a stranglehold against her chest before lifting to meet hers once again.

"How?" She relaxed her grip, felt the blood rush back to her fingertips as she placed the scrubs in his hand. "How did you know?"

"Spatial awareness," he said taking the clothes from her and immediately tossing the shirt onto the gurney. "That and you knocked on the door before you came in." He flashed that half smile again before stepping into the pants and tying the drawstring. "Thanks for the clothes, Rachel. I can handle it from here."

Immediately she looked down to see if he'd read the name from her badge, only to realize her crossed arms were covering her ID. Clearly, he knew her. So she looked harder this time, doing her best to ignore the chest—and abs and arms—and focus on his face. As she mentally stripped away the disheveled hair, the heavy scruff covering his face, the laugh lines around his eyes, the earlier feelings of lust were replaced by a sinking feeling in the pit of her stomach.

There was little doubt the man standing in front of her was the one and only Lucky James.